Dragan Velikić
The Investigator

Copyright © 2015, Dragan Velikić
Published by agreement with Laguna, Serbia

Translation © Christina Pribichevich-Zorić

First published in Serbian as *Islednik*, by Laguna, Serbia, 2015
The right of Dragan Velikić to be identified as the author of
this work has been asserted in accordance with the Copyright,
Designs and Patents Act, 1988

First published in 2025 by Istros Books
London, United Kingdom
www.istrosbooks.com

Design and layout: pikavejica.com

Printed by CMP, Poole, Dorset

ISBN: 978-1-912545-54-4

Supported using public funding by

**ARTS COUNCIL
ENGLAND**

Dragan Velikić

The Investigator

Translated from the Serbian by
CHRISTINA PRIBICHEVICH-ZORIĆ

A man feels none the purer after a confession than before. On the contrary. He feels like a rubbish bin.

Having rid himself of all the better versions of himself, he was left with the worst one, the one that never confesses to anyone.

BORISLAV PEKIĆ

PART I

1.

"You're always so relaxed about everything, at the expense of others. Somebody else pays for it."

That's what my mother used to say.

"If I were a saint," she would sigh wistfully, "I'd protect cooks, maids and servants. Saint Nicholas protects sailors; well, I would protect servants. Only they know what somebody is like within the privacy of their own four walls."

She would follow this up with one of the many stories that populated her memory. A certain Professor Lolić had a son, a medical student, who liked to eat in bed. He would spill the food all over his sheets.

Disgusted by the thought of soiled sheets, she would stop and say: "Tell me, who in his right mind eats in bed? True, the young man later established a career in London, but what good is that when he's a barbarian."

Or she would cite the example of the famous writer whose flat she had lived in for a while. "You should have seen that stove, that neglected oven. Charred black and stinking of grease. I don't trust a writer like that. Full stop."

All her stories came from the boudoir, from the servants' quarters, from the maid's room. Places where you lower your voice. Where shadows are never still. Where giggles alternate with sobs and sighs. The stories neither start nor finish in this natural den of iniquity; rather there is an endless *in medias res*. An interspace and interim. And the vestiges of other people's lives. Seen from down below. Living life through a peephole.

My mother talked to the world from her kitchen. It was from there that she delivered her messages. There that everything was in its place. The kitchen was her altar, her command deck, the place where, after marrying, she took on the role of acting as God's agent. She had no doubt that this devotion to justice and the battle for truth would be rewarded one day. That after her death she would be proclaimed a saint. She used the Italian version of her name, as if her real name would shatter the illusion.

"Violeta. Santa Violeta, the patron saint of servants."

She was already in the care home by then. She had ended up in the one place that she had rejected all her life.

"I'd rather kill myself than live in a home," she always said.

After she went to the home, left behind in her armoire were presents intended for future weddings, housewarming parties and birthdays. Because presents were bought whenever a good opportunity presented itself. She would stop in front of a shop window displaying a set of plates at half-price. She would think about it for a moment and then come out with the name of a relative who had just started school. The plates would be for her. The little girl never dreamt that she was already the proud owner of the porcelain dinner set sitting in our armoire.

A small fortune lay in those presents, with their neatly written notes bearing the names of the recipients, some of whom had long since died.

Things were bought in advance. Life was lived in advance. Everything was doable because nothing was left to chance. My mother's eyes carefully scanned the territory of daily life. Nothing escaped her control. Nothing happened just by or of itself. Even the spider in the corner of the toilet owed its existence to my mother's superstitions. The entire universe of our flat vibrated to the rhythm of her breathing.

"Household appliances love me because I take care of them."

She believed things and objects have secret lives that only the sensitive and serious amongst us can intuit.

And she despised wastefulness: She was a world-class economiser.

During her last years in the home, she spent her days reading newspapers and women's magazines. She became addicted to articles that glorified vulgarity and bad taste. She devoted at least two hours of her day to irritation. She was infuriated when she read that somebody had given a villa as a wedding present. She was appalled by luxury and waste. To her, spending a fortune on curtains or chandeliers was an unforgivable sin. And as for yachts.... All that money spent every year on their upkeep just to be able to spend a few weeks cruising warm waters! "The world will explode from all that vulgarity," she would say.

What irritated her the most was the idea of indulging in an easy life. She believed that enjoyment, when seen as the principal purpose of human existence, turned people into idiots. The trend towards making everything easier led to the degeneration of humanity and, ultimately, to the extinction of the human species. The world was not created for our amusement.

At the cinema, she would react loudly if people whispered, munched, slurped. I remember ushers coming over in the darkness of the movie theatre, warning my mother that if she didn't stop, they would have to ask her to leave. She often wrote letters to the management of the cinema where on Saturdays we attended premier showings, saying that they should ban food and drink from the place.

My mother couldn't stand the lackadaisical. She had a profound respect for ants.

Santa Violeta. She was so afraid of water! Always be prepared for the worst, was her motto. She believed that you could avoid danger by constantly invoking it. She took immense pleasure in saying that when she was a child, on several occasions she had almost drowned. She passed that fear on to my sister and me. We never learned to swim properly. But my mother took us regularly to the beach: to Valkane, Gorton cove, Fisherman's Hut, Golden Rocks…She preferred Stoja. It was a real city beach, with concrete paths to the sea, toboggans, changing cabins, showers, a restaurant. I would watch the swimmers with such envy. The unrestrained bodies on the diving boards. The mid-air pirouettes. They would disappear into the waves, only to resurface a few seconds later. The cries, the laughter.

I would flail my arms around, vainly trying to keep my head above water for more than two minutes. I practiced in the deserted cove, by the camping site, where there were few witnesses. I felt that the whole world was watching me. I liked the beach at Stoja. My school friends didn't go there a lot. They preferred public beaches, where they didn't have to pay. They went in groups, without their parents. If any of them happened to stray to Stoja, I would lose myself in the crowd of naked bodies or hide behind a hedge and wait for the danger to pass.

My mother despised anything temporary, be it a bathing spot or a TV aerial. She couldn't stand repairs or alterations. Anything chipped or scratched had no place in our house. The moment she saw a crack in a plate, glass or cup, she would throw it out.

At the beach she would glare at children who screamed, raced around, threw scraps of fruit everywhere. Sometimes, when they ran over our towels, she would shout at them. Their parents would smile benignly. When she told some of them off, my sister and I wanted to die of shame. She would scold them for sticking cigarette butts into the crevices of the rocks. She behaved as if it was her job to guard the beach. Once, in the street, I heard a woman say to her husband: "Look, isn't that the son of that crazy woman from the beach?"

They've won, Mum. The beach people have taken over the world. Indifferent, numbed by pleasure, they stagger to exotic destinations. They do not value anything. They hide their sorry souls behind the mask of freedom. Hordes of barbarians wearing brand name clothes, pulling brand name suitcases through hotel lobbies. Inundating airports and railway stations. Taking cruises. Swarms of tourists everywhere. They have polluted the entire planet.

It is immoral to spend your summer holiday on a Greek island without knowing at least one ancient Greek play. How can you travel around Spain without realising that the Knight of the Sorrowful Countenance and his servant Sancho Panza once roamed Andalusia on horseback? You want to go to London? First let's see if you know at least one of Shakespeare's sonnets. Or John Donne's.

My mother liked the unadulterated truth. Relating everything precisely as it happened, with the exact intonation, facial expression, gestures and *sotto voce* comments. Without any double meanings. Telling the truth to the world straight to its face. Not forgetting the stains on the bedding. Or the charred oven. It was all about the details. The innate instinct to recognise the essential behind the incidental, that was her gift. She would often mention some minister whose secretary, she this knew first-hand, would change his socks on the plane for him while he sat sprawled out in his seat like a pasha.

"That says a lot about a person. Anyone who wants to see clearly, will understand everything. And then people are surprised that primitives and fools come to power. There are always warning signs."

"It's easier to imagine life than to live it," she would say after long reflection. "God alone knows all the mistakes one can make in the throes of enthusiasm."

And then she would add, almost to herself: "It's easier to be honest than to be diligent."

After returning from a trip, my mother liked hanging the laundry out to dry on the balcony. "Every return lends new life to a house; we all feel renewed when we come back from somewhere," she would say while unpacking the suitcases and bags. She would put everything back in its place, and immediately decide where to put the new things she had brought back. She would run her hand over a figurine, or the television screen, as if stroking a household pet. She was moved by the gentle hum of the washing machine. The spin setting announced the end of the cycle. Everything would be back in order again.

"Children, I wouldn't swap the day we return home for anything in the world. It's the nicest day of all. Though, the day when we depart is nice too. And so is the trip itself.

Ultimately, it's the travelling that's important. Even if it's only from the kitchen to the balcony."

2.

I'm a year old. And I don't remember a thing. It's my first time in a hotel. In the background of the photograph, there's a stone fence and the dark contours of vegetation in the garden. The one-year-old little boy is standing in front of the wide-open terrace door. He looks frightened. He has just slipped on the polished parquet floor and is about to cry. But he is momentarily distracted by the appearance of the photographer, with his camera and flash.

He is already showing an ability to immediately forget anything unpleasant. A flash of light, a new frame. An initiation to the cinema hall. The dense vegetation in the background is in sharp contrast to the little boy's face. Time of day: twilight. Written in black ink on the back of the photograph: *Hotel Palace, Ohrid, 22 June 1954.*

Exactly two decades later, I will return to that same hotel. And pick up from the *Post Restante* in Ohrid my mother's letter where she reminds me of my first trip. I can see from her florid handwriting that she's made an effort not to omit anything. The attentiveness of a teacher. The photographic memory of an ordinary day. Was it a sensitivity to travel? Or was she already imagining all the things that could happen? How had the professional photographer come to be there just then, to take a snapshot of a little boy on the verge of tears. The mystery is resolved by the note accompanying my mother's letter: a film crew making a documentary about Lake Ohrid was staying at the Palace hotel. She was a past master at anticipating questions. In fact, she spent most of her energy answering questions that she asked of herself on behalf of others.

Why did she remember that day? And was it all exactly like that from the moment that she arrived in Ohrid with Dad and me? How could she remember so much? She had hundreds of biographies stored in her head. Some of these people she had met only briefly. Encounters on a train, a day or two of travelling together, but certainly long enough for them to recount their life stories. Everything was instructive. Nothing was superfluous. Everything had its *raison d'etre* in the righteous world of the teacher. She lived what she recounted. She was what she recounted.

A born encyclopaedist. She remembered a myriad of banal details. She celebrated the everyday. No priorities; everything was important. A lonely passer-by waiting at the pedestrian crossing for the light to turn green, columns of ants marching in the grass, a smiling glazier after a summer storm, the arrangement of the beds in the dormitory of the Teachers College in Šabac, the first car ride in a Citroen from Ruma to Bogatić.

For years, she kept a special notebook where she recorded all the hotels where she had stayed. The notebook was at the bottom of a caoutchouc box, along with bundles of letters. That box was one of the things that was stolen when we were moving from Belgrade to Pula, and our luggage compartment was burgled at the train station in Vinkovci. It is still a mystery why she didn't keep the notebook with her. The only explanation I can come up with is that she always found it hard to remove things from their long-standing place. So, the notebook had to stay in the box with the letters.

Many years later, when she was fading away in the care home, she whispered her favourite mantra – the names of the hotels where she had stayed. Was she perhaps trying to reconstruct the contents of her lost notebook? There were moments when she was completely unaware that I was right there next to her. I would ask her questions to bring her back from the depth of her absence.

"*Therapia*. What do you mean, where is it?" she said, surprised by my ignorance. "It's the nicest hotel in Crikvenica. The only language you heard in the lobby was Czech, it was like being in Hradčany. The Czechs loved Crikvenica."

She would be silent for a while, nodding her head. The expression on her face would change, as if she were greeting all those Czechs in the hotel lobby.

"Then they moved on to Pula."

"Who did?"

"The Czechs, for heaven's sake!! Have you forgotten that it was only the Czechs who holidayed at the Fisherman's *Hut*? In the annex across the road, on the edge of the pinewood forest. It was always clean there. The Czechs are neat and tidy. That's why a lot of people don't like them. I don't know why that is."

That magic word "annex" spoken by my mother. Before I even knew what it meant, I imbued it with whatever I could think of. I thought annexes were special hotel premises reserved for important guests. It took me a long time to accept that, in terms of comfort, an annex was basically a second class part of the hotel, solely a place to sleep, without any other amenities. Even when the rooms were more comfortable than those in the main building – which I had occasion to see for myself when I stayed in luxury annexes – I viewed that comfort as a sort of compensation for its secondary status compared to the main building.

I'm sitting in the flat on Erzsébet Körút in the centre of Budapest that June day that my mother dies. I say aloud: The *Lipa* Hotel. Our first address in Pula. A lightbulb hanging from the high ceiling. The weak voltage of the single-phase current adds to the sense of bleak despair and abandonment. A cold November morning. Flags fluttering in the street outside. It's a national holiday. I am standing at the window. I look out, trying to distance myself from the hotel room. Since early in the morning when the news came that our carriage on the train had been burgled in Vinkovci, my mother has been angrily rebuking Dad, saying he should have put a padlock on the door of the compartment instead of believing those people at Belgrade station's shipping office, who said that a leaden seal was perfectly sufficient.

"You're so naive! What planet do you live on?" she keeps saying. "They duped you. They're all in it together. That's what you get when you live in a country of thieves."

My father tells her to keep her voice down. He chews nervously at his cigarette holder, pacing the room in his blue naval uniform. The trunk containing his clothes was among the things stolen in Vinkovci.

A deserted Kandler Street. The bare branches of the plane trees in front of the *Lipa* Hotel. Flags and banners on the buildings. An occasional passer-by on this holiday morning. I can see it all clearly from the window on Erzsébet Körút four decades later, on that sunny June day when the news of my mother's death arrived.

The carriage burgled in Vinkovci — that is the first thing that comes to mind after her death. I say it to myself in her voice. I walk over to the window and look out at the cars and yellow trams hurrying down the boulevard. I try to ease the pain with a tried and tested trick. The principle is the same, whether I'm sitting in the dentist's chair or suffering from heartache. I take myself to another place, to a time long ago. The flash of the camera in the *Palace* hotel room at Lake Ohrid stopped the tears. That was the first time I had tried to escape pain.

I continue with my mother's mantra. It triggers images of hotel lobbies, anonymous people, squares and streets, facades of buildings, snippets of conversations, suitcases and bags on metal racks above the seats in the train carriages. I don't have the Ohrid photograph in my mind's eye just then. It is not until a year later, when I return to Belgrade, that on the back of the photograph I discover the date: 22nd June, the day my mother died forty-six years later.

How long do the voices of those we love echo in our ears? With their distinct intonations.

Some words belong only to them.

"For heaven's sake!" My mother's favourite exclamation. Always said in a raised voice. With pursed lips and narrowed eyes. Followed by strong disagreement, verging on an argument, with whomever she was talking to.

That morning at the *Lipa* hotel, she refused to go to the train station with my father. "For heaven's sake," she kept saying. "Go on your own! You have a list of all the things; it will be easy for the commission to establish what's been stolen. And bring me back my box of letters from the red trunk. That they didn't steal, I hope."

I suppose she didn't have the strength to confront the mess the thieves left behind in the burgled compartment. In her mind everything was numbered, hemmed, sewn, framed, symmetric. Nothing was just of itself. Everything in this world results from something else. The best defence against awkward questions is to have ready answers. In fact, my mother didn't converse, she answered questions that she asked of herself. That pathological need for order produced the greatest possible disorder.

That disorder has built up in me. All my life I have been trying to shrug off the heavy mantle of realism that my mother placed on my shoulders. I am incapable of understanding that someone or something always has to be somewhere And that I am not obliged to explain anything to anyone. For instance, it is enough for a bird to fly. It is not up to me to find it a branch to alight on. At every moment, I have the right to slam the door shut on the chapter.

I feel completely lost in the world of fantasy. Fairy tales have always made me uneasy. Any event that is without a rational explanation drives me crazy. One can't fly in from nowhere. And as for flying? Magic lamps, flying carpets and other nonsense. Even with a treasure chest, you never find it when you need it most.

At first, before I learned the alphabet, my mother would read me bedtime stories. That was when we were living in New Belgrade. I remember the fable of the ant and the bee. Later I looked for it in vain in La Fontaine, Andersen, the brothers Grimm. Most of the stories were about things and objects. I remember one about the doorsill of a house. Mistrustful of any newcomer, the old, creaky doors would imperceptibly move, causing the intruder to trip. Even now, I am still suspicious of people who slip or stumble when entering the house.

When my father returned from the train station and told my mother that her box had been stolen as well, she burst into tears. My sister and I fell silent. My mother sobbed that she would never get over the loss of the letters and notebook where she had recorded all her trips – the cities and hotels where she had stayed. And all those stories.

Two years after the *Lipa*, it was the *Slon* hotel in Ljubljana. My mother had stopped taking inventory. But I decided to remember and secretly write down the names of the hotels. We drove to Slovenia in a Fiat *Topolino*. My father had only recently passed his driving test. The roads were virtually empty. Every village square had an intersection. In the window of a bookshop in Ljubljana, I saw the novels of Karl May. That evening, while my parents were enjoying themselves at the bar of the *Slon* hotel, I lay down on the big bed and read *Winnetou*.

The wailing siren of the ambulance on Erzsébet Körút takes me back to that June day. One trip is over.

"Everybody has to be somewhere," my mother repeats, following me down the corridor of the care home. She mentions the Czechs who are so clean and tidy that they deserve to have a sea of their own. At least a little bay, like the Slovenes. "We had a wonderful time in Ljubljana; your dad and I listened to Lado Leskovar sing for two nights in a row at the *Bellevue* hotel."

"The *Bellevue* was in Split. You listened to Leskovar at the *Slon*. That's where we stayed."

"For heaven's sake! The *Slon* had a bar. And it was Marijana Deržaj who sang there. Only foreigners were allowed in. Foreigners and whores. At the *Bellevue*, Lado sang at dances. I remember it very well. Ivo Robić in Rijeka, at the *Blue Adriatic*, and Dobri Stavrevski at the *Palace* in Ohrid. Everybody had to be somewhere."

I repeat the mantra, but in her voice: the *Palace* in Ohrid, the *Lipa* in Pula, the *Slon* in Ljubljana, the *Neboder* in Sušak, the *Slavija* in Opatija, the *Therapia* in Crikvenica, the *Bonavia* in Rijeka, the *Bellevue* in Split, the *Grand* in Skopje, the

Evropa in Sarajevo, the *Union* in Belgrade, the *Esplanade* in Zagreb, the *Vojvodina* in Novi Sad, the *Admiral* in Vinkovci...

The Raša Inn.

The sign above the door of the two-story corner building. The bus from Pula suddenly slows down and turns onto the square of the small mining town. There is a fifteen-minute break.

I walk around the stage that is Raša. Because everything on this square is like a stage set: the station house, the church, the wide steps, the long fronts of the buildings, the framed slogans at the beginning of something that looks like a street; and then, just ten steps further on, the illusion vanishes at the edge of the stage. The town is eerily deserted. The passengers from the bus are extras in a play that has been momentarily suspended.

For years I would pass through Raša on my way to Rijeka or Zagreb. Fifteen minutes for a coffee, a cigarette and the men's room. I would head for the centre of the square. The cinema's gaping round windows reminded me of an abandoned ship. Always that same feeling of not having arrived anywhere. The soundtrack is switched off for a moment. Alone in a mute frame.

Sometime in the late seventies of the last century, the *Raša Inn* vanished from my horizon. But the word "inn" retained a special status in my memory. Denuded and mysterious, it evoked a time of poverty, of cheap soaps and smoke-filled waiting rooms at train stations, of sad window displays of ready-made clothes and of milk bars. Of suitcases without wheels.

When the light of the last star dies, the hotel becomes an inn. A bed, wardrobe and sink. A toilet in the corridor. And sleep.

In a hotel, I live in the third person. With a different head.

I leave traces. I don't make the bed. I revel in the luxury of disorder. In freedom. Because order is nothing other than the absence of life. The triumph of the grave.

"Don't think too much," I hear my mother say.

That meant just one thing: to think like her. I'd lost touch with myself. Then the complications started. And the anxiety that came with the start of the swimming season at the end of May. I had to think up a good plan for the beach. Be in a group without revealing the little matter of my feeble swimming skills.

My first experience of love was on a rainy August afternoon. The southern *jugo* wind had been blowing for days. It suddenly turned cold. The beaches were deserted. I was relaxed and happy.

3.

It is not unusual to step into a room and forget why we went there in the first place. The easiest way to remember is to walk back out through the same door. It has been scientifically proven that people are three times more likely to forget what they have come into the room for if they have already walked through the door. The reason is that our brain sees the door as the *boundary-line of an event* and the decisions taken in the room as interred there when we leave. That is why we can remember them again if we go back into the first room.

4.

The cellar of the Villa Maria is a *boundary-line of events,* a stage where an imaginary life unfolds. A place where all escapes are possible. A long corridor leads past padlocked doors to the huge laundry room. Big, barred windows on the two outer walls rise up to the ceiling. A deep cement sink for washing the laundry runs almost the length of one of the walls. In the corner, by the cauldron, is a chair with an upholstered backrest.

That boy in the laundry room is me. The malcontent, the rebel, the person from the cellar of the building, whose actions are directed by "that other one", his double on the floor above, the one who decides everything under the strict eye of the upbringing given him by his mother. A captive to the imperative of responsibility, utterly dedicated to the task of anticipating anything that might happen. Which is why, years later, his backpack contains an umbrella, a battery lamp, a clean T-shirt, and aspirin. Accessories to calm the rebel seated on his throne between the cauldron and the sink. He never made all the forty-three steps that separated the laundry room of the old *Central* hotel from the flat on the first floor. The door to the cellar remained shut.

For two years, the Villa Maria was a military hotel called the *Central,* and it housed English officers. During the war it was reportedly a brothel which, after Germany capitulated, overnight became a hotel for senior officers. In September 1947, power was handed back to the city. My father, a young lieutenant in the Yugoslav Navy, is standing on the deck of a landing ship at the entrance to the port of Pula. The Anglo-American troops are leaving the city. People are celebrating. The loud-speakers installed on terraces and lampposts are blaring out speeches, partisan songs and marches. Flags are fluttering. The walls are covered with banners. Posters with portraits of national heroes. Euphoria, immortalised in newsreels on cinema screens across the country which has finally secured its borders.

What you do not see on the cinema screens, or in the newsreels, are the individual fates of the people. The deserted city of Pula, vacated flats, future children conceived by local women with foreigners. One army had left, another had arrived. The refugee days of Istria's Italians in camps outside of Trieste and Udine. The past has been boiled in the cauldrons of the *Central's* laundry room. The laundry is clean again. No stains.

I sit in my refuge for hours. I sense that this is the heart of the Villa Maria. The cauldron and sink have been here from the very beginning. I wait for the residents of the *Central* to appear in the semi-darkness. I imagine impressive-looking English officers in their light-coloured uniforms. And women of dubious morals who remember the Italian and German uniforms. Some of them, now ladies of a certain age, can still be seen in the narrow passageways and on the steps of the old part of town at the foot of the Kaštel fortress. Malicious comments follow their footsteps as they disappear into the houses in Gupčeva and Kandler streets. They, along with their caustic biographers, are the heroes of stories that will never be fully told.

For a brief time, a year or two, the Villa Maria was a home for war orphans. And then, in the mid-1950s, new residents arrived – worthy veterans of the people's liberation struggle. We found ourselves amongst this communist elite after my father's transfer, when one November day in 1958 he exchanged the Danube for the Adriatic. Instead of going every morning to the *Sava* monitor anchored in the port of Belgrade, my father went to the *Muzil* barracks, which protected the port of Pula from being approached from the sea. After we moved, I soon became known by my peers as: the boy from the Villa.

I spread out my fingers. I count to ten. I try to grasp the notion of time. Each finger represents a year. The minutes I count to myself seem long. How much can fit into a year? How many people and events? I travel through time even when I am not in the cellar. Steps. Forty-three to the first floor flat. That's my father's age. When I go down the stairs to Prvomajska Street on my way to school, after every fifteen steps I stop on the landing, on those few metres of flat surface. I recap my journey. All the things I have seen through the windows of the houses. I have covered my own life, those ten or so years, before I reach the first landing. The rest of the journey belongs to the future. To the years that still lie ahead of me. Every day on my way to school, I traverse this still unlived life. One day, I have no doubt, I will measure my own life with three flights of stairs. I will be older than my father. I will be an old man of seventy when I reach Prvomajska Street.

I take the long way home from school. I go along Prvomajska to the Golden Gate, and then walk uphill, where there are no steps, to the house. It takes a whole hour. I stop, I look at the inner courtyards with their gardens, grapevines, fig trees and privets. Walls covered with laurel leaves. I read the metal name plates by the front doors to the buildings. The seed of my later passion for phone books. For a story, it's enough to have a name, a combination of syllables that produce a sonorous sound, sometimes just a roll of double consonants. In some places, instead of an electric bell by the front door, there is an iron ring affixed to a metal plate. Or a chain in the groove of the doorpost which activates a bell on the courtyard side. I was especially alert to surnames that did not end with the usual "ić", names with long vowels that I drew out even more, sensing there were secrets lodged in these melodious codes.

The old part of town, where the Histra fortress predated the arrival of the Romans, is crisscrossed with narrow passageways linking Prvomajska and Kandler streets to that even narrower ring of Gupčeva St. Way up, in the middle of the spiderweb, stands the 17th century Venetian fortress Kaštel. There are not enough fingers or steps to count off the time that separates a Roman legionnaire on his galley from my father, the young lieutenant of the Yugoslav Navy, scanning Pula's seafront from the deck of the landing ship. Their eyes meet in the darkness of the laundry room. There, on my throne, between the cauldron and the sink, the past lives in the present. The whole world pulsates in the head of the young rebel. Providence has ensured that everyone is there: the Roman legionnaire, and my father. And me.

And the English officers. Because nothing disappears just like that. Whatever was, exists forever. It floats in the chasm of the centuries. At the time, I still know nothing about the original owners of the Villa Maria. But they too are here somewhere, in the pockets of time. I pass by them every day. I sleep in the same room where they breathed. I sense their indestructible existence. The words that they spoke. The visions that they had. The world is a constant reforging.

One morning, Lizeta, my mother's friend from the house across the street, appeared at our door with an Italian woman, the daughter of the Villa Maria's former owner. Lizeta interpreted. My mother invited them in. She sent my sister and me out to play in the courtyard. Soon afterwards, Lizeta and my mother left the flat.

"You should have seen her," my mother tells my father that evening. "She asked me if she could see the rooms. She used to live in our part of the villa. Afterwards, she spent a long time on the balcony, gazing out at the surrounding landscape."

"It's a great loss, a house like this. Our burgled train carriage in Vinkovci is nothing in comparison," my father remarked.

I liked the way the Italian woman stood at the balcony railing, proud and distinguished, like a sphinx. I watched her from my hiding place in the leafy tree. She kept glancing at the shipyard and at Veruda. During the days that followed, I stood pensively on the balcony myself, my eyes straying to the distant Muzil barracks, the cement factory and the Church of the Lady of the Sea. I felt that only a loss could ennoble a face like the Italian woman's. It's not enough to have your carriage burgled in Vinkovci. It has to be a much bigger loss. I wished something like that would happen to me one day, something that would give me such a hard, embittered look.

Half a century later, I'm standing at the Kaštel fortress, looking at the courtyard of the Villa Maria. Through the trees I can see the house across the street, the windows of Lizeta's second floor flat. I discover that, in the meantime, two corner windows of the building have been walled up. The empty pupils of a blind man. There used to be a television set right there, between the two windows. One of the first in Gupčeva Street. The neighbourhood children would come to Lizeta's to watch cartoons. The older ones watched series and music festivals. Lizeta regularly watched the Italian programme. The San Remo Music Festival. Mina, Claudio Villa, Modugno, Rita Pavone, Bobby Solo. And Pula's Sergio Endrigo. The quiz shows on RAI. *Sette voci*. Pippo Baudo.

I spent a few days in Lizeta's flat when my nine-year-old sister was taking part in the *Children Sing – Zagreb 1964* festival. My mother accompanied her to Zagreb. I had classes in the afternoon. In the morning, as soon as Lizeta left for the market, I would get out of bed and start exploring the flat. For the first few seconds I would feel weak at the knees, because I knew that I was embarking on something forbidden. My penchant for voyeurism, born in the cellar of the Villa Maria, where the bare legs of the women hanging out the laundry briefly passed by the windows, came into its own during my stay in Lizeta's flat.

I would go into that other room, the one that Lizeta didn't show me, where she slept. On the walls, dozens of small, framed photographs. I would look at them more carefully later, after inspecting the wardrobes and dressers. A heavy smell of winter coats, fur coats and capes. Ladies' plumed hats. In the drawers – scarves, silk stockings, gloves. In a box, a man's pocket watch and a gold necklace. I didn't remember seeing them on Lizeta. She always dressed unassumingly. These things seemed to belong to a different person who had once lived here. And had left.

The photographs came later. An entire life laid out on the wall. Above the bed, on a wide corkboard, small, yellowed photographs and postcards with serrated edges, some of them already curling at the corners, becoming unstuck from the damp. Hard faces, knobby, hooked noses, dark eyes, fixed stares. Like physiognomies from another planet. The men wearing fezzes and kippahs. Cramped, overflowing market stalls. Shops. Fishmongers. Street scenes. Company signs written out in ornate, incomprehensible lettering. Above the big entrance to a building, a sign in Latin script: *Kinematografos Odeon*. A little girl in a white dress, with long plaits, standing on a pathway in a park. She appears in several other photographs as well. In one, she is sitting on the lap of an elegant man wearing a bowtie and boater hat. The same person, in a dark suit and derby hat, is standing in front of a two-storey building with forged iron balcony railings and big French windows. A sign on the front says *Xenodochion Egnatia*. Then, several black-and-white post-cards of the seaside town. Masts densely lined up in the port. Written in Latin script at the bottom of a sepia photo on a postcard: *Salonica*.

Footsteps in the kitchen. I quickly step away from the wall displaying the photographs. Lizeta appears at the door. She smiles and says something to me in a strange language. Susurrating words, as if she's speaking through leaves. She says it is Greek, the language of her childhood. In Salonica.

I'm surprised by her reaction. I expected her to scold me, or at least to ask me what I was doing there. The way my mother did when she caught me rummaging through her things. Whenever we went to visit someone, I would find a moment to sneak into an empty room and start exploring. That was my passion. I said that I was going to be an explorer when I grew up. To secretly open a drawer in someone's flat, to inhale the smell of a wardrobe, to touch objects, to absorb the scenes depicted in the photographs in a china cabinet, filled me with absolute wonder. Even now, I lose my breath when I stand in front of the half-open door of a closet, a storeroom, the iron bars of a cellar.

At the mention of Salonica, I tell Lizeta that my grandfather had been there, fighting in the war. All those who fought there are called Salonicans. Before that he was in Corfu, then in Tunisia, he was treated at the hospital in Bizerte after he was wounded crossing Albania. Lizeta is surprised that I can remember the names of all these places.

"It's not just the names of towns that I remember," I say. Then, without waiting for her reaction, I start listing the last names on the metal plates next to the front doors, in the order in which I see them on my daily walk to school, a musical keyboard of different tones.

During the following days, while my mother and sister are away in Zagreb, I often stroll through Salonica with Lizeta. We sit on the bed, facing the corkboard of photographs. It's like when I'm in the laundry room imagining the English officers. And it's not just the people in the photos who are with us, but also those Lizeta conjures up with her eyes closed. Sometimes, she becomes so lost in the moment that she forgets I'm there. As if in a trance, she says words in Greek. Then she switches to Italian, only a little of which I understand. She is not in Salonica anymore, now she's in Ancona; she mentions her ancestors, the Benedetti family. She shows me a crumpled photograph of a bearded old man. Ambroggi Benedetti, Lizeta's great-grandfather, who opened the first European hotel in Salonica, the *Albergo Benedetti*. Then she says: *Xenodochion Benedetti*.

The Bechtsinar gardens, says Lizeta. She used to play there. The tram passed by the gate to the park. Further on was the red light district with its hourly-rate hotels, like the *Aphrodite* and *Bacchus*. She wasn't allowed to go that far. Her world was limited to behind the old marketplace, with its array of shops: Kapon, Perahia, Modiano, Benmayor, Moreno. She played with the children of the Jewish tradespeople, who taught her Ladino. She did not go to the synagogue and did not have two names — one for at home and the other for outside — like her best friend Francesco, who at home was called Abraham.

She falls silent for a moment. "Mrs. Haslinger's boarding school for girls in Vienna," she says. She spent five carefree years there. She learned solo singing at the academy. When the war started, her parents sent her to stay with relatives in Trieste. She was supposed to wait in the shelter of this Adriatic city for the war to end. But a terrible fire broke out in Salonica. Her parents' entire neighbourhood burned down. And they disappeared with it. That city doesn't exist anymore. Another city with the same name is there now, but the streets and squares where she grew up are gone, the houses and parks are no more, nothing that she remembers exists anymore, except on this wall, and in her memory. Her parents don't even have graves. Their bodies were never found.

Then she talks about Trieste. She lived in the outlying neighbourhood of Servola. She shows me a photograph of her standing on the platform of a tram. Next to her is a young man in uniform. In the summer, she would take the open tram to the beach at Barcola. I repeat after her the names of Trieste's neighbourhoods. I memorise the sound, the intonation of the words I will use to unwind the mental rolls of film in my refuge, in the laundry room. Like when I say: Bizerte. I see my grandfather in the white light of Africa. Hundreds of days squeezed into nothingness. The scar on his hand left from the removal of a shell fragment. And the stiff right index finger.

Lizeta moves on, to the Istrian coast. After Trieste she lives in Rovinj, then on Red Island, until she finally comes to a stop in Pula. The corner house, by the wall of the Arsenal, where the tram slows down before making a sharp turn towards

San Policarpo. Later, she moves to Gupčeva Street. Narrow passageways and steps at the foot of the Kaštel fortress, small hidden courtyards and gardens, houses whose extensions have squeezed them all together. Everything reminds her of the Salonica neighbourhood of her childhood.

I loved the ritual of these journeys, strolling through Salonica's parks, streets and squares, whose names I remembered after our very first walk. Trained by the silence of Villa Maria's cellar, I was an ideal travel companion for Lizeta. From time to time, she would cast a gentle, absent smile at me, devoid of emotion. Just a slight weariness of life. Decades later, I recognise that vague smile on my mother's face as she walks with me down the corridor of the care home where she spent the last years of her life.

Standing on the wall at the foot of Kaštel Fortress in the winter twilight, I gaze at the Villa Maria. A light is on in my room. Who lives there now? Who is leaning on my past? The way I did with the English officers and that Italian woman. So many stories drive this powerful drama! When they have run their course, what is left? Blind windows. Moth-eaten clothes in wardrobes and dresser drawers. Anecdotes. Neatly packed lies, spawned by successive retellings of what had once been. Much had been wanted. Countless attempts had been made and even more had been abandoned. The ember of intention had glowed for a long time. One thought it would last forever. That no fear could cool it down, harden it into anxiety. It is no one's fault that everything turned out differently, that illusions remain the only sure manifestations of vanity. That is why it is healthy to look at the window that had framed his daily life for so many years. He might discover a missing detail, without which it was impossible to account for the cowardice, the failures. Nothing

35

should be ascribed to others. No big words to mitigate the confession; to enable yet another escape.

The hours drip by with the rhythm of an infusion.

When I think of all the friends, relatives and acquaintances that stayed in our flat! They would usually come for the weekend, to visit their sons at the barracks in Pula. I remember a certain Velizar, a sailor whose fiancée was a cousin of my mother's. They would spend hours in the room. I wonder if memories of the Villa Maria still linger in a corner of their mind. Or at least the smell of the laurel on the high wall by the Kaštel fortress. Just as I remember the rolls of carpets in the *Istra* department store. I can recall not only the stale air in the carpets and curtain department on the first floor and the golden reflections of the enormous perfume bottles on the ground floor, where fragrances were sold by the ounce, but also the voices from the nearby *Sljeme* community canteen. The impossibility of translating the notions of an era is the best proof of its authenticity.

Every era has its own smell.

Barić, my history teacher, said that the whole of the Middle Ages stank. You could barely walk in the street from the stench. People didn't bathe. They emptied their chamber pots out the window. They were surrounded by smells that were very different from what we know today. The air was different. The taste of water, meat, fruit. I can clearly hear him, ignoring our outbursts of laughter, in the raspy voice of an inveterate smoker calmly proceeding to explain the notion of the transitory: "Your grandchildren won't know what a drugstore is, or a steel works, or a paint shop. Bleach and wax will not exist. There will be no grocery stores. Only pills to swallow!" That last bit would be said in a menacing tone.

I told myself that I could, at any time, whenever I wanted to, slam shut the door of a chapter.

Bang!!!

5.

"Are you alright here? Isn't it a bit cold?" I ask my mother, just to say something, as we walk down the corridor towards the little courtyard.

"There's always something missing," she replies with a smile.

"And the people here?"

Through the half-open door of a room, I catch a glimpse of an old man in a coat. He is sitting on the bed, hunched over an empty chessboard.

"I like to go for walks in Sušak. The bridge over the Fiumara used to be the border between the Kingdom of Yugoslavia and Italy. Afterwards, everything got jumbled up."

"Yes," I say absently. "And the food, is it any good?"

"Dobri Stavrevski, is he still alive? He sang so beautifully that time in Ohrid."

"I don't know about Stavrevski. I recently saw Lado Leskovar walking along Terazije in Belgrade…".

"People in Rijeka live long."

"The air here is good…"

"The most important thing is to have a rhythm. That shows refinement. Every day, at the same hour, you have your café au lait, you read the newspaper, you water the flowers…Then you go to the market or out for a stroll…My landladies in Sušak, the Car sisters, Milkica and Irma, lived into their late nineties. They had a rhythm. Everybody in Rijeka has a rhythm; that's why they live so long. Their cemeteries are full of centenarians. When you lose your rhythm, you get sick. And then it's the end."

"Didn't they have that tobacco shop near the *Neboder* Hotel?"

"You can have a tobacco shop and still be refined. Irma spoke six languages. Milkica played the violin. They never married." She pauses. "They had a lot of time."

Neither of us says anything. While I try to think of another question, she suddenly turns serious.

"And what are you doing? Writing?"

"Yes. I'm writing a new novel."

"You're inventing things again," she says, with a reproachful look. "I don't like it that you make things up. A real writer doesn't make things up. There aren't many real writers around," she says.

I follow her eyes; they are sombre again, a film covering them as they stare at the top of the high-rise building across the street.

"What's important is to look within yourself. Then everything naturally follows. Like in the movies."

I don't say anything. I let her look within herself.

"I can't always remember everything, but that's what makes it fun, when you don't know what's awaiting you round the next corner. No need to rush. You are never relaxed," she says. And again, that reproachful look.

"You don't think that it might have something to do with you?", I reply irritably, already on my guard. "We were constantly rushing somewhere. We always arrived at the station at the last minute. We'd jump onto trains that were already leaving the station. Unlike everybody else, we never arrived at the cinema on time. We would sneak in through the dark, hunched over, everybody grumbling and swearing at us. I don't remember the beginning of a single film. That's why I now have to invent things."

"For heaven's sake!" she says with a dismissive wave of her hand. "Now it's my fault. I don't recognise a thing in your books. It's as if you lived somewhere else. How is it possible to forget so many things?"

"And what should I be writing about?"

"About what you know, what you've experienced, your life. Where are those people, those houses, those streets? If only I could recognise just a single person, even from afar. Where did you meet all those creatures?"

I hold my tongue.

"Do you remember Lizeta?"

Of course I remembered Lizeta.

"The morning we arrived in Pula...I'll never forget it. That evening, they burgled our carriage in Vinkovci; your father, rest his soul, as useless as ever, wouldn't listen to me when I told him to put a padlock on the carriage door. They robbed us dry. They took everything, everything that was mine..." she says, her face suffused with childish anger and sadness. "Lizeta was the first person who approached us. She took care of the two of you while your father and I fixed up the flat."

"I remember her rooms. The walls plastered with photographs."

"All sorts of stories were told about her," she laughs mischievously. "People are jealous of those who don't let life pass them by."

"I remember a lonely old woman."

"Old woman?" she looks at me, shocked. "You're inventing again. She wasn't much older than you are now."

Disconcerted, I say nothing; that can't be true. How many years had she spent on Red Island, at the Hiterots'? How had she wound up with them? As if reading my mind, my mother says:

"She was a friend of Barbara's, the baroness' younger daughter. They knew each other from Trieste. When Barbara decided to move to Red Island, she invited Lizeta to join her. Later, they each went their own way.

In a matter of minutes, she barrages me with the story of the unfortunate Hiterot family of Red Island, only to suddenly switch to the nearby island of Katarina, owned by the eccentric, debauched Count Milevski, who, in the wake of a murder, had fled his native Lithuania in a coffin.

"Where did you hear that?"

"When we were looking for a house to buy...Dad was working for Jugolinija and was at sea a lot; we had money... Lizeta went with me all over Istria, from Rovinj to Umag. Maleša, the watchmaker, drove us in his Mercedes. In those days you could buy wonderful houses for a song. On one of our scouting trips we went to Red Island. We also went to Katarina. It would take more than a dozen novels to recount all the things she told me at the time."

"In the end, you didn't buy anything."

She senses the implicit reproach in my voice.

"Your father was at sea, I couldn't make that kind of decision by myself," she says defensively. "Anyway, something unexpected always cropped up while I waited for him to come back."

I look at her, she's absent, her eyes fixed on the wall separating the courtyard of the care home from the desolate landscape of the high-rises. This is her final address. And no matter how much longer she lives, and how many more high-rises are built here in the meantime, there will always be the wall. Nothing will change on that screen anymore, until the end comes. I try to work out how much time I've got left until my own final address, when you know that no changes are possible anymore, that the only thing that awaits you is a miserable existence, with pain of one sort or another. To fall asleep in the embrace of dementia is God's reward for all the suffering and uncertainties of life.

"She had an affair with Count Milevski," she whispers proudly. "You remember, I took you to see his grave."

"Where?"

"What do you mean where? At the Rovinj cemetery."

"Considering all the cemeteries we visited, it's hard to remember."

"You haven't forgotten everything though, have you?", she says, her tone irate again.

"No. I remember the cemetery in Sušak, and the one in Split…"

"In Sustipan."

"I remember the Šabac cemetery. And the one in Sremska Kamenica, with Uncle Jova Zmaj's grave…"*

"Write about Lizeta," she interrupts me, annoyed by the ironic note she senses in my answer. "She was lively in life. Her life is a novel."

"Alright!" I say, just to say something.

"Why are you looking at me like that? One day, when you get your head straight, you'll realise that I was right."

She turns to look at the bench where two old women from the home are sitting. They are observing us. My mother nods at them. They respond by waving, first the one, then the other. Their unusual synchronisation makes me feel the

---

*   Jovan Jovanović-Zmaj, a Serbian poet best known for his children's poetry, affectionately known as Uncle Jova (All footnotes are the translator's).

full awfulness of the care home. Cemeteries are much nicer places. The dead are closer and more alive in their finality. We step away towards the enclosure of the courtyard.

"You've never written about the beaches I took you to. Where are Stoja, Valkane, Gortan cove? The cakes at the *Hungarian Cafe*? The presents I brought you from Paris, from Trieste...? Is there anything of real life in your books? What are you writing about now?"

"Hotels."

"Hotels? This here is a hotel too; it doesn't have many stars, but it's cheerful. Like the holiday camp in Selce. I used to take the schoolchildren there; that's before you were born," she says, and then, pensively, her eyes fixed on the bench where the two old ladies are sitting: "Lord, they look so much like..."

"Like?"

"Like the Car sisters. They're the spitting image of Milkica and Irma. Even the bench, it looks just like the one in Trsat. Don't you think?"

"I barely remember them."

"You don't remember Milkica? All those ice creams you had with her at *Slavica* by the waterfront in Rijeka. You don't remember that either?"

"I had cakes, I wasn't allowed ice cream because of my tonsils."

"For heaven's sake! What are you talking about? We removed your tonsils as soon as we came to Pula."

"You and Dad didn't remove my tonsils, it was Dr Slišković. In the hospital, I was in a room with two sailors, that I remember very well. But I don't remember Milkica. I remember their house in Vidikovac, near the church. I know from the stories I was told that she took me out for cakes. The ice cream came later. When only Irma was left."

"They broke into our carriage in Vinkovci. Dad wouldn't put a padlock on the door. They robbed us of everything," she repeats softly, casting a long, absent look at me.

"That I remember."

"So, write about that then."

I say nothing. My mother's eyes are fixed on the wall.

"I went to Pula for the first time in 1949, on business, just for the day. At the time, I was working in Rijeka for the Directorate of the Ports of the Northern Adriatic. I walked down to the park at the foot of the Arena, sat on a bench and looked out at the sea. It was the middle of the day and not a soul was around. Nobody walking in the park or along the waterfront. It was not until a good half-hour later that a cyclist appeared, coming from the Arena; he cycled down the slope and disappeared into the distance. And then there was nobody again. An empty city. Deserted. Had anybody told me that I would be spending a third of my life in that city, I would have said they were crazy. Ah, if only we knew what was waiting for us..."

And then, as if in passing, she mentions that the bus broke down just before the town of Raša. It was getting dark; the driver couldn't fix the problem. Some of the passengers who lived in nearby villages set out for home on foot. A big black car appeared and two men wearing leather coats and cloth caps stepped out. They told the driver that they would send for a mechanic. A girl asked them if they would give her a lift to Opatija. They agreed.

"When I saw the girl leaving with them, I went over and asked if they would take me to Opatija too. Actually, to Rijeka. They laughed. I realised that they were a bit tipsy. They reeked of garlic. The other passengers watched them in silence, not a peep out of anyone. The four of us left in the limousine. That was the first time I heard the name Hiterot. 'She's got good pick-up, this baroness,' the driver kept saying, extolling the quality of the car. The two men worked for the security service in Labin. They kept sniggering and laughing. They were more than tipsy. When we arrived in Raša, they invited us to dinner at the hotel."

"Raša doesn't have a hotel, just a miserable inn," I say.

"For heaven's sake! There was a hotel smack in the middle of town. The bus arrived, the passengers flooded into the restaurant and I somehow managed to get away. The girl from Opatija stayed with them."

I recognise the pause, that enigmatic moment of silence which comes just before the final act. In order to understand why the story was told in the first place. What had actually happened. How it had ended.

The girl from Opatija stayed with them.

An open ending to the story. To add something that is inappropriate to even think, let alone say. Just a hint, a vague outline. The passageways seem free, but all the doors are locked. Nothing is ever said clearly. That is how my entire childhood became inhabited by spirits, chimera and lies. Hence, when I grew up, my penchant for the provisional, the superficial, the drifting roads of the seductive women I fell in love with.

"Dad was in Pula too at the time," I say, just to jolt her out of her absent state.

"Everybody has to be somewhere. Everything has its own time. Dad and I met three years later, in Arandjelovac. But why am I telling you this? You'll make it all up anyway. I'm not interested in fabrications. That's why I don't read anything anymore. And just so you know, the world will go to pot not because of the hole in the ozone, or because of Martians, but because of lies."

She looks at me tearfully and says softly: "Off with you now."

6.

Everybody has to be somewhere.

That June afternoon in 2000, when my mother passed on to a better place, I am sitting in the flat in Erzsébet Boulevard in Budapest. Down in the street, yellow trams are weaving their way through the heavy traffic, rushing along the corridors, concrete boulders separating them from the car lanes.

Yes, it is important to note these concrete boulders, to register as many unimportant details as possible, to let one's thoughts escape into the banal, to suppress the news of my mother's death with whatever I can. My eyes follow the metal railing around the pedestrian area in front of the *New York* café; there's a woman gazing at a shop window, green road signs on the electric lamp posts, an advertisement for a travel agency on Blaha Lujza Square. Then, the trams again.

"The Stuttgart method," I can hear my mother say.

Stuttgart was the first city to introduce special car-free corridors for trams, which was later adopted all over Europe.

I try to grasp the point of this demented story. Because, one moment the Stuttgart method referred to trams, and the next to a certain gardener named Ziegler from Stuttgart and his landscaping of parks. Having long stopped giving credence to anything my mother said, I Google him: after the departure of the Ottoman Turks, he visited Belgrade to try to negotiate a job with the new Serbian authorities. The Serbian capital's green spaces narrowly escaped his plans. But nowhere is there any mention of the Stuttgart method.

My mother did her memory exercises every day. Boredom was an alien concept to her. She would take a box full of photographs, go through them slowly one by one, trying not just to recall the names of some of the people, but also the context, and their role in the infinite universe of the past.

Or she would spend hours rummaging through wardrobes and drawers, delighted when she discovered something she had completely forgotten about. She felt that she had rescued from oblivion an episode of her life. She was obsessed with wanting to have the full wealth of her experience at her disposal at every moment. That was why she had to keep remembering the life she had lived and vigilantly reign over its vast territory. Life would be meaningless without constant awareness of the road travelled. There is no need to invent, one just has to remember. Life is God's work, granted for temporary use. And that is why the past has to be reconstituted, so that it can live. My father sailed the seas, my mother sailed her life.

That June afternoon, after receiving the news of my mother's death, I try to find an answer to the question: Why am I here, in a rented flat in Erzsébet Boulevard in Budapest? Where did this woman beside me come from? These people around us. This me. So different from the model I was supposed to conform to. At first, everything was logical, predictable, clear. The world was like a catalogue. I started from there. And I found myself living a life that I didn't want, a life that wasn't mine. With habits and customs that were alien to me. Without a logical order to my daily duties. How did I come to eat things I don't like? Do things I don't like? Say things I don't think? This woman beside me knows how I feel better than I do. I live with unpacked suitcases. With one foot in retreat. Constantly looking for a fixed point where I can catch my breath, discover my mistakes, and then, re-generated, proceed in the right direction. Because what I am living now cannot be my life. Nothing is in its place. Objects, people and events have multiple shadows. What happened that I should now find myself where I wasn't supposed to be? An unsolvable question at first glance. Or should I, like my mother, without thinking, look for someone else to blame? For all the troubles endured, wrong choices and miserable circumstances.

I leaf randomly through the thick book of memories. Something is bound to leap out at me.

A photograph of the bridge on the Rječina, once the border between the Kingdom of Yugoslavia and Italy, taken from Sušak (Photo B. Fučić, 1947), one of the few pictures to survive the burglary of the train carriage in Vinkovci. It accidentally wound up in the small collection of family snap-shots that I brought with me when I left Belgrade at dawn on the 24th of March 1999. In the early afternoon of that same day, a few hours before the first NATO bombs fell on my city, I stepped off the train at Budapest's Keleti station; stretching out before me was the unending Fiumei ut – the Rijeka Road that passes by the Kerepesi cemetery. But people had started fleeing into exile well before that. The roads they had to take were traced long ago.

The blue lightbulb of the sleeping car on the Belgrade-Pula train has been glowing ever since that November night in 1958. That was the first time that I stepped into the inter-space between two homes, the one in New Belgrade which I had left forever the night before, and the one in Pula where I was heading. A tinge of fear that the journey might never end, that we would forever remain in the limbo of night.

That blue light has been burning for half a century now. It determined what I read, the worlds I inhabited, the heroes who would become closer to me than my own blood relatives. I recognise them unfailingly at our first encounter, just as Steiner did on page eighty of Remarque's novel *Love Thy Neighbour*:

He stopped under a streetlight and took out his passport. Johann Huber! Labourer! You are dead and rotting somewhere in the soil of Graz, but your passport lives on and is valid in the eyes of the authorities. I, Josef Steiner, am alive; but without a passport I am dead in the eyes of the authorities. He laughed out loud. Let's swap, Johann Huber! Give me your paper life and take my paperless death. Since the living won't help us, the dead will have to do it!

Johann Huber, alias Jozef Steiner, had become my inseparable companion long before NATO's bombers set off from Aviano for Belgrade. Years earlier this same Jozef Steiner had queued up with me in front of foreign consulates, filled in forms by my side, watched, not without trepidation, as uniformed men at border crossings suspiciously checked passports issued in the East. It was with him that I discovered that inalienable territory inside me, where visas and passports don't apply. Where there are no flags or border guards, no coats of arms or anthems, where what reigns is the silence of one's own conscience. Therefore, beware of big words, fiery speakers, false poets and greedy priests, beware of dining tables where policemen and criminals feast together and fraternise, where the poor of spirit preach, where people, their pockets full, speak about patriotism.

To return to the point of departure, to that November night in 1958, when both the uniformed men and the travellers spoke the same language. On an engraving in the lobby of the *Lipa* hotel, gun carriages buried in the sand in front of the city walls. A deserted Kandler Street on that holiday morning. The indestructible ramparts of the city that give refuge to new inhabitants every half a century. They move, eat, sleep, quarrel, make love in flats where, only yesterday, a different language was spoken.

Telling fortunes by reading the coffee grounds in a cup. During a May Day excursion to Bled, my mother visits a fortune-teller who is allegedly consulted by high-level Slovene officials. In the evening, pretending to be asleep, I listen to my parents talk. I hear that I am destined to go on a long trip, that I will cross the ocean and live in America. I will be rich and happy. My decision to opt for maritime studies after high school dates back to then. And to embark as soon as possible on the journey predicted by the fortune-teller in Bled.

In the Benedictine monastery on Mount St Mihovil in Pula, Dante Alighieri contemplates the graves he will mention in *The Divine Comedy*. With a whole universe compressed into tercets, into neatly arranged dossiers, he envisages for each thief a place in one of the nine circles of hell. Before returning the book to the city library, I copy out a few short excerpts. I do it systematically, in separate notebooks: landscapes, dialogues, descriptions of towns, love. I arrange my daily life using the Stuttgart method.

My mother cries out in the night, a few days before her departure for the care home. I walk over to the half-open door of her room. She is sitting on the armrest of the chair, naked. All three drawers of the big dresser are open. Leaning one arm on the edge of the top drawer, she is looking down, as if searching for something on the floor. Something important is missing in this terrible scene.

Like a replay of another night, only then there had been no cry. I peer through the half-open door of the room where

Grandma Danica is performing her pre-slumber ritual. She puts a few drops of hawthorn tincture into a glass of water, stirs and swallows it in one gulp. Then she removes her head-scarf and lets down her long grey hair, whispering something throughout. She repeatedly goes over to the icon of St George. She takes a package out of the wardrobe, a beige woollen vest, and places it under her pillow. The vest has three holes in it, from the bullets that, during an ambush one November night in 1943, killed her younger son Dragomir, my father's brother, the commander of the partisan detachment of Sićevo. At first, they said that the Bulgarians had killed him. Then it was the Serbian Chetniks.*

Six decades later, I learned that he had been killed by his fellow partisans, a victim of jealousy and envy. The woman who had supposedly been the cause of it all lives in a house on the edge of the village. I walk over to the fence. I take a picture of the scarved old woman digging in the garden. Hearing the camera click on my mobile phone, she straightens up for a second. Her face is rough, sunburned. Like an Indian warrior's. That is the face that my uncle kissed. I quickly step away. Up on the hill, behind the village cooperative, is a monument to Dragomir Velikić.

Sitting with my grandfather in the motel by the Sićevo dam, I touch his stiff index finger, a memento from the Salonica Front. Drunk together for the first time. I resist the feeling of disgust that his body arouses in me. He has always smelled of sweat and brandy. His wrinkled neck shows the clear line where he ended his morning shave. A hairy chest can be detected under his collar. He talks to me about Bizerte. Brothels under the tents. He mentions the murder

---

* A Serbian royalist, nationalist movement, parts of which collaborated with the occupying forces during World War II.

of a prostitute. A Serbian soldier shot her just when the poor woman had started performing fellatio on him. His defence in court was that he thought she wanted to bite off his male organ.

Twelve years have passed since that June afternoon in Budapest when I received the news of my mother's death. There are more and more unknown people in my address book. Names that I can't connect to faces, situations, stories. I walk around aimlessly, letting the road guide me.

Whenever I am in Rijeka, I go to the Governor's Palace and look for the building where we were supposed to move after my father started working for *Jugolinija*.* One rainy afternoon during summer vacation, we went to Rijeka to see our future flat. A week earlier, the Rijeka family had come to see Villa Maria. As far as they were concerned, they had already made their decision to move. They were now waiting for us to decide. However, after seeing the huge flat in the noisy street by the Governor's Palace, my mother had numerous reservations, which she laid out to my father in detail on our way back to Pula. The flat is dark and damp, she kept saying. She had also noticed that there was woodworm. That wasn't good news for our furniture. My sister was dozing next to me in the car. I closed my eyes to hide my tears. Every kilometre was taking me farther and farther away from Rijeka, from the noisy streets and magnificent buildings of this city that was not to be mine, and from a very different kind of life that I would have had there. And now I was leaving it forever. It was already dark by the time we arrived in Pula. It looked deserted, sad, like a prison I was being condemned to.

* A Yugoslav shipping company.

Change always made my mother panicky. Because it implied changing the usual order of things where everything was in its place and life unfolded exactly as she envisaged it. To move meant to enter unfamiliar territory, meet new people, re-establish oneself, recreate one's life story all over again. She always took a long time when preparing to step into the outside world. It was a ritual that occupied all of her attention. She was more concerned about what wasn't there than what was. Every outing was a performance. She had only so much time to send everyone a clear message, to create the self-image she wanted to project in an unkind world.

Moving to another city created countless unsolvable problems. It caused headaches over banal things like how to find reliable repairmen. Because, in my mother's mind she was already facing bursting water-pipes in that dark flat near the Governor's Palace. Fuses blowing, windowpanes breaking, the balcony railing teetering, the cellar broken into, and tomorrow it might even be the flat. How to find a seamstress who could make her look slimmer, a cobbler who could design a shoe that hid her bunions, a hairdresser who would find the right hairdo to suit her face?

To step out of a new flat into an unknown world caused her the kind of anxiety that left her feeling helpless. In the ensuing years she managed to prevent two other moves. She opted for the safety of backing out. And so, I remained a prisoner of Pula.

After *Jugolinija*, my father sailed for a long time on a cargo ship belonging to a German company from Flensburg, but it wasn't a regular line, rather in each port the crew was told its next destination. These ships are known in maritime slang as "vagabonds". They carry only loose cargo.

The Stuttgart method. The world floats in a sweet state of semi-slumber. Without fear or anxiety. The warmth of dementia.

I can finally mention the bird without having to find it a branch to alight on.

7.

The world I lived in at the time was the only possible one.

I can still see the wasteland of New Belgrade, viewed from the window of our old flat in 15 Pohorska Street. The view before me now offers a very different scene: the cranes of the naval shipyard, the outlines of the barracks in Muzil and the high tower of the maritime church. Lizeta calls it the Church of Our Lady of the Sea.

Once night falls, Gupčeva Street is deserted. Owls cry out from the walls of the Kaštel fortress. Every now and then a car or motorbike passes by. After midnight, the bells of the Church of Saint Francis ring the hour.

In the summer, you can hear the same conversations drifting out of the open windows. The taste of the Malvazija wine in the glass flagons on the kitchen tables is the same. In the shop windows on Prvomajska Street, the choice of styles and colours on display is modest. The same newsreel is showing in all four cinemas. The only difference between the newspapers is their headlines. No one doubts official opinion. The people are in power. I think that everyone in every village has the same food on the table. And they all say what they think. And they all think more or less the same thing.

Once a month, the watchmaker Josip Maleša comes to our house for dinner. My mother makes *gibanica*,* the way they make it in Mačva. Mr. Maleša is from Šabac. He came to Pula right after the departure of the Anglo-American administration. He acquired a shop across the way from the market building. Maleša maintains the clocks at Tito's residence on Brioni island. Once a year they send a car for him. He spends the whole day there, sometimes even two, until he finishes cleaning and checking all the clocks. He closes his shop while he is away.

The watchmaker Maleša is a generous man. He lends money interest-free, and in cafés he pays the tab for everyone. Charming and entertaining, he's full of stories, retelling those he's heard elsewhere. Over time, he has invented many of his own as well. A fine connoisseur of clocks and watches, a keen hunter, a man who loves the night life, he couldn't live without making things up. It was all fine and good as long as he squinted with one eye, either to take aim at a deer or to examine the inner mechanism of a watch with his magnifying glass; the problem started when he looked with both eyes. Then he didn't see so well. He often changed mistresses. Women were a mystery to him.

I saw it as divine justice for all those rabbits, deer and pheasants he killed. He always gave the dead game to his friends. At least once a month, he would come to us straight from the hunt with his bird-dog Dis. Being muddy and wet, he wouldn't enter the house, he would just hand his haul to my mother at the door and advise her about how to marinate the rabbit or prepare the grouse or pheasant. After he left, I would be faced with a picture of still life: rabbit ears drooping onto elongated, rigid bodies, a brace of vacant-eyed

* A layered cheese pie.

partridges and snipe. I would touch the moist, cold bodies with a fearful hand. The next evening, the watchmaker would come over for dinner. There would be lots of people at the table. One of the constant subjects of conversation at these dinners was when would Maleša get around to finding himself a wife. The inveterate bachelor said he would get married like a shot if only he could find a woman like my mother: hard-working, devoted to the children and to the house. Everybody agreed with him. My father smiled. But the subject was never raised if Maleša brought one of his mistresses to dinner. They were all very young, tall, real beauties. I knew that the watchmaker was lying, that he was not even thinking about finding a woman like my mother, because it was much easier for him to meet somebody like her than somebody like one of his conquests.

My mother and Maleša have similar political views. My father merely smiles and says nothing. Just to irritate him, she mentions the lawyer Djordjević, who emigrated to the United States right after the war. She bought the yew wood bookshelves from him. The bottom shelf held my father's complete blue leather set of the *Maritime Encyclopaedia*, along with lexicons and books on navigation. Djordjević also sold her the huge dining table, along with six chairs. Before leaving for America, he gave her a lamp with a yellow caoutchouc lampshade. It stands on my desk. Under the glass desktop is a map of the world. The city of Akron, Ohio, where the lawyer Djordjević now lives, is not on it.

Whenever Maleša comes to dinner, the same stories are always told. That's to drum in the moral of the tale. Unlike my father, my mother knows the other side of the coin. She doesn't see any difference between pre-war reactionaries and today's communists. The watchmaker shares her opinion.

"History is the story of property," he says. "It's all about the spoils."

The watchmaker Maleša has a bird-dog named Dis, from a litter belonging to the Queen of England. I can't figure out how the dog got here all the way from England. Or how the watchmaker, whose father belonged to pre-war reactionary circles, now goes to Brioni to fix Tito's clocks.

"Wealth is indestructible, it just moves around, like dust," says Maleša. "You can remove dust as much as you like, it's always around somewhere. It's the same with wealth. It just moves somewhere else."

"Those fifteen days at the residence in Paris were enough for me to see that nothing, absolutely nothing, has changed, it has simply moved somewhere else," my mother says, and then, after waiting to see my father's reaction — because it is he who pays the price of the regime's anomalies and injustices — she returns to her stay with Irina, her old schoolmate and now the wife of the Yugoslav ambassador to France. "All those family jewels, portraits, rugs. If I didn't know the miserable poverty she grew up in, I might even believe her. But how can you expect anything to change when it all comes from the top. It makes me sick when I hear them say *in the name of the people*. Penniless communists have become collectors. Lizeta put it well: some people are happy in houses that aren't theirs."

"Lizeta was one of my first clients," the watchmaker says. "More than once I found her buyers for her clocks. People say all sorts of things about her. She could have lost her life because of the Hiterots."

"That's because she knows where the riches from Red Island were taken," my mother says. "Where the baroness's curtains are now billowing. Who is driving her limousine…"

She pauses for a second; she's spotted me standing at the door, listening to their conversation. She tells me to go out and play with my sister and Dis. These stories are not for children.

I remember sitting with my parents and sister around the radio one evening. Tito was giving an interview to the Americans. Asked if Yugoslavia would change its flag, Tito says firmly that the nations and nationalities of Yugoslavia had fought under this flag, that many fighters had laid down their lives for it, and that therefore the flag would not be changed. My parents' faces light up. "Good answer," they say in unison.

The world is monolithic to the mind of a ten-year-old. I share my parents' enthusiasm for Tito's response. The vandalised train carriage in Vinkovci has yet to cast a pall on the scene. I don't know anything beyond the story I inhabit.

What world did my parents belong to? It all looks so sad from today's perspective. Sad that a little boy can naively believe that justice exists. A banal statement by the sovereign is elevated to the status of profound wisdom. The little family assembled around the radio has demonstrated its loyalty. For the moment, the heresy of socialising with the watchmaker Maleša is swept under the carpet. We have no past. There are no unpaid bills or dirty money in our house. We have a clear conscience. We will not change the flag.

For three years, I share a bench in primary school with Hrz Avdo. His father has a shop for shining and dyeing shoes. It is one of a string of shoeshine and umbrella repair shops in the steep street that leads to People's Square. Lizeta calls the square Piazza Verdi. She doesn't call even my school by its real name, "Moše Pijade". She calls it "Dante Alighieri".

Hrz Avdo bites his nails. He is tense and silent. A poor student. He still spells out his letters. One winter, when he falls ill, I go for several days running to see him after school. Avdo is slow when copying out his lessons. A little courtyard separates his father's shop from the flat where the large Hrz family lives. They come from Sandžak*. I remember the big red enamel pots with white polka dots, standing on the kitchen stove. And the colourful scatter rugs. They walked around the house in their socks.

Years later, every day on my way to high school, I pass by the steep street where the shoeshine and umbrella repair shops used to be. With the demise of the shoe dyeing trade, that little colony of people from Sandžak dispersed across Istria, taking up other kinds of work.

I go to my friends' houses. The world outside the Villa Maria is expanding.

Storelli Mario, whose family had opted not to go to Italy after the Anglo-American administration departed, lives in a huge flat in Omladinska Street. His father is a model constructor at the shipyard. Within a few hundred square meters, I discover a world very different from the Hrz family's. Another civilization. There are no awkward silences like in the Hrz household, no void left by the unsaid. Could it perhaps be because of the Italian language's long vowels which sound cheerful even when quarrelling? Or because of the music that is constantly playing on the radio?

Wherever I go, I immerse myself in the intonations, gestures, smiles, shadows, placement of things, looks, smells, words. Many years later, when my country was disintegrating and the middle class, with all its very different worlds, was

---

* A region in Serbia and Montenegro where a plurality of people identify as Bosniaks

gradually disappearing, I would decipher this entire period from the impressions archived in my memory. Archives holding essential facts that had not been deciphered for decades. The boy's memory preserved the originals, unadulterated by sterile interpretation, and, thus protected, it carried them through time, until, when the moment came, another brain could connect all these once unimportant impressions and turn them into a coherent picture of a bygone time.

The invisible foundations on which such different lives flourished were crucial for the survival of that world. Legacies, legends, centuries-old traditions, personal histories – plunged into a socialist reality whose rituals and propaganda held that world together – bubbled under the surface of everyday life. Not only in my city, but across the country, small family factories were producing values and illusions night and day. Hidden in the false myths were the failed lives of the weak and the unhappy. Always looking for those to blame, they consoled themselves by complaining to the wrong address. And though they all had skeletons in their closets, they obstinately kept counting the minutes of the Renaissance and the Baroque in their God-forsaken backwaters, celebrating defeats and counting the centuries of celestial life, constantly arguing over where life was lived *à la mitteleuropa* and where *alla turca*. Anxiety and fear filled the heads of children.

The worlds intermingled.

I summon up the names of the children in my class. Their last names, then their first names, the way they were listed in the attendance book.

Baf Mirela. Her long legs had caught my eye. She was the first girl who sexually aroused me. In eighth grade she moved to Dubrovnik. I dreamed of us moving somewhere too. Of discovering a new milieu. In my mind, I would walk the streets of Rijeka, climb the steps of Trsat and look out from the fortress at the ships in the port.

Bućan Boško. I just remember the sound of his name, his ruddy cheeks and his green schoolbag which he always dragged along with him. I can't remember his face. His father was a tailor in Prvomajska Street. Later they too left Pula.

Suton Dolores, Rosanda Denis, Recchiuto Sergio, Piton Vesna, Pugar Goran, the Alfeldi sisters...

The Alfeldi twins, Noemi and Doris. They lived in one of the alleyways between Gupčeva and Kandler Streets. Their father was Hungarian. We were in the same class for four years. Whenever they planned to cheat, they would come to school identically dressed. While the teacher was writing down the mark in his gradebook, they would quickly swap places, and it was always the twin who had studied for the lesson who went up to the blackboard.

It was with them that I smoked my first cigarette. Later we chewed a laurel leaf to mask the smell. One evening, during summer vacation, I had my first kiss by the wall of the fortress designed by de Ville. Was it with Noemi? Or with Doris? I never found out. Because, the next evening, when we were playing hide-and-seek and I went up to one of them thinking it was her I had kissed, she began to scream. I pulled away, embarrassed and scared. That autumn the Alfeldi sisters left for the school at Monte Zaro. We didn't see each other anymore. I no longer passed down their street. With time, they vanished from my horizon.

Forty years later, on a March afternoon, I arrive in Kecskemét Street, my first address in Budapest. On the ground floor of the building is the *Alfeldi* restaurant. Its walls are covered with framed photographs of its famous customers. Of the hundreds of faces, the only one I recognise is my writer friend István Eörsi. The others are all part of an era defined by a small circle traced on a map of the city: *Budapest's Best Restaurants*. Just like the ghosts on the walls of Lizeta's room – the inhabitants of Salonica a hundred years ago.

The instant one's consciousness is compressed, distances briefly disappear and the whole of existence is condensed into a single point; the living and the dead float in the infinity of the present. There then comes a moment when the entire journey travelled appears in one chunk, and no matter how long the future lasts, the circle is closed, the story told. Nothing of importance can be changed anymore. The paths are traced in advance. It could not be otherwise.

In my mind, I visit the places that my parents had mentioned only in passing. Maps of their lives before they met. The legacy of a whole geography. I detected, by sound as well as by sight, their commas and question marks, parentheses and footnotes, the secret syntax where they hid their unfulfilled lives. After carrying out their biological duties, they remained prisoners of untold stories, powerless to establish a closer relationship with their children.

A scene from a Melville film: a windy autumn afternoon on the waterfront in Pula; my father, in a trench coat and hat, is showing me where the landing ship that had first brought him here had stopped. I remember the scene in black-and-white. But something much more than words, looks and gestures etched itself into the consciousness of the boy who had just started school. The next frame during my walk with my father shows the windows of the flat in Omladinska St, where he'd rented a room from an Italian woman. The soundtrack for this image is one of profound silence. The place has survived, intact, for half a century. The only thing that must have changed is the interior of the flat behind the large first floor windows, where I think traces of my father's presence must still exist.

It is around then that my mother comes to Pula for the first time as well. It amuses me to think that they might have passed one another in the street before she returned to Rijeka that same day. The bus breaking down on the road, then the drive in Baroness Hiterot's car, the stop-over at the little inn in Raša, the secret service men. Four years later, they are both in Selce, my father in a new post and my mother as the head of a school holiday centre. They have yet to meet.

I reach the age they were when I lost interest in them. Everything possible had already happened to them. Their lives were reduced to the simple repetition of rituals. Every gesture, every thought, had its well-honed continuator. For the two of them, living in a small flat, full of bulky armchairs and shelves and dressers and lamps, with thick carpets and tapestry pictures on the walls, was like living in a cupboard. Since nothing was thrown away, the flat looked smaller and smaller with every passing day.

Like his father before him, my father buttoned his shirt all the way up to the top. The wrinkled skin of his neck hung over the collar. Under his chin you could see the spots that had escaped his razor. When talking, my mother would scoop up invisible crumbs from the table with her hand. Whenever she reprimanded me, she would purse her lips in restrained anger, glare at me for a few seconds, and then, with an air of resignation, nod her head and wryly smile.

Superficial and disinterested as I was, I thought that these were signs of old age. Today I know that they were simply trying to tell me something before they departed for the other world. I should have been patient, I should have waited for the deep images to surface, like during that windy afternoon with my father on the promenade in Pula. I should have let them confess.

After all these years, I now possess long measurements of time. When I shut my eyes, I can imagine ten, twenty, thirty years. I have in me exactly five octaves, sixty keys, six decades of a life lived. What an impressive keyboard! I easily encompass half a century. I can clearly see that morning at the Pula railway station, when my mother, father, sister and I stepped off the *wagon lit* of the train from Belgrade. The same stretch of time links that November morning to me today, and the inhabitants of Pula to the start of the twentieth century. Large blocks of time open up – pontoon bridges across which I can reach any distance that comes to mind.

There, at the beginning of the twentieth century, James Joyce is walking along Campo Martio on his way from his flat in Via Medulino to the Berlitz School in Piazza Porta Aurea. He passes by houses that half a century later will be home to shoeshine shops. The buildings in Grafton Street flash by in his mind's eye as he tries to remember people from his childhood in Dublin.

The same time distance, but now all the way south, in Salonica, the sepia city. Little Lizeta is gazing out at the bustling city from the window of the family hotel in the French quarter. The tram appears for a few seconds between the Elias Moreno department store and the Odeon cinema. She isn't allowed to play with the local children in the park next to the Bara district. She is the little girl at the window. A few years later, she will leave her hometown for Mrs. Haslinger's boarding school in Vienna's eighteenth district. There she will have another observation post, the dormitory's tall window, overlooking the pleasant landscape and serenity of the elegant outskirts, a serenity broken periodically by the bell of the number 38 tram to Grinzig. Then, there are the windows of her relatives' flat in Servola, a suburb of Trieste. Her first experience of falling in love. Everyday life now unfolds in wide shots, but the frames remain the same. Even the years of an indiscriminate life with Barbara Hiterot in Trieste, Red Island, Brioni and Opatija fail to dislodge the shadow of the observer. In the mid-thirties of the twentieth century, Lizeta again takes up her post at the window, this time in a modest flat in Veruda, opposite the Naval Park, where the tram track follows the wall of the Arsenal before turning towards San Policarpo. And finally, the last observation post, on the second floor of the house at the foot of the Kaštel wall. Lizeta Benedetti, married name Bizjak, a tireless observer of life. The woman at the window. The first in Gupčeva Street to own a television set.

How do I know all these details? So many remembered toponyms? Is it possible that I remember everything from our strolls through the streets of Salonica, when Lizeta would fill the gaps between two photographs with the name of a store, a restaurant, a hotel? She would draw squares and streets on invisible maps. Not only had I not forgotten anything, but with the passage of time, more and more details emerged. Memory reproduced itself.

The frozen image in the photograph taken at the seaside was enlivened with a flow of words, conjuring up the road that runs along the port towards the White Tower, or, on the other side, towards the train station. It brought to life various scenes. The fiacre with her as a three-year-old sitting on her father's lap. She shows me where the wide pathway in the Bechtsinar Gardens ends, the pathway where she is talking to two girls, classmates from music school. And so this spectral sepia-toned city, this magical Salonica, came to occupy more and more space, filling the blank gaps on the wall of Lizeta's room with imaginary scenes.

We would continue our stroll on the other wall, where time suddenly accelerated. The girls from Mrs. Haslinger's boarding school in Schönbrunn. Ten years later, the platform of the tram to Bagni. Standing next to Lizeta, a young man in uniform.

"That's me with Giorgio in Trieste," she says, quickly moving on to the next photograph, taken on the terrace of the Adriatik hotel in Rovinj. "That's Barbara, her cousin Bruno and me."

I don't know who Giorgio is. Or Barbara. Or Bruno. I am just a silent partner on these strolls, a witness that it was all true, regardless of whether the story unfolds in Greek, Italian or Croatian. At the end of the series of photographs, I recognise the intersection at Veruda. She points to the house where she lived. She says that the tram used to pass by there on its way to San Policarpo.

When I project the half-century of time towards the future, towards the space inhabited by my son's life, where at some point I will depart from this world, the acceleration is so fast that I forget everyday things and objects. Now I understand my mother and why, at one of our last meetings, the appearance of a small leather suitcase moved her to tears. That morning, what emerged in the whiteness of her memory was a travel accessory from her trips as a young girl.

"Amazing how things suddenly disappear. I bought that suitcase, imported from Belgium, in Sušak, before that other war. It must have disappeared along with the things they stole in Vinkovci. But I can't swear to it."

8.

There were always lots of words in our house. An overabundance of words and sentences. Whole paragraphs that once belonged to someone somewhere. Fallen from the frontage of someone else's life. My mother would shower words upon whomever she was talking to. She was a collector of hundreds of replies – that is how she remembered the people who had said them.

"Nothing happens by chance. Even something bad can lead to something good. Lizeta was right when she said: when a door closes, a window opens."

She would stop for a second, as if searching her mind for that opening window. I can see her walking around the flat, and later in the corridors of the care home, looking for a sentence that would make her happy, that would always make her see the bright side of things. She never allowed herself to become despondent. She was convinced that weakness harboured all sorts of evils.

During her brief quarrels with my father – he was usually her punching ball – she would come out with the most incredible arguments and always had a ready answer. An actress who was just waiting for a propitious opportunity to come out with a monologue from a play that had long since been taken off the repertoire.

My sister and I are sitting at a little table, each of us with a picture book, each of us still. Porcelain figures. That's how we look in most photographs from those days.

"How can you always be so flustered? Don't you see anything at all?" my mother says. "Me, as soon as I come somewhere, it takes me just a second to read the situation, to register people's habits. Everybody would want somebody like me for a guest."

"Only for a guest," my father observes ironically.

"My, aren't we witty!" my mother says, launching into a tirade. The reasons were always banal: a glass left on a polished table without a coaster, a cigarette butt left burning in the ashtray, suds on the rim of the sink.

Any trace annoyed her. A witness to a presence. You had to step away silently from where you'd been. She was the cleaner of traces. An Indian warrior who marched in the middle of the stream to cover her own tracks. She liked going to cemeteries; there life was finally buried. Graves aroused in her a hidden joy, an awareness of the triumph of order over the confusion of life. Birth and death certificates were the only reliable testimonies. Everything in between — one's life on earth — was nothing but great suffering which could be endured by constantly deferring it. My mother lived a deferred life. Which is why she never carried out a single big plan, be it a trip to California to see her best friend from her youth or filling the photo albums that for years languished in the wardrobe, still in their cellophane wrapping, next to a dozen boxes stuffed with photographs.

My mother was a past master at postponement. A prisoner of rituals. Twice a year, for New Year and before the summer, she would open the trunk containing the toys and clothes that regularly arrived in huge packages from California. They were little family celebrations during which my sister and I would each be given a few toys. We were eager to see what else was hidden in the trunk. However, my mother believed that the best way to develop a sense of values in children was to show them that they couldn't have everything they wanted. There always had to be something they couldn't have.

Slow to make big decisions, she was quick to fulfil her daily duties. The one clashed with the other. Unless her zeal in everyday matters was merely an alibi for her lack of resourcefulness in life? The thousands of photographs kept in the boxes were convincing proof that life had, after all, been lived to the full. Smiling faces and embraces testified to a full life, a life of pleasures and joy.

Whenever we arrived in a town, my mother would remind my sister and me of some distant relatives who were no longer alive. That was an excuse to go to the cemetery. There we were free. She would let us roam among the graves. We would stop in front of family tombs, admire the marble, stone and plaster statues and the ornate wrought-iron railings.

"What a family!" she would say to herself. "Who says there is no such thing as eternity?"

My sister and I would gaze at the porcelain photographs. We amused ourselves by reading the unusual names, looking for who was the oldest. We competed to see which of us would be the first to find someone a hundred years old. But when we passed by the graves of children it was in silence; there we did not stop.

At the cemetery, my mother was relaxed, free of the tension that kept her slight body atremble. A constantly running engine.

I remember the cemetery in Varaždin, the tall cypress trees and the flowering magnolias, the geometrically shaped boxwood, the statues of angels.

"Like in Versailles," my mother sighed.

When we went to Rijeka, to visit my father on the ship, we always went to the cemetery in Trsat. For a long time, I thought that we had relatives buried there. In Split, we walked every day on the southern side of Marjan hill, all the way to the cemetery in Sustipan. A few years later, the cemetery was gone. They told us it had been moved outside the city.

"Terrible," my mother said with a shiver, "to be buried twice. See? Even the dead die."

Hidden behind her cheerfulness was a loneliness.

She was constantly looking for a story. That is how she forged her friendships. One of the most important was with the Milićes, a retired couple who spent their days making reproductions of tapestries. I never learned how they met, but one evening, my mother walked through the door talking excitedly about these magnificent tapestry pictures.

"You must see them; it's like a miniature Louvre. Velasquez, Goya, Rembrandt. Wiehler's tapestry picture of The Four Seasons. Mythological scenes embroidered in thirty-six shades of blue."

She developed a passion for collecting. After every visit to the Milićes, the walls of our flat would be covered with more of their ghastly creations in gilded plaster frames. She bought them at a very reasonable price, payable in instalments over several months. It must be said, however, that in those times of general poverty, the Milićes would have been hard put to find many customers. They gave her their latest works without asking for a deposit. When my father returned from one of his voyages, the Milićes were paid what they were owed but the rampant buying continued. A series of scenes by Dutch masters made their way into the room I shared with my sister. I have the Milićes to thank for waking up to Vermeer every morning. The first thing I saw when I opened my eyes was *View of Delft*.

My mother was quite cultured. She read, she went to the theatre. But her taste in paintings wasn't exactly the best. Aesthetically speaking, that was her weak point. In fact, she did not understand paintings at all. She sold a Kolesnikoff landscape for a song, the only painting we had in our flat – a present from the lawyer Djordjević before he left for America – so that she could buy a series of still life tapestry pictures... She was convinced that, with time, the value of her collection would only grow. Which made her disappointment all the greater when a Rijeka antiques dealer told her that no one was buying tapestry pictures anymore, they had fallen out of fashion.

When we moved to our new flat in Veruda, some of the tapestry pictures remained in the trunks. There were no high walls or long hallways, like in Villa Maria, where my mother could hang her whole collection. Years later, with the disintegration of the country and our return to Belgrade, the tapestry pictures, like so many other things, disappeared. Only the series of mythological scenes in thirty-six shades of blue was preserved.

When my parents left Pula in October 1991, they entrusted the keys of our summer cottage in Pomer to the Milićes, who had spontaneously offered to take care of the house and pay the bills. "Nothing is as strong as our friendship," they repeated as we left.

The siege of Vukovar was in full swing. War was raging in Slavonia and Lika. Our trip back to Belgrade, via Skopje, took a full two days.

A year later, the Milićes returned the keys to our cottage via someone who was passing through Belgrade. In a short letter, they told us that at the moment it was dangerous to take care of a Serbian house in Croatia. My mother saw the return of the keys as a betrayal of a long-standing friendship. When I asked her why she hadn't given the keys to the watchmaker Maleša instead, she replied that he had been away on a trip at the time. Anyway, the Milićes themselves had offered to take over the keys, and plus they were Croats.

Refugees moved into abandoned Serbian houses, obtaining the addresses from the police. A volunteer from the Slavonian battlefront installed himself in our house. My mother would wake up in the middle of the night, imagining herself following the intruder as he rummaged through the wardrobes and dressers. Everything was strewn about. And while houses were in flames in Slavonia, she was worrying about her porcelain in the china cabinet in Pomer. She couldn't forgive herself for not taking to Belgrade the cobalt blue figurine of the violinist that she had bought in an antiques shop in Sušak before that other war.

The break-in into our train carriage in Vinkovci had preceded our arrival in the city where I would spend my childhood and youth. With our departure from Pula, the intruder in our summer house simply marked a logical end to the cycle.

Everybody had to be somewhere. Only it was better if that "somewhere" was where they came from.

I wasn't angry at the Milićes. They belonged to that vast majority of people, the connective tissue of every society, who behave in the same way at all times and on all sides; they were the people who let the war happen; they make themselves out to be the ones who have to suffer events, whereas in fact, by doing nothing, it is they who engender them; by not participating, they participate in their advent.

And what does the petit bourgeois do? Instead of broadening the context, he narrows it. He believes that he can distance himself from the turbulence of history, protect his four walls, his bank account, the geraniums on his windowsill, and that this has nothing to do with the people starving in Africa or climate change, with the Milky Way or the neighbour who was taken away the previous night by unknown men.

Life had picked up speed. An era was on its last legs. Yesterday had become increasingly vast. People counted less in months and years. The unit of measure was now a decade or two. A lived life greatly reduced the territory of tomorrow. Palimpsests of past lives surfaced. Geography had changed in the blink of an eye.

The border on the Riječina River, which, when my parents were young, had been the dividing line between Sušak and Rijeka, between the Kingdom of Yugoslavia and Italy, between this world and that world, moved far back to the east.

As my father and mother aged, so the state shrank. And I was reaching an age which, for me, marked the beginning of my parents' declining years.

After my father's death, my mother gradually descended into dementia. Her speech became rambling. When she moved to the care home, she thought she had left Belgrade. She started using *ijekavian** when she spoke. When I visited her, she would often urge me to leave so that I wouldn't miss my train. In her mind, she had moved from one city to another. The last time I saw her she was living in Rijeka. She had partly adopted the city's dialect. She asked me when I was going back to Belgrade. What hotel I was staying at.

As I was leaving, she took my hand and said: "The next time you come, don't forget to bring my notebook. It has the addresses of all the hotels. I can't travel anywhere without it."

---

* A dialect spoken in Croatia, Bosnia-Herzegovina, Montenegro and parts of Serbia.

9.

"To visit the past is to constantly improve upon it, invoke it and live it, but because we *read* it in the traces it has left, and these traces depend on chance, on the more or less fragile material in which it is communicated, on different events in time, that past is then chaotic, random, fragmentary...I know nothing about one of my great-grandmothers, not her face, or her character, or her life, nothing, except that on 16 June 1669 she bought two ells of cotton and ginger. All that is left of her is a yellowed piece of paper covered with numbers and figures, and a note in the margin asking Mr. Szolt to buy two ells of cotton and ginger when he returns from Remigole. Ginger and cotton, just that, nothing else," writes Witold Gombrowicz in his diary.

10.

In May 2012, I spent a week in Salonica. I arrived in the late afternoon and stayed at the Luxembourg Hotel. I took the hotel brochure from the reception desk for my collection – a residual of my mother's penchant or her mythical notebook stolen in Vinkovci.

For years I dreamed of writing a novel about hotels. I wanted to reconstruct the itinerary of where I had stayed in these places of dislocation, places where we stop repeating our daily routine defined by old habits. No friends and family around, no familiar objects. A step into the unknown, where at any moment there might be an encounter that will open the door to a completely different life. A hotel is a place of anticipation and inspiration, life in the false bottom of fantasy. For just a while, one lives in the interim. It is not by chance that people who live double lives in novels are people who travel a lot – travelling salespeople. For them, the temporary is permanent.

I had only just left another hotel, to be precise, my novel *Bonavia*, where the story ends in the hotel of the same name and where I was probably conceived. I can still see the setting where I spent four years writing *Bonavia*. When I arrived in Salonica I wanted to discard as quickly as possible all this material which continued to steer my thoughts down a beaten track, where familiar situations awaited me. I yearned for other impressions and experiences so that I could slowly lay the ground for my next novel. I hadn't the slightest idea what it might be, but I was sure that at some moment it would come to me of itself.

When I stepped onto the balcony of my room on the third floor, the streetlights were already peeking through the mandarin and citrus trees. The town was settling down in the warmth of the vernal night. From the nearby outdoor cafés came the soft murmurings of the evening. To the right, you could hear the noise of the cars and the siren of an ambulance on one of Salonica's main streets, where the taxi I had picked up at the airport had taken me only half an hour earlier. And completely to the left, you could see the purple outlines of the gulf. Around there was also a piece of the seaside where, about a hundred years ago, dense rows of sailing ships had rocked in the water.

Suddenly, the wall of Lizeta's room emerged from the darkness like the bow of a ship: scenes of Salonica from the sepia postcards, black-and-white photographs of family gatherings, idyllic scenes from photography studios, the rough faces of ancestors wearing fezzes and hats. I lifted my arms as if to sweep aside the scenery of the houses, turn the pocket of time inside out in one fell swoop, and in the empty space once bordered by the Odeon cinema and Elias Moreno's department store, extend the stage across the whole of the Ladadika district. The inventory of the childhood of Lizeta Bizjak, née Benedetti, is to be found here: Jewish children from the neighbourhood, bearing two names, Sunday strolls in the Bechtsinar gardens, tram rides from the customs house to the White Tower, crowds of people at the Kapana market, afternoons at the music school in Kuskura Street.

A century later, it is the same indivisible space, separated by transparent rings of time, its existence indestructible. And yet, the chemical composition of the air in 2012 is not the same as it was at the beginning of the 20th century, when somewhere here, a mere hundred or so metres away from where the Luxembourg hotel stands today, little Lizeta was standing on the balcony of the Xenodochion Egnatia family hotel. The background sound is different as well: the dull, constant noise from the foundry by the seafront; the whistle of the train at the railway station; the tram wending its way along the narrow streets; the hustle and bustle around the stalls on the wooden walkways in front of the tightly packed shops. And the smells? What would Professor Barić say? It smelled as bad as in the Middle Ages. If we ride in horse-drawn carriages, if the horse-drawn tram passes through town, there must be stables somewhere nearby. Hay is brought in, and manure taken out, I hear the professor's raspy voice saying in the Salonica night. When Lizeta was a child, not all the houses had plumbing or water yet. The city walls had just been destroyed; the air was still fetid. Smells came from the slaughterhouse and tannery, from the cattle market, from the fish market in the port.

I wander through the streets of Salonica like a spy. I stop at street corners, run my eyes over the facades of the build-ings, read the names of the streets: Dodekanisu, Spondoni, Rogoti, Egnatia, Ermu, Salaminos, Mitropoleos, Frangon, Esopu... I turn around and try to remember the way I had come. I go back to my hotel several times in the course of the evening and then, fortified by my experience, I step away, widening the circle, moving increasingly westwards, to where, before the great fire of 1917, the notorious Bara district had once been, a great anthill of bygone streets, the Egyptian market, the Bechtsinar gardens and the Vardar Gate.

I can distinctly hear Lizeta's voice, the words that seem to be rustling through the leaves of afternoons spent with her in the early sixties of the last century. Dislodged from the everyday, from the lull of rituals, I can see my own life more clearly, with the dispassionate eye of a pathologist. The past is ever deeper, the future ever shallower.

During that week in Salonica, presenting the Greek edition of my book *The Russian Window* at the Book Fair, I gave an interview to a journalist who kept insisting on autobiographical details, wanting to know the degree to which the book's protagonist, Rudi Stupar, was my alter ego. To avoid repeating myself, to pull free from the power of sterile mystification, I rummaged through my past in search of images and words, but all I found were painful episodes from my own adolescence.

Later, alone in the café, still under the impression of these suppressed scenes, I asked myself what the most important thing in my life had been.

To live different existences simultaneously. That is why I write, because it is the only way that I can access these lives and indirectly live them.

Why do you occupy yourself with these imagined lives? Why do you imagine them at all? Isn't it more logical to delve into your own inner self? Have you lost touch with real life? Why this taboo about looking at your own life? And what are the consequences?

A missed life.

Slow down. Beware of big words, they are here to camouflage. Anyway, even a missed life is a kind of life. No distance is big enough to take that big a leap. Life is too broad a notion.

A missed youth?

That is something you can examine. But the crux of it lies deeper than that. It goes back to your childhood. Somebody took away your right to dwell on your own thoughts; somebody separated you from yourself. Hence, this escape into parallel, imagined lives. You refused to live your own life. You were under the thumb of your mother's strict ideas about upbringing. That boy from upstairs in the Villa Maria split himself into two and fled to the cellar, to the exile of the laundry room. Do you remember all the dreams you had, sitting between the cauldron and the sink?

I fantasised that I was adopted. I dreamed of a mother like Lizeta. Of the wall in Lizeta's room telling my story. Those seven days with Lizeta while my mother and sister were in Zagreb were for me an oasis of freedom. Without anxiety and without discipline. It left a deep mark on me, the knowledge that life could be so carefree.

Lizeta. What do you think of when you say her name?

Of goodness. Without reservation. No false bottom. Everything is as it appears and as it is said.

And your mother? What is the first thing you think of?

Caution. That's how we were raised, my sister and I. That nothing is as it seems, that the world is fraught with danger, that deceit lurks in every corner. That it is a sin to be naive. And that our intelligence serves to discover people's real intentions on time.

And then a breather. A week with Lizeta. No taboos, no admonishments. Like in a blissful dream. And then, the return home.

An invisible weight bore down on me.

Later you tore down the walls. Your mother retreated, she stopped forbidding you and your sister from doing anything.

My mother's world was a world of imps. When my sister and I grew up, that world collapsed all on its own. It was fragile because it did not belong to a higher order. My mother's strictness was due to her fear of the world. She used discipline to try to obtain what she did not have in her life. Love, above all else. In the end, she wound up alone.

Everyone winds up alone in the end.

No, no. It is not the loneliness of a wasted life. It is the loneliness of a substitute life.

You then became your own mother. You pushed away everything profound and pure, you pushed away emotion. That is why you are always justifying yourself. You hold in reserve a ready answer to explain every intention. Forever the accused. Stop putting yourself on trial.

I left the café and headed west, in the direction of Zeitenlik. I crossed Vardaris Square and walked down the long stretch of Lagada Street, towards the military cemetery mentioned by my grandfather. He was once part of a delegation of veterans of the Salonica front who had come to lay a wreath at the Memorial to Serbian soldiers. He talked about Salonica, which, half a century later, he couldn't recognise. This was not the city where he had spent four months upon his return from the hospital in Bizerte.

And so, on that warm May afternoon, we walk, my grandfather and I, along the city's endless Lagada Street. Life is much more than daily obligations and senseless activities, than documents and testimonies, trials, legacies and conspiracies. My grandfather, a marginal figure in my childhood, as was his son, my father, suddenly grabs my attention. I grew up and was raised in a matriarchy. That is why I have this need to compensate for the absence of a male figure. Asymmetry developed certain instincts. There where I should be weak, I became strong. Endowed with prudence, patience, perceptiveness, all the traits missing in my male ancestors. I am the unifying descendent, the one who corrects the genetics.

I see the stiff index finger of my grandfather Milan, a corporal in the Serbian army, who, before breaching the Salonica front, spent four months under military tents somewhere here on Salonica's shore. So, this is not the first time I am in this city. There are traces of our DNA wherever our ancestors passed by. I wonder, as I walk, what destiny had in store for this corporal who all his life carried a pocketknife with him, using it to cut bread into symmetrical squares before putting them into his mouth one by one, and then slowly chewing them. At the mention of the Turks, his face would suddenly darken and his eyes would flash. My grandfather's first experience of abroad was during the Balkan wars. Then came Albania, when Serbian troops made that insane crossing of the Prokletija Mountains, just to avoid a capitulation that no one wanted to sign.

Talk about sticking your head in the sand, running away from reality, the inability to face the given situation! Shifting the responsibility onto our ancestors who speak through us, for whom we are simply a resonant voice box transmitting their words, has become a recognizable way of encamping the *nation* outside the realm of reality. Of living in a myth, camouflaging cowardice with madness, squandering the future of our descendants. Of atavism surviving in doctors of science, historians, politicians, writers, sculptors and *yurodivy*, or holy fools.

The people stayed in Serbia that tragic year of 1915. After crossing Prokletija in the snow and ice, half-dead, starving, frozen, wounded by Albanian tribes, Serbian troops reached the sea, at Durrës and Vlorë. It would be some time before the allies, indecisive and unprepared, had them transferred to Corfu and Bizerte. Thousands of them would die of typhus and exhaustion in the hospital on the island of Vido, just off the coast of Corfu. They were buried in the depths of the

Ionian Sea. For half a century Greek fisherman avoided the area.

There exists an anthological photograph from 1915 of King Peter of Serbia, affectionately known by the people as Pera, sitting on an ox-drawn cart in a camp. When the American film director John Ford saw it fifty years later, he decided to make a movie about the saga of the Serbian army. Negotiations with the Yugoslav authorities didn't get anywhere because rather than this Albania story, they proposed that he make a movie about one of the partisan offensives during World War II instead. In the end, the celebrated director abandoned the project. A quarter of a century later, Serbia gambled away all the historical points it had scored in two centuries of fighting for its independence. For the first time, it was not on the right side; rather it followed a false Messiah into the darkness of violence and crime.

I remember my grandfather appearing one autumn like a ghost in our Villa Maria flat, carrying a crate of grapes from Sićevo. He had travelled all night. My sister and I were awoken early in the morning by the sound of his voice. Still sleepy, we ran into his waiting arms. Rigid, a man of few words, his eyes gleamed with joy. Timidly, I touched the white scar on his stiff right index finger. He smiled, saying it was a souvenir from the Salonica front.

He was entitled to travel on the train for free. He would often appear unannounced, spend a few days with us, and then take the night train back to Belgrade, and continue on to Niš and Sićevo. He wouldn't let anyone accompany him. Once the watchmaker Maleša drove him to the train, because it was raining and very windy. Afterwards he told us that my grandfather had arrived at the station a whole two hours ahead of time. I am the same – I spend hours roaming around airports and train stations, waiting to leave.

That afternoon at the Zeitenlik cemetery, where the Serbian army's main field hospital once stood, I walk among the graves, reading the names of the dead soldiers. Živojin Janković from Lučani, plot 723, private in the 4th company of the 1st battalion of the Timok regiment. In the next row, under number 703, Danilo Radojčević from Sićevo, reservist soldier. Behind each number lies a story. Most of them untold. I tried to imagine them during those walks in the cemeteries, when my sister and I competed to see who would discover the most centenarians, while my mother looked for the grave of some alleged relative. As I wandered down the gravelled paths in Sustipan, Trsat, Sremska Kamenica, Varaždin, using just the names and dates of birth inscribed on the marble stones, I made up stories about them, I invented their lives. Wherever we go, we are already stepping upon the territory of other people's lives.

There are no centenarians in Zeitenlik. The graves hold only interrupted stories.

Buried here in this garden of marble crosses is Toša Zaka from Vršac, an Austro-Hungarian soldier who was taken prisoner on the Russian front. My grandfather told me his story a number of times. They were in the hospital in Zeitenlik together. Toša surrendered to the Russians in Galicia, ended up a prisoner, and then in Odessa joined the 1st Serbian Division of Volunteers. With the outbreak of the revolution in Russia, transport on the Salonica Front went via Siberia all the way to Vladivostok, Port Arthur, Singapore, and then through the Suez Canal to Alexandria, and finally to Salonica. My grandfather often mentioned the sites of Toša's adventures. I remembered the names and later would say them out loud, breaking them up into syllables: Vla-di-vos-tok. Sin-ga-pore. A-lex-an-dri-a. That was my way of entering these cities. I made my way between the syllables into the obscurity of unfamiliar streets and squares, came to river-banks, strolled along endless promenades. All I needed to travel was the name of the city, the touch of hard consonants and big vowels.

"What a trip!" my grandfather would sigh. "And then you end up in Zeitenlik. Toša's wound didn't look too bad at first. Mine was much worse. They barely managed to save my limb from the shell fragment in my lower leg. Toša was quicker to recover. And then, suddenly, he didn't feel well. The light in him died out like a candle. To cross the whole of Asia only to wind up in Zeitenlik. What a fate!"

The next day, I spend the whole morning under the arches of the Modiano market. Built after the great fire of 1917, it certainly wasn't etched in Lizeta's memory. Outside the main building of the market are rows of stalls selling souvenirs and Chinese ware. All the way in the back, I come upon a flea market. All sorts of things discovered in attics and basements are laid out on a long counter under an awning. Figurines, medals, porcelain plates, crystal glasses, silverware, com-passes, candle holders, tapestry pictures, lamps, covers, jewellery, daggers, wristwatches. There is a box containing bundles of letters, old photographs, postcards, maps, various documents. Some of the photographs are mounted. I pick up a rectangular framed photograph. Under the dirty glass, three girls are in a fake boat in the photographer's studio.

Fotographion Thanasis, Thessaloniki.

On the back of the photograph, a few handwritten lines. The ink has almost faded, only the odd word is legible. It is in French. Reading my mind, the vendor hands me a magnifying glass. I slide it slowly across the text. I understand only the first word: *Salonique*. The date is blurred and the only word I can decipher is *juillet* and the date 1908. I briefly ponder whether I should buy the photograph. Because, after half a century I have finally arrived in the sepia-toned city from the wall of Lizeta's room. At the time, she was a little girl, like the three in the fake boat. Maybe they knew each other? Attended the same school? Played in the Bechtsinar Gardens? Or merely crossed paths when strolling along the seaside promenade?

Three smiling little girls, who had long since passed on to a better life. I decide against it. I put the photograph back in the box and return the magnifying glass to the vendor. I quickly leave the market. However, the uneasy feeling aroused by the indistinct faces of the three little girls in the photograph stays with me. It is still there even half an hour later, when I am sitting at the terrace of the Negroponte restaurant in the Ladadika quarter. Strangely, whomever I ask about the Bechtsinar Gardens just shrugs their shoulders. Lizeta surely didn't invent them. I must have misremembered the name of the park. After half a century, all of Salonica's toponyms from Lizeta's wall have become so modified to my ears that I don't even try to find them anymore. It's impossible to walk through the sepia city.

My table is no longer in the shade. After lunch I doze in the May sun. I am relaxed. No obligations. I have discarded the crutch of senseless tasks that I systematically give myself when I arrive somewhere. It is a way of reassuring myself when faced with the void of freedom. Here, in Lizeta's town, I feel like her envoy. I am not in a breathless hurry to do something; I have no advance plan. I close my eyes. From the depths of my memory comes an image of that morning when Lizeta, back from the market, found me in her bedroom. The drawers of the wardrobe are open. I stand there scared, just a step away from the wall with the photographs. She speaks to me in Greek, smiling the entire time. An unexpected wave of relief fills me with joy. I wish I could stay with Lizeta forever. That is why being carefree evokes the smell of her flat. That is why Lizeta's shadow has remained in my memory all these years.

What is this divine intention that at the beginning of life offers a vision whose meaning is incomprehensible? Could it be that the explanation of the puzzle, written in childhood, is waiting somewhere along the way? The world is full of signs. The burgled train carriage in Vinkovci merely signals another event fifteen years later, when I would come within a hair's breadth of dying in a car accident on the outskirts of that same city.

"Vinkovci again?!" my mother cried out when I told her about the accident.

Writing is nothing more than deciphering the signs in the fabric of daily life. Those few days at Lizeta's, when for the first time I felt that life could be serene, etched themselves in my memory as a territory worth steering myself towards. One day, everything would fall into place. Nothing happens by chance. We are in this world to understand both the good and the bad. All those senseless deaths with no culprits, just silent enactors. To accept fate. And the infinity of the water one can sometimes even walk on.

That May afternoon, on the terrace of the Negroponte restaurant in the Ladadika quarter, I feel so relaxed. All the deadlines have expired, all the dates gone. Everything that had to be done according to a natural order, has been done. I am overwhelmed by a feeling of peace, by a quiet joy, because everything has a beginning and an end. Because nothing is forever.

I reached the age that Lizeta was when I first saw her at the window of the house opposite the Villa Maria. I was standing at the fence, leaning on the terracotta lion, watching the sailors carry the furniture from the military truck to our upstairs flat. An older woman appeared at the window of the house across the road. That November afternoon, while the sailors were moving our things into the flat under my mother's strict instructions, and my father was checking the electrical switches and sockets (my mother had a pathological fear not only of water, but also of electricity), my sister and I were to meet Lizeta. We spent the evening in her flat, in front of the television. It was the first television set we had ever seen. The programme was in Italian.

"Write about Lizeta, her life is like a novel," I hear my mother's voice say. "I'll tell you everything. You just have to put it together."

Yes, that is what she said that afternoon in the courtyard of the care home. Perhaps that was her strategy to distract me from the idea of writing about *her*? Truths are definitive, established once and for all, like the arrangement of the furniture in our Villa Maria flat. Standing like obstacles in front of all the windows were armchairs, dressers, shelves. It was important to block the view of the street, to safeguard peace from the outside world. To have everything packaged and logged.

I look down the Salonican street. Africans coming and going, selling eyeglasses, wristwatches, mobile phones, socks, fans. They come in waves. Nobody buys anything. Still, they keep pestering passers-by. When they approach the restaurant terraces, the waiters chase them away. These African refugees simply want to find a crevice where they can exist and survive their years on earth. There was a time when pedlars, quack doctors, entertainers and cheats of all kinds, from harpists to stargazers, roamed Europe; today, it is African and Asian refugees besieging its borders.

I go back half a century into the depths of time. I enter the courtyard of the Villa Maria. This is my Bechtsinar Gardens where, at the close of day, I play hide-and-seek with the local children. I can feel Lizeta watching as I hide in the bushes of boxwood. I just need another stretch of half a century to catch sight of Lizeta as a little girl, standing on the balcony of the family hotel in the French quarter. To accompany her to the music school in Kuskura St and on her Sunday seaside strolls with her parents. I am here where Lizeta once was. And yet, I see not a single house that dates from the time when she passed by here. Absolutely everything is missing; the intonation I need so as to hear the buzz of the city pictured on the sepia postcard, the cry of the vendors at Kapani market, the words spoken in Turkish, Greek, Ladino, French, Bulgarian, Italian. There is no rumble of the train, no siren of the steamboat, no bell of the tram. I don't even know how Lizeta left for Vienna. Whether someone accompanied her on that long trip. She lived in Frau Haslinger's boarding school in the eighteenth district and studied solo singing. She dreamed of a career as an opera singer. The war broke out. Lizeta temporarily took refuge with her relatives in Trieste. Three years later, the entire area where she had grown up burned down in the great fire; her parents disappeared, along with all traces of her previous life. She never went back to Salonica.

"For heaven's sake! Where did that come from?" I hear my mother say again. "You keep inventing things. Yes, she was in Salonica, right after the war. She went back to Trieste, horrified by what she had seen back there. She'd been through hell."

This is followed by stories from the boudoir, from the sub-surface of other people's lives. The Hiterots, Count Milevski, Diona Fažov all parade by. Where on earth did she collect all these episodes from? And what was it about Lizeta that so fascinated her? A life that she could only dream of, because Lizeta was everything that my mother wanted to be. And yet, she never displayed any signs of jealousy, the way she did with other women who had a turbulent past. They had both been rejected by their mothers. Their boarding school experience brought them closer together. They behaved like conspirators. They communicated through signs only they understood. They pulled the bedsheets tight in the same way. In the morning, with just a few movements, they made their beds with military precision, as if they were still at the boarding school in Vienna and Šabac.

By the time we moved to Gupčeva Street, Lizeta was no longer teaching solfeggio at the music school. She had also stopped giving private lessons. Her successor, Professor Fažov, lived a hundred metres down from the Steps, in Ribarska St. She had coached my sister for the 1964 *Children Sing* festival in Zagreb. People said that after the war, during the Anglo-American administration, Diona Fažov had played for the officers at parties at the Villa Maria, called the Central Hotel at the time. She reportedly had an affair with an English captain. The watchmaker Maleša claimed that Lizeta had also taken part in these parties. That she had sung songs from operettas. Although the watchmaker Maleša arrived in Pula after the departure of the Anglo-American army, he considered himself as a witness of those times. He told stories he had heard from others with such confidence that with time he turned into a first-hand witness. There were very few real witnesses. The city became deserted in a matter of months. Most Italians left after the partisans came to power. But that did not stop malicious tongues from spreading rumours, giving free rein to their jealousy and hypocrisy. And endangering the lives of those Italians who stayed.

"Everybody is a writer," my mother maintained. "There isn't a person on earth who hasn't invented at least one story. That's why there is such confusion."

An African quickly approaches the tables, offering fans. As soon as the waiter appears, he moves away. The fans look as if they have come out of Lizeta's dresser drawers. Silk hankies, scarves, stockings, brooches, bracelets. The smell of lavender. It's all on offer. The watchmaker Maleša's dinners of game, Lizeta's photographs, my father's enigmatic smile as guests at the dinner table praise my mother, the inventory of items stolen in Vinkovci, and my mother's words: "One day, when you get your head straight, you'll understand that it is only what you remember that belongs to you."

I reach the age of Lizeta Bizjak, and by tomorrow maybe that of Milkica and Irma Car. I could go with them for a walk, arm in arm, down the Trsat Steps to Rječina, and then to Slavica's for an ice cream. My mother is right: rather than invent, it suffices simply to look within oneself long enough. It is time for me to locate where *there* is. To approach it from a different angle. To relive every second preserved in my memory. I have acquired some new perspectives.

The advantage of old age is that you have nothing to lose anymore. All the cards are on the table. The soft touch of dementia is the reward for the road travelled. I am the same age as my mother was when her mind started periodically going.

"You and I are the only ones left of our entire generation," she said pensively. "That's probably because we are well-organised, so everything is within reach and life doesn't exhaust us."

It's time for me to submit my report to my mother.

The people from the beach have taken over the world. You remember how those fine barbarians trampled on our beach towels at Stoja and Valkani? They'd snicker, call out to each other, stub out their cigarettes in the crevices of the rocks. They'd nibble sesame seeds and crack jokes in the cinema. Relaxed and stupid in the eternity of the present time. In its mad race for comforts and pleasure, the world has been perverted by abundance. The past has disappeared. No one remembers anything anymore. Speed has erased memory. Desire is a weakness. Memory is defeat. Having unfulfilled desires is shameful. Feeling carefree lies in oblivion.

It is not true that if you are well-organised everything will be within reach. On the contrary, nothing must be within reach. Thrift humiliates, stops one from breathing, creates a slave-like mentality, moves the unpredictable further away.

A new era is coming. I can barely catch my breath in between each flight of steps. Havens of beauty and quiet have disappeared with the free-wheeling construction of buildings. Everywhere you look there are building contractors with their fake papers, bank clerks with their fake smiles, a menagerie of police and informants and criminals. Terrified of being unmasked, they all put on a confident air. Climate change is ruthlessly destroying people's characters, narrowing the mind, relativising morals. The hinterland has taken over and covered the cities. Citizens are being pushed back by followers of the *nation* and the subjects of international capital. What is being established is a civilization of managers, gallery owners, advertising agencies, dubious experts, logorrheic journalists, corrupt judges. Scams have been legalised. Dictionaries are empty. The necrologist is left with only a few adjectives that haven't been worn thin.

That afternoon, on the terrace of the Negroponte restaurant, I decided to listen to my mother, and take myself over *there*. To testify.

Only by remembering will I be able to stand up to the people from the beach.

11.

"Only a small part of our brain is accessible to our consciousness, like, say, a small section of a circle. That is where all our knowledge lies, all our current memory, in short: all that we live for. As for the rest of the surface that is unknown to us — what does it contain? Perhaps memories of bygone centuries, knowledge of forgotten languages and a host of things that lie in a millennial-long lethargy. And if only one day we could know it...", wrote Gaito Gazdanov in his story *Memory*.

12.

Ever since returning from Salonica, I keep thinking about just one thing: to go, as if for the first time, to the town where I was born.

To come as a stranger, to immerse myself in the darkness of the past, like the hero in one of Melville's films. Without contacting a soul.

To arrive without a map. To have no plan. To unwind. To stroll down streets that remember shadows from two or three thousand years ago. To slip into passageways at the foot of the Kaštel, to climb up to the tower of the meteorological station. To take in the town in a single breath.

I spend a long time on the internet checking out Pula's hotels. I look for a quiet place that is centrally located but secluded. I will be taking the night bus to Pula. Dawn will be breaking when I arrive and head for the city centre. I thought first of the Riviera, Pula's oldest hotel, a luxurious building dating from the Secessionist period, with parks separating it from the nearby sea and the amphitheatre. A repository of the saccharine Austro-Hungarian period. Sufficient unto itself. For almost half a century, film stars would grace its magnificent terrace overlooking the bay. After the collapse of socialism, the legendary hotel was downgraded to just one star. I'm not in the mood to invoke the past with stale marzipan sweets. I cast a quick eye at the column that lists its category. I'm horrified to see it's been reduced to a simple inn.

I continue to surf the internet. And then, noticing a familiar building, I make my final decision.

I opt for the Skaleta hotel, near the amphitheatre, just a step away from what was once the Istra cinema. What tipped the scales was the look of the building. I had passed by the two-storey edifice countless times. In the meantime, it had grown taller by another floor and become a hotel. These are buildings where I feel safe, whatever town I'm in – Pula, Ancona, Monfalcone or Rijeka. I feel at peace behind their simple facades the colour of dust, their windows framed by white stone. Modest and solid.

I look absently at the photographs of the rooms, restaurants, lobbies, because my mind is drifting away from my screen, up the Steps, right along the metal fence of the amphitheatre, all the way up to the square where the film festival is held. Gianfranco, a friend from music school, lived there. That was also where, one afternoon, after class, I was shocked to see him quietly place the core of his apple on the table, while I held mine in my hand, reluctant to leave it on the gleaming polished surface.

There were no taboos in that house. I remember his father, an artist, a painter, who would spend the whole day in his studio, reachable by stairs leading from the large loggia. Their flat was a veritable labyrinth, furnished differently from the socialist aesthetics of the 1960s, which consisted of having a wall unit in the living room, crocheted doilies on the side tables, framed tapestry pictures, a Venetian gondola on top of the television set. Gianfranco's parents' flat had a different aesthetic. Large areas without superfluous furniture or objects. His mother's slender figure, as weightless as a sheer curtain, would emerge from somewhere to say in her soft

97

voice that fruit and cakes were waiting for us in the kitchen, and then would disappear into one of the shaded rooms. The shutters in that spacious room were always pulled halfway down. Semi-darkness reigned both summer and winter. Gianfranco once told me in passing that his mother suffered from bad nerves and that the light bothered her. I envied him this peace and quiet. This freedom. This fluttering mother. The father who was always around somewhere, yet absent. Both were already in their fifties. At school Gianfranco was teased that it was his grandparents who had given birth to him. He just smiled indifferently. One time he told me that he had two brothers, one through his father, that one lived with his biological mother, and the other through his own mother, who was already grown up and lived alone. I wondered if there were any secrets in that house. Or was it simply that Gianfranco hadn't yet learned the technique of a tacit family agreement that clearly stipulated what should not be revealed to others.

I look at the Skaleta Hotel. The Istra cinema is only a minute away from this corner of the street. As usual, we arrive late, the ticket office may have already closed. My mother manages to persuade the cashier to sell us the tickets. The usher appears with a flashlight. We follow the beam of light, and, hunched over, squeeze our way through to our seats. Around us people grumble, whistle, swear. I want to die of embarrassment, to get out of there are quickly as possible, to lose myself in the film which has already been showing for the past quarter of an hour. And when the film ends and the lights go back on, I rush for the exit, leaving my mother and sister far behind. I know what comes next. My mother will keep stopping, appalled by the trash left behind by careless movie-goers. Meanwhile, people in the middle of the row complain that somebody is holding up their departure.

"It's like a stable in here, not a cinema," Mum says again loudly.

"So, take a broom and clean it," somebody calls out to her.

There's an outburst of laughter. I hurry towards the exit, as far away as possible from the comments pouring down from all sides.

I wait for my mother and sister at the foot of the Steps that lead to Monvidal. The Skaleta hotel stands on the corner where the Zagreb restaurant used to be. Yes, this is the right place for the encounters that await me during my journey, begun six months ago in Salonica, the journey into my own life.

It is then that I receive an invitation to the Book Fair in Pula. And nothing turns out as planned.

Guests at the Fair are put up at the Pula Hotel in Veruda. On the very first day I go to the Skaleta Hotel and book a room for the following week. I am sticking to my original plan. Once the Fair is over, I will spend some time in my town. I'm not going to invent anything; I am on a discovery trip.

I choose a room on the second floor, overlooking the Steps, right above the corner where I waited for my mother and sister in the 1960s. This is the starting point for my future journey. Going to Rovinj is a must, visiting Red Island, looking for traces of Lizeta. Finding the watchmaker Maleša, of course. If he is still alive, after all he must be in his eighties now. Criss-crossing the city which at every step offers a split image. I look at what is. But I also see what was.

The outcome will be a story that I didn't invent, the kind of story that my mother would enjoy reading. Her story. The kind she herself wrote when she was young, to reinforce her memory of the world she had lived in for years – the boarding school of the Teachers Training College in Šabac.

To discover as many details as possible, every hunch has its place, nothing is there by chance. The important thing is to note it down. Later, there will be the hotels and boarding houses, all those addresses where she would live her daily solitary life. This was territory where she reigned supreme. Things and objects have their own secret lives. The bee and the ant are in love. Justice always triumphs in the end.

This is the world where I was conceived. There must have been a note about the encounter without which I would not exist. And a whole range of events coded in a few words in the notebook that disappeared at the train station in Vinkovci that November night in 1958. An experienced investigator would start with the burgled carriage. He would have not only recorded the stolen items but also asked the injured party for the names of the hotels that she had so assiduously noted down. Every detail was important. Perhaps the addresses of future events are here. This notebook is the birthplace of many an illusion that my mother would bequeath to her children. The deferral of pleasure. The fear of satisfying a desire. An obsession with cemeteries. The firm conviction that forgetting is merely a variant of remembering, the supreme conservation of a legacy for one's descendants.

I booked a room at the Skaleta hotel and then headed for the seaside, crossing a little park. I look for the stone bench where my mother sits, looking out at the sea. She'd told me so many times about that first visit to Pula in 1949. She's distressed to see that the city has been abandoned. Wherever you look the country's flags are fluttering in the air. The banners on the buildings are in Italian and Croatian. Some are written in Cyrillic. She's spent the whole day at the Municipal Committee and in the half-empty offices of the Port Directorate. She had to select the most complicated files and take them to the Directorate of the Ports of the Northern Adriatic. She could hardly wait for the bus to Rijeka to come. To get as far away as possible from this city, which she would never return to. That's what she told herself as the bus stopped every so often to pick up villagers along the way. Then the bus broke down, leading to the episode with the security men from Labin. Dinner at the hotel restaurant in Raša. The curtain is suddenly lowered. The performance is interrupted.

She continues her trip on the bus, which had suddenly appeared, like a *deus ex machina*. She satisfied the cannons of her own drama, found a place for every banality, answered superfluous questions, leaving the main course of action without a denouement. I recognise this insane method of arranging the world, which I have inherited: overload the story with the superfulous, move away from the essential. My mother always looked for reasons to justify her actions. And kept missing her set goals.

Everything she refused to imagine, everything that horrified her, invariably happened to her: marriage to a military man, life in Pula, old age in a care home. And, in the end, departure for the beyond not in an urn but in a coffin.

What does she see, sitting on that bench? The shipyard, the cement works, the outlines of the barracks on the Muzil peninsula, the rail tracks along the seafront. And another life.

Everything has changed since then, but the rail tracks along the seafront are still there. The family story in Pula waited a decade before restarting at the very spot where my mother had had her first encounter with the city: by the seashore, at the foot of the Arena.

Half a century later, I come to write the epilogue of a story that began before its real beginning, the way all stories in life start, in the wake of certain seemingly entirely unimportant circumstances. Because, before an event occurs, it is presaged in the form of a slight disquiet triggered by something seen, by a name or a sound, by a sensitivity to certain words that surface when one wakes up, the intonation of unfamiliar voices, the fall of a pine cone on the gravelled path in a park, or the flutter of a nocturnal bird's wing. They are all signs of a higher order whose meaning escapes us, and so, in the absence of an explanation, we talk about chance and coincidence.

Over the next few days, I run into people who for years have played only marginal roles in the bottomless pit of the past. After a literary evening at the Makina gallery, a largish man, sixtyish, with grey hair and thick eyebrows, comes up to me. Smiling, he waits for me to recognise him, which I do as soon as he starts to speak.

"Don't you remember me?"

Instantly, I recognise the deep baritone and it casts me back into the depths of time.

"Goran Ban," I say my high school classmate's name aloud.

"This is yours. I'm returning it to you," he says, handing me a small hard-cover book.

After exactly forty years, he was returning to me the logarithm table I'd lent him for our finals when we were seniors in high school. I recognise my handwriting on the margins. I'd find it easier to understand hieroglyphics than this series of figures, these endless lines of numbers in parallel columns on the booklet's two hundred pages.

"I can't believe that I ever knew how to use these figures," I say to Goran, after we sit ourselves down in a nearby eatery behind the temple of Augustus.

We toast our reunion after forty years with a glass of Malvazija wine. I learn that Goran is a surveyor, an expert in capillary moisture. A damp specialist. He treats humidity in old houses all over Istria and the Kvarner islands. He tells me that a few years ago, he worked on a building just across the road from the Villa Maria.

'I'm looking for somebody who used to live in that house," I say, excited now. "She lived on the second floor. Maybe in the very flat you mentioned."

"Do you think she still lives there?"

"No, she must have died a long time ago. She was probably around sixty when we moved to the Villa Maria."

"Like us now, old fellow."

"Yes...Lizeta Bizjak, that was her name. What about that watchmaker across the way from the open-air market? Maleša. Is he still alive?"

"Josip Maleša! Last summer he celebrated the sixtieth anniversary of his shop."

"Don't tell me he's still working!"

"He comes in every day at noon, but his son has been running the place for years now."

"He used to visit my parents. He was an avid hunter. He used to bring us pheasants and rabbits."

We fall silent for a moment. I look around. These men, local drunkards, could easily feature in an etching. The area around the temple of Augustus was always buzzing with life. The taverns and cafés were full. Here, near the port, passengers would wait for the *jugo* wind to die down, for it to turn into a storm, and then, their sails full, they would continue their voyage to the Bay of Kvarner, or further still, towards the lagoons of Serenissima.

They are all here. Indestructible. Shadows waft over Kandler Street, disappearing down the steep passages at the foot of the Kaštel fortress.

I hurry after a small figure making her way through the deserted town, having finished her work at the Municipal

Committee. She is carrying a bag laden with office files. She'd stopped somewhere for lunch. Foodstuffs are still being rationed. You buy them with ration cards. She probably lunched at the canteen in Prvomajska Street, there where the People's Restaurant would later stand, and where we, after arriving in Pula, would often go for family dinners.

But when my mother first arrives in the city, people power is quite new. American tins, cigarettes, nylon stockings, penicillin are all bought on the black market. There have been too many changes of power over the previous ten years and moral resources have already been largely depleted. Mountain people have created a nervousness in this tranquil city. My mother distrusts uniforms, she is good at looking like an innocent girl who is no longer that young. Her boarding school experience has taught her patience and modesty. When she came to Rijeka from Belgrade in the autumn of 1948 and started working at the Directorate of Ports of the Northern Adriatic, she lived at the *Jadran* hotel in Pećine for a few weeks. Later she moved to the *Bonavia* hotel in the city centre. Most of the guests were single. The atmosphere at these temporary lodgings, before she found a room at the Car sisters' in Sušak, reminded her of the boarding school in Šabac. The pungent smell of disinfectants, the thin blanket, hot water only in the mornings.

It is around then that she starts keeping a record of her hotel stays. She organises her daily routine according to the strict rules of a single woman who, as she approaches the end of her third decade of life, continues her inner struggle, torn between the role of mentor and that of protégé. During her brief outings, she gives free rein to her cheerful disposition. On her return from Pula she must have entered into her notebook the name of the hotel in Raška, which, two decades later, with the closing of the mine, would be downgraded to an ordinary inn. The bright neon sign of the *Raška Inn* will be extinguished forever at the beginning of the 1970s.

"Logarithms are signposts to the truth," Goran says, startling me.

"All her life my mother had looked for signposts, ready-made solutions leading to ultimate truths. She was convinced that something of the sort existed. To go through life with as few problems and as little discomfort as possible."

I ask him to tell me a little more about logarithms.

"They are diagnostic evaluations of numbers that help to bring the unknown to the world of the known. Not to respect these diagnostic evaluations is to sink into a profound lie. Logarithms are numbers that simplify the complex."

"That's already better. To diverge from these signposts, you say, is to sink into the world of lies. That's enough. I get the idea now."

Goran quickly reverts to his favourite topics of humidity, the Austro-Hungarian villas in Veruda, projects that address the issue of dampness, where his company *Folan* will be one of the lead partners. As I listen to him, I see the villas I passed every day on my way to school at the end of the 1960s, when we moved to a newly built area near the military hospital. Expelled from a place that held my past. Suddenly I found myself outside, unprotected, with no residents who had lived there before me, with whom, in a way, I shared the same space. There were no traces in the new flat. No stories. Everything smelled new: the varnished parquet, the woodwork, the kitchen cabinets on the wall, the gas stove. I was alone. Later, deciding on the route I would take to school, I gradually started noticing details on the facades of the Austro-Hungarian villas, I mentally transported myself to those rooms which were so different from the monotone flats in the new buildings. I avoided my old neighbourhood.

Whenever I found myself back in Gupčeva Street, my heart would start pounding. I would rush to No. 14 and stop in front of the Villa Maria, captivated. I was that Italian woman with the proud look of a sphinx.

"I envied you for living in the Villa Maria," Goran said, his words jolting me out of my reverie.

"Well, the house where you lived had a pedigree of its own."

"Can't be compared. If you remember those two-story buildings further down my street, where there used to be shops for repairing umbrellas and shoe-polishing, that's where my office is now."

"How could I forget! My friend from primary school, Hrz Avdo, lived in the courtyard behind one of those shops."

"I don't remember Avdo. By the time we moved into that huge first floor flat, the shoe-polishers and umbrella repairers had already gone. The shops were closed for a long time. Afterwards the lawyers came."

Like a born cataloguer, Goran continues to list Pula's streets and squares. Occasionally, a face emerges from the depths of time, like Laštiko, a ticket tout in front of the *Beograd* cinema at Saturday previews. He used to read the subtitles out loud during the screening. Irritated, people in the audience would walk out in the middle of the film. The ushers' words of warning would be in vain. He was two metres tall and no one dared to approach him. The only way to get Laštiko to keep quiet was to pay him, which the cinema's management allegedly did. And some of the city's older inhabitants made their own donations as well. He would stand by the entrance and say in his dialect: "Give Laštiko a bit of money for food."

Four days later, having installed myself at the *Skaleta*, I went to Rovinj for a meeting with the director of the town's museum. Sitting in the half-empty morning bus, my eyes were glued to the window. I was waiting for the spot where the bus turned off onto the road for Rovinj, at the edge of the park, to see for just a second the stone bench from the days of the Italians. I imagined that it was here, at this now mythical place in my family lore, that my mother recapped the journey she had made and, as always at moments of respite, made her final decisions, which the relentless twists and turns of daily life were to quickly shatter.

13.

I arrived in Rovinj an hour early for my appointment with the director of the museum. I bought a copy of the Istrian newspaper *Glas Istre* at the kiosk, and went to the café at the *Adriatik* hotel.

Like every neurotic, no matter where I was, I would fill any short period of free time with silly rituals. I would take out my notebook to jot something down or make a shamanic drawing. I would open and close my backpack, leaf through my address book, glance at the book I was reading, check my pockets to make sure I still had my documents and money. Because it was important to keep busy, even if it was only rustling around, maintaining the illusion of the outside world's static state. Everything was exactly the only way it could be, sound and stable. To someone looking from the outside, this behaviour may have seemed crazy and stupid, but, without the connecting tissue of rituals, the inner world of any neurotic would fall apart.

I ordered a coffee and started leafing through the newspaper. Every so often I would look out the window at the other side of the square, where, among the row of tightly packed three-storey houses, was the one that my mother had wanted to buy when she visited the Istrian coast with

Lizeta and the watchmaker Maleša almost half a century earlier. The houses were narrow, with one room on each floor. The row stretched down towards the sea, ending at the clock tower, which looked like a big chess piece. Waiting for my father to return from his seafaring, and formally agree to buy the house, my mother was already mentally working on her renovation plans. She allotted my sister and me a whole floor each. I managed to get the room under the roof. Although we still hadn't seen our future Rovinj house, my sister and I amused ourselves by imagining going up and down the narrow wooden stairs. I would tell my sister that from my window you could see the ships out at sea. This house was within our reach, like the trunk with the toys from America. Something had to stay out of reach. Desire fortifies the spirit.

However, these plans were upset by the arrival of a music conductor from Belgrade, who bought the house from right under my mother's nose. In the late 1950s, Rovinj had become the favourite destination of Belgraders, especially among artists. They bought, at a reasonable price, national-ised houses whose owners, mostly Italians, had left for Italy in 1945. Half a century later, with the break-up of Yugoslavia, Belgraders would sell their houses for a song and leave Rovinj forever.

My mother was extremely disappointed when the pur-chase of the house fell through, and quite angry at the whole of this small coastal town; in her resentment, she turned her back not only on Rovinj, but on the whole of Istria's western coast. She started visiting the eastern coast. When my father returned from sea, they bought a house in the village of Pomer, in the Bay of Medulin.

I look at the row of houses with cafés on the ground floor. One of those houses could have been ours. Only the watchmaker Maleša might remember which one it was. We missed the chance to live on this square solely because my mother always insisted on my father being formally part of any important decision to be made. That was her strategy to make him wholly responsible in the event of an adverse outcome. Is he still alive, the conductor whose rush to buy the house deprived me of vacationing in Rovinj when I was young? That would have been a different life, though not really. Because here I am in Rovinj all the same. Everything is unfolding according to a seemingly elusive order of events, controlled by the subconscious. What lies inside that ninety-five percent of the terra incognita of our brain? Chips transported from millennial depths are locked inside the archives of our head.

I pick out the narrowest house in the row, next to the Batana café. I run my eyes over the façade all the way up to the roof. There is my window. On this December morning, after the previous night's rain, the air is so crisp, the visibility so perfect, that from my observation point I could count the cypress trees on nearby Katarina island. I stop this journey into the past and focus on the newspaper. A headline at the beginning of the Pula Chronicle catches my attention.

EXCAVATORS DIG UP HUMAN SKELETONS
Quite unexpectedly, while installing gas pipes and reconstructing the water supply grid in Preradović Street, in the centre of Pula, behind the wall of the old general hospital, excavator shovels "snagged" parts of subterranean graves and from a depth of just 30 centimetres brought to light fragments of human bones. This spot, where the Austro-Hungarian fortress dating from the second half of the 19th century used to stand, was once the site of the St Mihovil monastery. The place where the graves were discovered under what is today Preradović Street was probably once the

monastery's medieval cemetery. Since Pula and the cemetery are mentioned in Dante's "Divine Comedy", it is possible that this cemetery inspired him to include it in his great narrative poem. Dante was probably in Pula between 1304 and 1308.

When I was a boy, Eugen Poropat lived in this street. In the early 1960s, my father bought his first car from him, a navy-blue Fiat Topolino convertible. I can clearly see the faces of Eugen and his wife Sergia, and their garden where my sister and I played. Nothing was forbidden at the Poropats'. They had no children and they let us do whatever we wanted. There were two fig trees by the back wall of the garden. From the taller one you could see the hospital courtyard where patients in their pyjamas and robes would stroll in the quiet of the summer afternoon. They looked like the soldiers of a ghostly army. Just like Dante Alighieri – dressed in a long red cape, with a book in his hand – when I saw him for the first time on a picture in my Italian language textbook. So, the poet of "The Divine Comedy" had something to do with the courtyard of the Pula hospital; it is here, from the wall of the Benedictine monastery, that he looked out at the city. Inspired by the necropolis at the foot of the wall, he would evoke the view of the open graves in his tercets.

Cemeteries are indeed a place where one grows up. At every moment the bones of the past surface somewhere.

Half an hour later, I am sitting in the office of the director of the city's Museum, who receives me at the recommendation of Goran Ban. I try to learn something about Lizeta by mentioning the Hiterots.

"They had many visitors on the island of St Andreja," she tells me. They left behind a wealth of correspondence. Not all of it has been documented yet. It wasn't until 1927, seventeen years after the death of Baron Georg, that the baroness and her younger daughter Barbara moved to the island permanently."

I tell her my conjectures about Lizeta's long stay on the island of St Andreja between the two wars. She knew Count Milevski; allegedly, he was her lover.

The director bursts out laughing. She asks me where I got this information. When the Hiterots moved to the island, Milevski was an old man, abandoned and crazy. There are all sorts of stories about him. He led a turbulent life. Duels, adultery, kidnappings. Allegedly, he fled from his native Lithuania in a coffin. But historiography isn't literature. She suggests that I look at the photographs that are among their effects. She points to a monograph about the Hiterots, saying this is only the first volume. The second and third are planned for later.

"Why?" I ask.

"Because of living witnesses."

"Witnesses to what?"

"Looting. There are still valuable objects to be found in Rovinj houses that were stolen from the Hiterots' castle at the end of World War II."

"Wealth is indestructible, it just moves around, like dust," I say, repeating the watchmaker Maleša's phrase.

"No one knows that better than archivists. Almost ten years ago, a pile of unrecorded archive material relating to the Hiterot family was discovered," the director goes on to say. "There is no complete documentation about how certain objects from the Hiterots' estate made their way to the museum's depository. Who knows how many more unclassified objects lie in other museums and institutions, let alone in private collections. Baron Hiterot was the Japanese consul in Trieste, he travelled the world and brought back exceptional works of art from his travels."

The director gets up and takes a folio-like book from the shelf. It is the story of the Hiterots, everything she and her team had managed to discover and classify. She gives me a copy.

I take the heavy luxury edition into my hands. On the cover is a scanned picture of the Hiterots' red wax seal – a subtle message to readers that they are entering the private world of a family. I leaf through it at random. Hundreds of pages. Endless lists. Bills. Maps. Photographs of antique furniture and exotic objects from China and Japan. Signatures authenticating thousands of letters and objects of art. Catalogue cards of the Hiterots' books. Family photographs.

"There are lots of private things here," says the director. "We weren't sure until the very last day whether we should publish the details of the Hiterots' estate. Would they want that if they were alive? Since the weather was extremely unstable at the time, and St Andreja and Red Island are always in the path of storms, we said to ourselves: if the weather is good tomorrow, they would have wanted us to do it; if it is bad, they wouldn't. It seems that even the Hiterots couldn't agree until the last moment. The next morning it rained cats and dogs, and the sky was leaden. Just two hours later, a strong wind blew in, chased away the clouds, the sun came out and by the evening the puddles were dry."

"And so you published the dossier about the Hiterots."

"Yes. And that's only a small part."

Before parting, the director again says that I absolutely must visit Red Island. She was curious to know how the Hiterots would be depicted in my novel.

"I'm not sure whether I'll include them," I say. "I'm still just thinking about it, groping in the dark. Writers see things that are not even in the archives."

I leave holding the weighty gift in my hands. Waiting for the bus, I wonder why I am so intent on chasing after the daily lives of other people. After all, the everyday changes like a snake shedding its skin, layers sink into the depths of memory. They disappear. Habits alternate with rituals. And it is only at moments when the senses are briefly left isolated, and the eyes listen while the palate sees, that a forgotten scene surfaces, a spectre in the night, only to disappear right after. Jolted awake, we stare into the void. We cannot retain anything, embrace it, anchor ourselves in the bay of fond memories, and wait there for the end.

What is man if not a collection of habits and routines which he maintains; which maintain him? They are the skeleton on which he leans with every movement he makes, with every thought he has, regardless of whether he is picking grapes in the vineyard, pulling a fishing net out of the sea or typing on the keyboard of his computer. I try in vain to remember at least the pair of shoes I wore in primary school, to recall the smell of the leather straps on the *settimo soprani* accordion during hours of rehearsals with the orchestra of the music school in Pula, to list all the towns of our tour of Czechoslovakia in the summer of 1967, to remember where I washed my laundry when I was a student, when it was that I switched from smoking 57 Filter to Winston cigarettes.

Half an hour later, I am sitting in the bus for Pula. The heavy book with its green cover and red seal, is resting on my lap. Through the window, I see for a second, off in the distance, the dark cedars of the Golden Cape. In my mind, I start walking beside the sea, following the necklace of bays: Lone, Škaraba, Kuvi, Polari. The Hiterots' tourist empire. As the bus reaches the coastal highway, I begin to leaf through the book, slowly entering the world of a family which, a hundred years ago, turned the wasteland around the small fishing town into a paradise.

And so, in following the Hiterots, I break the seal on my own archive.

14.

Right at the beginning, a photograph of the Hiterot family: Georg, Mari, Hana and Barbara in the courtyard of the castle in St Andreja in 1906. Smiles over a hundred years old.

Over the next forty minutes, which is how long the bus ride from Rovinj to Pula takes, I browse through the daily life of the Hiterot family. The titles of the neatly signed and dated letters – whose contents lie in the darkness of the archives in Pazin – sound like verses: Sunday on the Island, Business in Trieste, Purchase of a Radio Set, Arrival of Mari and Georg in Hong Kong, Hana's Visit to the Ophthalmologist, Mussolini's Call to Work the Land, Obtaining a Yugoslav Visa, Founding a Children's Summer Camp. Building Hotels in Rovinj, Playing Bridge, Reflections on Marriage, Barbara's First Aid Exam, Plans to Sell the Property, Thanks for the Truffles, Sluggish Mail, Description of the Past Day …

Photographs, notes, bills, dates and daily jottings. The bulk of the book is devoted to a catalogue of the museum-worthy objects that form part of the legacy they left. In addition to photographs of an ivory comb, a parasol, candelabra, opium pipe, bamboo flute and samurai armour, each item is given an archive number and general description. All these documents, whose endless columns of numbers look like logarithm tables, are only the first volume of a possible monograph about the Hiterot family.

"Because of the tragic end that awaited two members of the family, Mari and her daughter Barbara, who disappeared right after the Second World War, we often, if not always, hit a wall of silence and mistrust. That is why we decided that to start with we would devote ourselves more to their estate than to them themselves, because that estate is not a story of comings and goings, but rather a trustworthy document of staying," says the preface to the monograph.

A lasting document about staying: the everyday coded with seemingly unimportant facts, with the ashes of hours burned in identical days. All of that was a life, a string of time spent, sealed with a long smile in front of the camera lens. Births and deaths, marriages and divorces, meetings and partings, wealth and bankruptcy are merely seconds on the earthly road, and in the endless everyday of life where seemingly monotonous rituals fill it with pleasure and sadness. Sediments of unmemorised days enlarged the past. And then, suddenly, for no reason, through an unexpected drift of the conscious mind, a scene, a face or a voice would surface, upsetting the order of usual events, bringing into question the meaning of the road traversed.

As I comb through the Hiterot archive, I have an image of one of my last visits to my mother at the care home, when, as we approached the exit, and contrary to her habit of constantly stopping in the hallway to delay the inevitable moment of parting, she suddenly started walking faster, as if wanting to be alone as soon as possible. While walking, she looked at me and said: "You know, maybe I should have married Vesko Krmpotić."

The Hiterot monograph lying on my lap made me think of my mother's notebook, the one that disappeared when the train carriage was burgled in Vinkovci one November night in 1958. Faced with an abundance of dates and index numbers, titles of hundreds upon hundreds of letters recording the material of a family forgetting, I wanted to have my own *lasting document about staying,* written in my mother's hand, to find among the notes about hotels and lodgings the secret entry "Vesko Krmpotić – a name my mother had mentioned only once; to stop in the lobby of Crikvenica's Terapija hotel, where people spoke Czech, to catch my breath by the sea in Pula and sit on the marble bench dating from Italian times, to recognise the outlines of the Raša Inn in the fable about the bee and the ant; to grasp, if only by enumerating them, my mother's moments of enthusiasm, be it for the mysterious lawyer Djordjević or for Professor Lolić, whose son liked to eat in bed; to visit regions of a long past future, there where, at a given moment, I came into the world. Because examining my mother's notebook would make it easier for me to understand my own actions, anxieties and fears, to understand all the residue I had inherited and the stray paths of genetics.

I continue my stroll outside the Hiterot family circle. The war has only just ended and Red Island – still St Andreja – isn't in Italy anymore, it is now in communist Yugoslavia. People power is now in place. In an excerpt from a letter, I come across a Decision from the People's Liberation Committee for Istria, notifying Countess Hiterot Barbara, property-owner, residing in Rovinj, of German nationality, that all her movable and immovable property is being confiscated. She has the right to lodge a complaint with the Ministry of the Interior of the Federal Republic of Croatia within eight days of receiving the Decision.

The Decision is dated 1 June 1945, and, according to the director of the museum, Barbara Hiterot and her mother

Mari Hiterot were condemned a day earlier, by summary procedure, without trial, and executed with a bullet in the back of the head. Their bodies were thrown into the sea by the rock of Banjole. Their only sin was their wealth, which passed into the hands of the people's authorities.

I can see them at dawn on the deck of the patrol boat, tied up, casting one last look at their realm, the forest of dark cypress trees of Punta Corrente, and the coast of the little island of Maškin, all quickly disappearing into the distance.

According to the testimony of some Rovinj residents, all night long before the execution, cries could be heard coming from Red Island. Maybe the Hiterots were already half-dead by the time they left the next day on their final journey.

There is endless correspondence between different boards and committees, offices and commands, military adminis-trations and OZNA.* The people are in power. The era takes on new rituals, phrases and slogans. Yet another temporar-iness is in the making, within the scope of which millions of people will spend their time on earth. The majority will believe in the immutability of the stage set.

The comrades from OZNA Labin are particularly active in nationalising Countess Hiterot's property. The preserved documents show how bit by bit, various things disappeared from Red Island: boat engines, carpets, paintings, silverware, pieces of porcelain. There are receipts for six tennis racquets, seven tennis balls and two nets, a Neumann sewing machine, a motorboat, 20 naval flags, a bicycle, an Underwood type-writer, a guitar, a pocket watch, an ivory chess set, two legs of ham, four kilos of bacon, five kilos of cured meat. One list also mentions a "Chinese memento, 60 pairs of socks, two cows, a calf, a variety of books and other unusable objects."

---

* OZNA – Odeljenje za zaštitu naroda (Department for the Protection of the People), the Yugoslav Security Service.

Mario Licul, one of the custodians of the Hiterots' property, reports that "our guards on the island had to tend to those three heads of cattle (two cows and a calf). Before, when we had civilian guards, a hen died and a chick drowned." At the end, Licul wrote: "Please answer my question because I'm left without a companion, and I can't stay here without a companion, because I can't both do my job and prepare myself something to eat, and so for the moment I need a companion."

The Regional Administration for the People's Goods keeps telling the People's Liberation Committee for Istria to return the goods appropriated by irresponsible comrades from the confiscated property of Countess Hiterot. These objects are considered works of art and therefore nothing can be confiscated. The headquarters of the 43rd Istrian Division sends a note to the Regional Administration of the People's Goods for Istria, saying that following a comprehensive investigation, the location of the said objects could not be established, and therefore it is proposed that they be deleted from the inventory.

But then, serious experts arrive on the scene, professors Branko Fučić and Aleksandar Tuhtan of Zagreb. They will make a list of all the immovable property on Red Island, along with Countess Barbara Hiterot's movable property.

"Baroness Hiterot's castle is on the island of St Andreja, near Rovinj. The entire property consists of seven to eight little islands and the tip of the cape opposite, where she had a garage with two automobiles," write Fučić and Tuhtan at the beginning of their detailed, roughly twenty-page report.

They also write the following: "It is evident that those who came to the castle before us rummaged through, ransacked and turned inside out every room, every wardrobe, every drawer. We understand OZNA searching the owner's house after her arrest, but was it necessary to empty the drawers, toss onto the floor underwear, dishes, private correspondence, books and photographs? It was literally impossible to step foot into some of the rooms because there were so many things on the floor. Leftover food, wine bottles, broken glasses, empty jewellery boxes, in short a ravaged castle. Discovered at OZNA were parts of one of the castle's most expensive dinner sets. As well as rugs, which now cover the office floors in OZNA. A small Persian rug is already in a lamentable condition because it has been placed in the corridor by the front door and serves as a doormat."

The report goes on to say that OZNA appropriated the silver cutlery (291 spoons, 182 forks, 90 knives), the People's Liberation Municipal Council appropriated a typewriter and sewing machine, and an electric cooker, while the Headquarters of the 43rd Istrian Division, located in Pazin, far from the sea, confiscated all the fishing gear, a record-player with twenty records and a pocket watch.

As they compile an inventory of the books at the Hiterots' castle, Fučić and Tuhtan note that "based on all the evidence, this is a very diverse collection of books, consisting of the best works from all branches of literature. It is worth mentioning that the nature of this collection is *anti-fascist*. It includes not just Zweig and Mann, and anti-fascist German literature, but also works published in the allied countries during the war."

Next comes the report of another custodian of the island of St Andreja, Milan Šestan, addressed to the Administration of the People's Goods for Istria. "I hereby inform you that I went to look for all those things that are with OZNA in Rovinj, because I heard that they are holding many of our things, but they replied that they have nothing of ours; however, I am certain that they have our boat and engine, and the new black-and-green Lancia car, which is with OZNA in Labin. Whatever I found of ours that was of value, I put in a padlocked room and notified Vesko Krmpotić of OZNA in Opatija. Death to fascism, freedom to the people!"

The bus was entering Pula. As if hypnotised, I kept on my lap the book that never once mentioned Lizeta Bizjak, née Benedetti. But Vesko Krmpotić's name came up. Was it pure coincidence that this first and last name had appeared twice within a matter of just half an hour, neither name being that common or usual? It wasn't an ordinary Nikola Marković or a Marko Nikolić. And why was it that, leafing through the book about the Hiterots, I suddenly remembered my mother's passing remark that maybe she should have married Vesko Krmpotić, whom she had never mentioned before, only for that same name to appear some ten minutes later in the monograph? True, the book about the Hiterots made me think of the notebook stolen in Vinkovci, but the name Vesko Krmpotić in that fragment of the report written by a semi-literate person could not have appeared by chance.

I have always been interested in the marginal, the unimportant. When I was a child, I would spend hours reading the names in the telephone book, user manuals and warrantees for electrical appliances, as well as whatever brochures came my way. The booklet about the development of Pula's municipal network — found on top of a pile of discarded books next to the trash bin — was my favourite kind of reading.

Even today, the most valuable item in my collection is a notepad with the letterhead of the Garibaldi hotel in Venice, which, as was my wont, I took away with me. Several weeks later, I discovered among its empty pages, two sheets of dense notes handwritten in German. The notes, by a previous guest at the hotel, were about Alzheimer's disease. Perhaps they were written by a participant at the symposium of neurologists in Venice. Or maybe they were just the draft of a lecture. Or maybe it was a student revising for a course. These notes, in the middle of the empty pages of the notepad, probably meant that their author had suddenly had an idea, grabbed the notepad and quickly jotted it down, later forgetting to tear out the pages.

I have a feeling that these senseless facts, seemingly unrelated to our lives, presage events and encounters that await us. There are no superfluous notes on the cosmic music sheet, it sets out every tone, every pause, nothing is left to improvisation. Was it by chance that my logarithm tables, which I had completely forgotten about, were returned to me forty years later? Secret gestures, whispers, side looks register on our conscious mind much more than orders and commands. The unsaid resonates much louder than the said. My search for Lizeta is merely the consequence of substituting one thing for another, my inability to come to grips with this delay mechanism, this constant of my life, to confront my fear of accomplishment, of success, of ultimate triumph. And just as I use a towel to wipe off traces of the act of love from the bedsheet, so I cover up my laziness with fits of mad ardour. Do anything that excludes risk. Read for the umpteenth time the user instructions for the blender or coffee machine. Go in search of Lizeta instead of my own self. It doesn't matter that Lizeta lived on Red Island; but it would be good to learn why I banished myself from the beach. Why I cuddle up with boring books. Why I dream about the quiet towns of Pannonia as safe havens, where a bumblebee buzzing on the trellis is an event. Why I have all this consideration for the inhabitants of small worlds. What the point is of this restraint, this hesitant step, this breathlessness.

To be smaller than oneself — the real size could hurt those around.

That is my double upstairs at the Villa Maria talking, the one who would like to foresee everything, pre-empt any unpleasantness, neutralise the rebel in the laundry room, sitting on his throne between the cauldron and the sink. The only sure way to protect oneself from life is to take refuge in autism. To organise life so that you abolish it. The end result is: the absence of life, in the name of life.

And so, finally free the rebel from the basement. Take a deep breath, face failure. Cowardice is the worst of sins.

Leave the herbarium, to which I have been pinning my life for more than half a century.

15.

Late in the afternoon, I head for People's Square by the marketplace, which Lizeta called the Piazza Verdi. A man who looks about forty is sitting behind the counter in the watchmaker's shop. I observe him through the front window. Even at this distance, I recognise on his face the features of watchmaker Maleša. There is no doubt about it, this is his son. As soon as I walk in, he stands up.

Unlike the director in Rovinj, who needed time to understand the reason for my visit because, in my desire to be clear, I had complicated the situation to the hilt, this time, I explained to Josip Maleša's son in just a few sentences why I had come. He said he was already used to journalists. His father was a mythical figure in Pula. A Slovenian television crew had recently come to do a story about Tito's watchmaker, as the film introduced him. When I mention my parents' names, Maleša junior smiles and says he knows about them from his father's stories.

"My father is nearly ninety, but he has all his marbles, still plays the harmonica, still drives his car. The only thing he's given up is hunting. He lives alone in his house at Monvidal. He's got a good memory. He can hardly wait to find someone new to talk to. He lights up as soon as he's asked if he can remember something. It's unbelievable how much he remembers. I'll announce you as a special surprise. I'm sure he'll recognise you."

"It's been more than thirty years since we've seen each other," I say. "Where does he live?"

"At the top of Skaleta, that's up there by the old Istra cinema."

"I'm staying at the Skaleta hotel."

"Well, then you're neighbours. I'll phone him right now and we can arrange a meeting. I'll just tell him that someone from the distant past is looking for him. He'll want to see you straight away, this evening."

And he was right.

That evening, I left the hotel and walked up to the top of the Steps. The watchmaker Maleša was waiting for me at the door. He'd seen me coming from his balcony. He recognised me right away. He said I walked like my father. And asked if he was still alive. And your mother? He punctuated my replies with a short silence. He led me into a spacious living room. Four hunting rifles were displayed horizontally on the side wall, one under the other. I mentioned Dis. He was surprised that I remembered his favourite dog. It was a good moment for me to resolve the enigma.

"How did Dis get here from England?"

"He comes from a litter belonging to the Queen of England. I got him in Brioni when he was a puppy. You know that I used to go there regularly to maintain the clocks."

He offers me a glass of Teran wine from Vižinada. We clink glasses. I tell him that I'd been to Rovinj that morning. I ask if he remembers the house that my parents had wanted to buy.

"Of course I remember. Across from the Jadran hotel. That was an opportunity not to be wasted. Today that house would be worth a fortune."

"Wealth is indestructible, like dust, it just moves around," I say, watching for his reaction out of the corner of my eye, to see whether he will recognise the phrase he had used so often at those evening get-togethers at the Villa Maria half a century ago.

He is silent for a few minutes, lost in thought.

"Yes, yes, you're right, exactly, like dust," he says, quickly changing the subject. "The Jadran hotel was a real rat hole in the early sixties, you can't imagine. The only hotel that was worse was the one in Raša. I never went there but I did once spend the night with a woman at the Jadran. I remember that they didn't even give you breakfast. The whole of Rovinj was like that hotel – dilapidated and abandoned. I hear that the Jadran has become the Adriatik again, they've restored its sheen from Austrian times."

As I listen to Maleša rediscover and take visible pleasure in enumerating the filigree details of everyday life from half a century ago, I can't shake off the strange feeling that he's forgotten that phrase of his, that wealth, like dust, is indestructible. How could that phrase, which he had used so often and by which I remember him, have disappeared from his mind? Can habits too waste away and disappear as if they never existed, only to be replaced by other ones? New sayings, new gestures. We can't remember everything, reconstruct everything, even when we try to evoke a precise moment from the past.

Maleša's voice interrupts my thoughts. He remembers how one summer, sometime in August, comrade Pepca Kardelj came into the shop with her daughter. She brought in her husband Edvard Kardelj's* watch to change the strap. In those days, watchmakers had a meagre selection of watch-straps and comrade Pepca wanted one made of snakeskin.

* A politician and close collaborator of Tito's.

While she was in the shop, her husband strolled around the square, under the discreet protection of two dark-jacketed security men. He walked to the corner of Lenin Street to look at Pula's new supermarket, one of the first in Yugoslavia.

"I promised comrade Pepca that I would get a snakeskin watchstrap for comrade Kardelj in seven days. She asked why snakeskin watchstraps were the most durable. I told her it has to do with our body's natural temperature, which is much higher than a snake's. The body temperature of a snake depends on the temperature of the environment. There is an ideal contrast between a snakeskin strap and the skin of the human hand."

"In the summer, top officials would come to me from Brioni," Maleša continues. "Always the same story, water in the mechanism. Blockheads! They would swim wearing watches that weren't waterproof. Ranković* sent his adjutant. He didn't have a waterproof watch either; few people did in those days. Only Tito had high-end watches: Patek Philippe, Certina Grana, Schaffhausen. The most expensive watch I ever held in my hands was his Marvin, a special model. He'd been given it as a present by Finland's president, Urho Kekkonen. The watch had a double lid. The inside one opened into two, but only an experienced professional could tell. On the back of the watch I saw a code, a combination of three letters and four numbers, hand-engraved, clearly post-production. It wasn't factory-made."

Maleša's eyes turn bright. He is waiting for my reaction. I ask him: What could that mean? Did he jot down the code?

"Yes, I did. I wrote it down. I have it somewhere. But why am I telling you this? All this business about bugging Tito is absolute nonsense. Bugging Tito? Some foxy character who engraves a code on the watch without me discovering

* Minister of the Interior at the time.

it? For several years after his death, all sorts of stupid things were written about him. Even that he was co-owner of the Imperial hotel in Vienna! But, like everywhere, there was no code. I wanted to go to Belgrade and find one of the people handling his estate. To tell them about the secret lid on the Marvin. But then the war started, and I gave up," says Maleša.

I remember the political pacts my mother and Maleša made half-a- century ago, consulting the cards after a dinner of game, their hushed debates with my father, a naval officer, who duly took the official line. Allegedly he was a Titoist and they were some sort of reactionaries. Relative categories that the inexorable march of time returns to their proper place! Within the constellation of all the tragedies that have hit the subjects of the former Yugoslavia in the past quarter of a century, the owner of the Marvin and supposed co-proprietor of Vienna's Imperial hotel is a historical figure who alone possessed the secret code of co-habitation in these seismic Balkan lands. He was succeeded by highway robbers, thieves and small-time crooks, mercenaries in the service of big-time players, executers of yet another modification of the cadastre.

"Seiko caused a real revolution when it launched its in-expensive waterproof watches; then came Cassio, Fossil, Swatch, Festina, but they're all toys compared to the *Swiss*," he says, stopping for a second as if wondering where he was going with this.

Is that the way to stay in shape and keep a clear head in old age? To turn yourself into a memory machine, focussing only on details, sinking into the superfluous and the ephem-eral, and thereby, in all this endless nonsense, to protect yourself from daily stress, from profound emotions that de-stroy the soul. Because when Kardelj's snakeskin watchstrap lives on in the memory for more than half a century, and not just the strap but also the two security men in their dark jackets, boiling outside in the August sun, then being light-hearted is a permanent condition and nothing can disturb this blissful state anymore.

The watchmaker opens the pockets of time as if they were watches. When I ask how he manages to stay in such good shape, he says that the secret is sleep.

"Eight to ten hours of sleep, that's the secret. When I was younger and went hunting on Sundays, I had to get up at three in the morning; but I never had a problem going to sleep early in the evening. I don't know the meaning of the word insomnia, though recently I have been having some strange dreams." Here he stops for a moment, as if wondering whether to continue. "I often dream that a man and a woman are trying to convince me that they are my parents. It's terrible! I try in vain to prove to them that they are not my parents, I offer arguments to support my case, I ask them awkward questions. Oddly enough, they know everything, they describe every detail of our house in Šabac. Imagine, our house! Even the place where we hid our gold coins during the war. I wake up in a cold sweat. Such an awful dream."

He almost looks through me and then continues. He says he's obsessed with all sorts of crazy ideas. For instance, isn't it stupid that we leave this world just when we have come to understand so much about it? I nod in agreement.

"Sometimes I think that we've been raised somewhere in outer space. Earth is simply a huge farm with all sorts of human specimens. They take us as needed. I don't mean that they eat us, but I increasingly think that we serve some purpose of theirs."

With a dismissive wave of his hand, he says that he must be getting senile to be talking such nonsense. He asks if I am doing any writing. He's heard that I've written some novels about Pula and that I mention him in one of them. I promise to send it to him.

"I went to Rovinj because of the Hiterots," I say. "I plan to write a novel about them. As far as I remember, Lizeta, our neighbour in Gupčeva Street, knew Baroness Hiterot and her younger daughter Barbara, with whom she was friends from her time in Trieste. I think that Lizeta even lived on Red Island for a while."

Maleša seems slightly thrown by my question, or else he needs a few minutes to shift gears and embark on a different story, outside of his usual repertoire.

"Lizeta? Now she was something, not exactly like Tito, but a whizz at getting out of any situation. When I came to Pula in the autumn of 1947, right after the English and Americans left, Lizeta was reputed to be the best black marketeer around; she could get you anything, from silk stockings to penicillin. She wasn't young anymore, but she was still beautiful, one of those women who never age, who is indestructible, like Swiss watches. Generally speaking, Greek women are not beautiful, but when they are, they are real goddesses."

"I remember her as the pensive woman at the window; the local kids adored her. I find it hard to believe those stories that she slept with German and Italian officers at the Villa Maria."

"And later with English officers, and with our comrades, at least that's what was said," says Maleša. "I sold several of her luxury watches on the black market."

"What did she live off? Did she have a pension? As far as I know, she taught solfeggio at the music school right after the war."

"She inherited her husband's pension."

"Her husband's? She was married?"

What followed was a story that surprised me: Sometime in the early 1930s, Lizeta left the Hiterots' and moved to Pula. She had allegedly come into an inheritance. She lived in a four-storey corner building, opposite the Naval Park and the wall of the Arsenal, where the tram turns for San Policarpo.

According to the story, she fell in love with a musician, a local Don Juan several years her junior. After they married, he continued to run after women. All of Pula talked about his adventures with a young tram conductor. When she was making her last round, she would blow her whistle as the tram passed by Lizeta's window. It was an agreed signal. He would run out of the house to meet her. Just before the war, he disappeared from town. Nobody knew what had happened to him, until, in the mid-1950s, Lizeta received an official letter informing her that she had inherited her husband's pension. He had died in Split. Lizeta moved to Gupčeva Street.

"That was a time when people from all over Yugoslavia started moving to Pula. The city came back to life again. Many things suddenly changed. There were fewer and fewer witnesses to those bygone times," Maleša says, winding up his story.

Again I mention the Hiterots, and the monograph about them. They built the Jadran Hotel, they did up the seafront, enlivening the whole of Rovinj, only for them to end up with a bullet in the back of the head.

Maleša looks at me for a few seconds, as if hesitating.

"Eh, if that had been the case, it would have been an easy death," he says. "I know how the Hiterots came to their end. They were tortured for hours and finished up by being bludgeoned to death with cudgels. The next day, their bodies were loaded onto a motorboat, taken out to sea, and tossed into the water near the small island of Banjole, where the sea is at its deepest. It was a team from OZNA, in charge of executions. Their boss was a certain Pulčinović. With him were Baba, Spalato and Benusi from Rovinj, whom they called Four-Eyes. You're wondering how I learned all this? From Lizeta. She had often recognised the value of the objects that the Hiterots brought her to resell. Rovinj was in Zone B, under the control of the partisans. Her customers were mostly English officers from the Villa Maria. When the English and the Americans left, Pula became a part of Yugoslavia. Lizeta was arrested several times, but she always managed to get out of it. She had a powerful protector, somebody named Krmpotić, the head of OZNA for Opatija.

"Krmpotić!"

Maleša looks at me in surprise.

"You've heard of him?"

I tell him that I found the name in the book about the Hiterots. Maleša immediately starts giving me details, as if reading from a file on this powerful man with a weakness for women. But he must have made some terrible mistake because suddenly he was fired. This was the time of the Cominform* and of widescale denunciations. Comrade Vesko Krmpotić finished up on Goli Otok.** Two years later he came back looking like a shadow of himself, gaunt and sick. He lived quietly in Pula for a while, and then moved to Labin.

"When your mother rejected the idea of buying the house in Rovinj, I suggested Rabac. One Sunday she and I went with Lizeta to Rabac. It was a little fishing village at the time, with a wonderful beach and just one hotel dating from Italian times. Amazingly, we immediately found a house for

---

* The Cominform was a co-ordination body of Marxist-Leninist communist parties in Europe which existed from 1947 to 1956.

** A prison island in the Adriatic for pro-Stalinists in the 1950s.

sale right by the sea. The price was more than reasonable. We went to the hotel for lunch and to drink to her coming purchase of the house, when suddenly, whom did we see? Krmpotić! The once all-powerful man had become the director of the hotel. He told us that in a few years' time Rabac would be an elite tourist destination, and that houses by the sea would be worth a fortune."

"So, what happened? Why didn't she buy it? How come instead of Rovinj or Rabac, she chose a hole like Pomer?"

"I have no idea. Probably because it was close to Pula. Rabac was too far away for your mother," says Maleša, an absent look in his eyes, as if he didn't know what we were talking about anymore.

"Maybe its nearness really was decisive," I say, casting him a wry look.

He doesn't react to my allusion; he just waits silently for my next question.

"So, what happened to Krmpotić?"

"He got involved in some shady business; for a while there were rumours of scandals, but in the end, he became a top hotelier. He spent his old age in Opatija. He died sometime before the war."

The story then opens up. I learn that Krmpotić's only son was a well-known optician in Rijeka, a fact as important to me as the dark jackets worn by Kardelj's security men.

"With genes like that, no wonder his son became a leading optician," says Maleša.

I want to be on my own, to get to grips with this image of my mother's unexpected encounter with Krmpotić at the hotel in Rabac. Did she manage to cover up her reaction with that frozen smile she employed whenever she faced an unpleasant surprise – a smile as terrible as a deep scar, an indelible trauma from my childhood? And what about the mystery that I sensed was coming? A name in a book that just happened to fall into my hands. However, the fact that my mother had only once mentioned his name in my presence gave it epic importance.

She spent most of her last years in the care home examining versions of the life she should have led. I heard so many times about the lawyer Djordjević, who had moved to America a few years after the war. She should have left with him. No doubt about it, that had been her best option. The fact that then my sister and I would never have been born didn't concern her in the least. She would often remain deeply immersed in her imaginary lives until the end of my visit, continuing to tell me the everyday details of her life in faraway places. I would hug her goodbye and leave under different names. Once I was even her long-dead half-brother.

"And to end like that, without a trace," Mališa's voice jolts me out of my thoughts.

"Who? The optician?" I ask, perplexed.

"What optician! Lizeta. I'm talking about Lizeta!"

I learn that in the early eighties she moved to a care home, the Villa Idola, in Valsaline. She was diagnosed with Alzheimer's. Two years later, she disappeared.

"Another one of those unsolved cases," says Maleša.

When I ask him if my mother knew how Lizeta had ended up, he says that they visited her at the home that summer, a few days before she disappeared. She didn't recognise them.

"You had already left Pomer, I remember. I phoned your mother in Belgrade and told her what had happened."

It is way past midnight when I leave Maleša. As soon as I step out into the cold December air, I feel the effect of the *teran* wine from Vižinada. I take a walk to Monvidal. The sky is clear. No lights in any of the windows. Just the full moon glowing in the icy dark.

I think of Lizeta. How come my mother never mentioned that she had disappeared? Or that she had visited her, with Maleša, at the Villa Idola? Was it because she was superstitious that the same thing might happen to her? Or, as she slipped into dementia, had that fact been erased from her memory, never to surface again?

She had a horror of care homes. I don't remember that my sister and I ever went to the beach at Valsaline when we were little. Because we would have had to pass by the Villa Idola to get there.

And so, I gave up the idea of going to the Pula cemetery. Like her parents, Lizeta has no grave. All roads are open.

The world is so vast. I walk through this town with my mother evermore present inside me – her habits, thoughts, fears, desires, dementia. My father is there somewhere too, always at a slight remove. His power lay in his absence. It is time to clear up all this confusion; there is no need to be afraid. No one is to blame. *Behold what quiet settles on the world*; I hear Mayakovsky's verse in my head.

Had the boarding school, that glacial nowhere, that provisional address substituting for some kind of home, that nowhere like a hotel or boarding house, marked my mother's life? That nowhere, that place for preparing for the life awaiting her outside, like an expensive dress in a shop window. Leading to her obsession with hotels, with these interim times that brought illusions of a better life which she certainly deserved considering her exemplary conduct at the boarding school. Later, living on her own in rented rooms, hotels and lodging houses, she would dream of a family home as she imagined it, with clearly defined duties and rituals, where there was no room for deceit or lies, where life unfolded carefree. Everything was just the way it looked from the outside. An idyllic image of a doll's house. She was captive to the petit-bourgeois ideal of being able to achieve, once and for all, a perfectly organised life, where everything was in its place, and where this organised life would continue without any ruptures, any problems, any upheavals.

Did I become a writer because of the disappearance of my mother's notebook in Vinkovci? She never got over that loss. As for me, I just wanted to continue the family chronicle of stays in hotels. I was impressed by the importance of keeping a record of the nights spent away from home. My first piece of writing was a short note with the names of the hotels where I had spent the night, written one night in Ljubljana in a notebook with a yellow cover. The list is quite short: the *Palas* in Ohrid, the *Lipa* in Pula, the *Slon* in Ljubljana. I quickly gave up keeping a record. I started collecting the brochures of hotels where I had stayed.

Twelve years later, on the first day of spring in 1974, after a car accident on the outskirts of Vinkovci which left me with a few bruises and scratches, I find myself at the *Admiral* hotel in the centre of town. I call my mother from the reception desk, and in a few words tell her what happened.

"Vinkovci again!" she cries out, her voice frozen with fear.

I assure her that I am fine, that there is no need to worry. I will spend the night in the hotel. To cheer her up, I finish by saying that the next day I will try to track down her notebook.

After listening to Maleša's stories, all sorts of ideas enter my head during my walk to Monvidal. For instance, to sound record the dreams of those asleep right now, just a few metres away from me, behind the thick walls of their warm lairs. Maybe, like the watchmaker Maleša, they are having heated conversations with strangers who are trying to persuade them that they are their parents. Or they are making love, whether in their dream or in reality. They are breathing. Some will never wake up.

The constellation formed by the inhabitants of Pula that night in December 2012 is unique. If it could be transcribed onto a graph, with the positions of each of them, what a fantastic design it would make! And then, to walk through the nocturnal archive of the city. To leaf through the files. To peer into the darkness of 1947, when columns of future refugees are leaving their houses and flats, lugging their things, heading for the waterfront, where the ships Toscana and Pola are waiting for them. A last goodbye to the city at dawn.

To slip into the November night of 1958 while the Belgrade train is rushing across the Slavonian plains, cutting through the fog of Slovenia, between Zidani Most and Postojna, and in the early morning to drop anchor on the coast of Pula. Farther away doesn't exist. Because farther away is the sea. The end, and the beginning.

At the reception desk of the *Skaleta* hotel, I take the key to my room. I quietly climb up to the second floor. In the darkness of the room, the moon casts a pale light on the high ceiling. Yet another tardy sleeper in Monvidal is being inscribed on the map of the night.

16.

The next day, the weather turned, bringing the southern *jugo* wind. When I opened the window around ten o'clock, an unhealthy heat hit me. All the energy I had accumulated during my deep sleep disappeared at the touch of this warm air. In my mind's eye I suddenly saw those bygone mornings when the *jugo* made it doubly hard to leave for school. I walked the wet streets of Pula, my eyes colliding with the run-down facades, and envied the people who briefly appeared at the window or on the balcony. They are at home, I thought, enjoying their leisure, while I am heading for the uncertainty of yet another day at school.

I stood in front of the window of the Skaleta hotel, situated on the corner of the building; the view from the room stretched all the way to the Punta on one side, and to the Arena on the other. I took deep breaths. I could smell the rain. It hadn't arrived yet, but all those years spent living here had sharpened my senses. I imagined that, like an animal, I could sense any change in the weather approaching the seven hills of Pula. I was the city's guardian spirit, sensitive to the pulsations carried by the wind of the centuries. I devoured old calendars and magazines, maps and engravings,

I scrutinised photographs that showed a vanished city, with anonymous witnesses who happened to be at the place that the local photographer was about to immortalise. I roamed through the deep layers of the past, through the mythical period of the Argonauts who, while searching for the Golden Fleece, had stopped to rest right here in the bay of Pula, on the peninsula of Stoja. Amongst the ruins of the Roman amphitheatre at Monte Zar, I listened to the voices of the legionnaires. And later, to the cries of the Ostrogoths and Byzantines, the Venetians and Genoese, crossing the flame-engulfed city. The centuries passed. I can see Dante's shadow in the cemetery of the Benedictine monastery, there where now stand the police station, department store and Croatia Insurance. All sorts of things grow in a cemetery.

On this December morning, the empty terrace of the hotel restaurant on the other side of the street reinforces the impression of abandonment. Like a nest embedded in the dense vegetation that provides deep shade in the summer, it once had a good reputation and was the only place open until midnight. There was no hotel there at the time, just a restaurant, called the Zagreb. Along with the Riviera and the Delfin, it was the favourite meeting place of actors, directors and their fans during the Film Festival. But for me, as a regular at the Istra cinema who constantly passed by this way, the terrace of the Zagreb restaurant served as a precise meteorological instrument. When it suddenly turned cold at the end of August, and the northeaster gave way to the southern *jugo*, bringing wind and rain, the sight of this deserted place, of the tables and chairs strewn with wet leaves, was a remorseless reminder that the summer was over. That meant that the next school year was soon to begin. And with the August *jugo* my anxiety grew. It was then that I understood the Venetian administrators who three or four centuries earlier had sent desperate letters to the Doge of Venice from malaria-infested Pula, begging him to bring them back as quickly as possible to the city of lagoons.

During those gloomy high school years, I dreamed of the day when I would leave this boring town once and for all. And I did leave, but I took its dimensions with me. Along with the anxiety imprinted on my soul by the people at the beach, the sound of their voices, the free-falling naked bodies, the laughter and casualness.

The three big towels, spread out over the smooth rocks of the Stoja beach, constitute our family territory. There we are exposed to the eyes of others. Wherever I go, that towel of mine follows me, the magic carpet of my childhood, and the tiny figure of my mother, her smile as horrible as her cry in the night thirty years later, sitting naked on the edge of the armchair, staring into the maw of the open drawer.

Fearing disaster all my life, everything I do is simply an attempt to protect myself against it, to find a safety lock. To hide in a solitary cell of order and calm. To prevent making the wrong choice by wisely withdrawing into myself. To defer new distractions. To slow down the moment of free choice with a long *fermata*.

That is why I never went to a brothel. Like a stray dog, I prowled the areas frequented by ladies of the night, watched them from a safe distance, timidly approached the doors of brothels and pay-by-the-hour hotels. It was always the same story, whether in Berlin, Munich, Budapest, Vienna or Bremen. At the last moment, I would change my mind, beset by an avalanche of all the possible consequences of that brief moment of pleasure.

In mid-January 1993, I was part of a group of writers from the former Yugoslavia who had been invited to Literaturhaus in Hamburg. We were put up in nearby hotels and in lodgings along the lake. Aleksandar Tišma and I were at the Miramar.

"The majority of hotels in this area are run by former prostitutes. They invested their savings on time," Tišma said while we sat in the lobby, drinking coffee.

"Where did you hear that?"

"Have you noticed their eyes? They're like X-rays, they register everything. You can't hide a thing from them."

"I think you're exaggerating."

"You've never been to a brothel?

"No."

"I was watching you at the station yesterday, with that huge suitcase, as if you were going on a trip around the world. I had a smaller suitcase when I went to India."

"What has that got to do with brothels?"

"Luggage, my dear Velikić. It's impossible for you to get rid of superfluous things."

"You can't know in advance what is going to be superfluous."

"You're like my Sonia. I bet your larder is full of tins."

"My flat hasn't got a larder."

"But you have one in your head."

"What's wrong with me wanting to anticipate things?"

"Nothing, it's just pointless. And dangerous. One day you'll wish you had a life in reserve. That's how it goes."

A few years ago, I noticed a tall brunette in the forecourt of Novi Sad's Catholic church. It was nightfall and the streetlights had just gone on. She was pacing back and forth, turning around as if waiting for someone. I stood there in awe. I couldn't take my eyes off her body, clad in a short dress, with a deep décolleté. Suddenly, a fat fifty-year-old man appeared, walked up to her and, after a brief conversation, they went into a nearby house together.

"Your prey is gone, my dear Velikić," I heard Tišma's voice in my head.

I was in his town. At dusk, when outlines lose their sharpness and desire takes hold of both body and soul, finding no place where it can be appeased. Walking, just aimlessly walking. All those people that I passed, the women that I secretly observed, the building facades and shop windows, the parks, squares, quays, have left a lasting trace in Tišma's books. And though it's been years since he was laid to rest in the Novi Sad cemetery, his protagonists continue to exist in everyday life, under other names. They come into the world, long since inscribed in Tišma's register.

Like a hunting dog, I went out into the night, roaming the narrow streets and passageways around the Catholic church. I kept seeing Tišma's face, his mischievous smile, half-restrained, until his interlocuter might perhaps feel, God forbid, a bit of warmth.

I kept repeating to myself the word "prey" that Tišma had repeatedly used that evening in Hamburg. Everything he said was razor-sharp, straightforward, He would repeat a barbed remark several times, waiting for my reaction. I tempered his comments, as if I too was responsible for things being the way they were, mostly bad.

"You keep complicating things. Is that why you can't go to a brothel?" he said, a devilish gleam in his eyes. "And yet, you'd like to? Right?"

I gave a dismissive wave of my hand and reached for another cigarette.

That morning, at breakfast, he told me that he had stopped smoking long ago. Whenever I lit a cigarette, his little eyes twitched. And so, I smoked a lot; with each cigarette

I sent him a message that I was in my best years, carefree; that I didn't fall for his provocations; that a whole lifetime separated the two of us. He seemed to guess the reasons for my rudeness. Peevishly, he wouldn't let it go.

"Nobody is spared. Everyone more or less experiences what corresponds with his inclinations and abilities. Anyway, everyone determines his own place. We did not wind up somewhere by pure chance."

"You mean to say that everybody allows or does not allow himself something?"

"Exactly," said Tišma. "For instance, you didn't allow yourself brothels."

"If that were true, everyone would choose fame, money, women…"

"The order you put them in is interesting," Tišma interrupted me.

"That's because I'm hiding what I care about most. Not to jinx it. I'm superstitious. Otherwise, I'd put health in first place."

"And that's why you smoke, for your health. I see, you'll be more of a misanthrope than I am."

"How do you know that?"

"At some point one has to unburden oneself of the unsaid. If that weren't true, then why would we write? But you can't get down to doing it, can you?"

"How do you know that? Have you perhaps read my books?"

"No. But I've read what you've written in the press. You are very naive."

He stopped for a second.

"Why do you invent?"

The same words my mother would say four years later in the corridor of the care home, words that she was to repeat many more times during our painful meetings, at moments when we would both fall silent, and when I could hardly wait to leave that antechamber to nothingness.

"Do you sometimes look down at the pavement when you walk? Listen! There are so many things to hear," said Tišma. "You could write a novel about pavements. Think about it."

In the meantime, my luggage has been getting heavier. I invent less and less. Thinking through my lived experience, my ears often ring with the phrase said by both my mother and Tišma. What an encounter that would have been! She, a weave of all sorts of complications, fears, fibs; and he, maskless, forthright, impertinent. Who knows, maybe their paths once crossed in the street during those post-war days when Tišma lived in Belgrade and would walk around the Sava docks at night looking for a good catch, around the Bristol hotel and the steep streets leading to Zeleni Venac, where the newspaper *Službeni list* had its offices where my mother worked when she came back from Rijeka.

Whenever I find myself in a city I don't know, I start aimlessly walking around, calm and anonymous, almost invisible; with each step I slip deeper into some sort of reserve life which could have happened here; I delve into the labyrinths of stories that preceded me, into the endless book of genetics where every fact about my ancestors' lives is written with encyclopaedic precision. They walk alongside me, wordless and silent; with a sixth sense I explore this immense legacy which one cannot refuse just like that, but rather accepts with every lived second; and so I become yet another in the series, in this sequence with no beginning which staggers from the depths of existence into the next day.

There are many lies, anxieties, delusions and fears. The same sorts of confusion that trouble both the young employee of the Rijeka-based Directorate of Ports of the Northern Adriatic on her brief business trip, while walking in the deserted streets of Pula, and her son twenty years later, who doesn't know not only whom he had shared his first kiss with, but whether that kiss with one of the Gupčeva Street twins had happened at all. It was to be the same that rainy August afternoon, when the people from the beach suddenly disappeared, and he felt tranquil and free for the first time. But not for long, because the very next day the sun reappeared, the beaches were full, and the fearful swimmer retreated to his fallback position in the pinewood forest, with a rather uncertain memory of his first experience of love.

Or else this is the logical consequence, more precisely the anticipation of that shadow in the middle of the skull, revealed by the magnetic resonance imaging; the spreading void shaped like a four-leaf clover signalling Alzheimer's, as the anonymous guest at the Garibaldi hotel in Venice had noted down several years earlier. After returning from my trip, I find the note among the empty pages of the leather-bound notebook that I had appropriated from the hotel because of the small purple metal ballpoint attached to it.

The road from autism to Alzheimer's is not long. The structure imprinted by one's upbringing, through a daily drill, through never fully articulated allusions, produces a particular picture of the world, full of warnings: don't let the body relax, be constantly on the alert, anticipate from the starting block what is coming from behind the bend the very next second.

Bites of food rolling in my mouth, unbearable noise pulsating in my head. I strain my ears. Terrified that I might stop breathing, that my swallowing mechanism might stall. Without the presence of another person the food is tasteless. I lose my appetite. It's my mother in me that is refusing to enjoy it, swallowing unchewed food like a seagull. I need to leave this soup kitchen in this phantom city as soon as possible. At the next table, two men are staring at her. She feels a bead of sweat slowly trickle down her spine. She will never come back here. She calls over the waiter, pays the bill and walks out into the street. She heads for the bus stop, in the direction shown her by a passerby. But it is a winding street, she can't see the end of it. To the right, some kind of lodging house, one of those neglected buildings that can be found all over the new State; it can't compare with the prewar hotels in Dubrovnik and Opatija. Or with the Terapija in Crikvenica, where in times past only Czech was spoken. The Roman amphitheatre finally appears in the distance. The bus stop must be here somewhere. She slows down. Crossing the little park, she finds herself by the sea. She sits on the bench and waits for the bus. She notes her tasks for the next day, a habit from her five years at boarding school in Šabac. The columns where she records her tasks shape her thoughts. Completing these tasks is the only guarantee of a sure and happy future – the advice given by the teachers at the boarding school in Šabac, the irrefutable postulate of her philosophy of life. Thus, she denied herself what she desired the most: love. She insisted on doing things her way, incapable of relaxing, of taking deep breaths, of being open to meeting someone; instead she overwhelmed suitors with a torrent of words, erected barriers, talked when she should have remained silent and let their eyes do the touching, but there was no column in her notebook for that and so it remained unrecorded, a mere possibility of something that could have happened. But it hadn't. Not because she had done something wrong, but because the world is made so that pure souls are condemned to being alone. It was not her fault, she thought. One's actions neither produce nor influence the circumstances, rather the circumstances are set by fate. And fate had reserved major challenges for her, but her faith was strong. There was no goal she couldn't achieve by dint of her inexhaustible energy, perseverance and patience. The pulsations of the unsaid will form layers. Her descendants will carry the burden of this mortgage.

The anxiety I feel when I sit down alone at a table in a restaurant, the panicky need to finish my meal as quickly as possible and rush outside, had as a result that in the next generation my son unconsciously avoided eating his meals alone. He always goes to restaurants with friends. He would go on to study the symptoms of family neuroses at university clinics in Singapore, Stockholm, San Diego, listen to the mute language of dementia, detect the first symptoms of Alzheimer's in his patients, following the methods of Professor Dalask. Over time, geysers of the unsaid, buried deep in the limbo of the subconscious, run dry, leaving behind a void, a black hole of nothingness. That is why it is important to activate in time the millions of neurons needed when searching for fugitive memories; to constantly confront the dangerous legacy of one's ancestors; to face, rather than avoid, disturbing scenes which suddenly flash randomly before our eyes; to activate the dense network of transmitters through the persevering work of the memory; to extract from the memory images, noises, smells, touches; to arm oneself with the patience of an archaeologist, because what else is memory if not digging? The imagined is merely a shadow of something that has already happened.

Hence Lizeta, Tito's watchmaker, Lado Leskovar, Remarque's heroes, the Hiterots, Tišma, Vesko Krmpotić, people known and unknown who merely pass by the lens of the conscious mind – they are all part of the architecture of a life. Just as that life is a material, more or less visible, in countless other lives, or merely the outline of an anonymous figure in a photograph taken by a Japanese tourist in Saint Mark's Square in Venice.

What else is a novel but an attempt to place a number of everyday scenes in a cause-and-effect relationship, revealing the story within, like a sculpture in a block of rough stone. We all carry within ourselves an invisible library, a body of unwritten novels.

The pavements and train tracks are buzzing.

Towards the end of August 1991, I was returning to Belgrade from a holiday in Pula on one of the last trains still being run by the Yugoslav Railway. Somewhere after Zagreb, when the trains justified their adjectives "rapid" and "express", and finally picked up speed in the Slavonian plains, a lady of a certain age seated in the corner of the compartment, said:

"You're Dragan? Buba and Voja's son?"

We were alone, a couple had just left the compartment. Approaching the station, the train suddenly slowed down. Over the ensuing four hours, the woman, who introduced herself as Radmila – the wife of an Air Force major about whom the only thing I remembered was his name, but I had a vivid memory of the big balcony of their apartment in the centre of Pula, where my sister and I used to play – evoked a series of scenes from life, constantly changing the optics. She had been an adolescent, boarding at the Teachers College in Šabac, where she had shared a clothes cupboard with my mother, and the next minute she was prophetically sketching out what the world would look like after the war which was just about to break out. Then, in an absent voice, as if talking to herself, she noted that my mother had been pathologically pedantic, and that once she had burst into tears when their clothes cupboard wasn't declared the neatest in the whole boarding school.

She recognised me immediately from the way I lit a cigarette in the corridor of the train. Just like your father, she said. Her Vlatko had died the previous year. A heart attack. She was going to her sister's in Stara Pazova to get some documents. Suddenly dropping her voice, making it sound very confidential, she told me that it was so sad how everything had ended the way it had. I didn't react, so she repeated several times that she would never understand why my mother had broken off their friendship without any explanation. Did I know that my parents might never have met had she not literally dragged my mother to an excursion to Mount Fruška Gora organised by the *Official Gazette*. For a while I tried to follow the story of this person to whom I allegedly owed my birth.

At one point, Radmila told me an odd story and I immediately doubted the truth of it. I ascribed it to her being hurt by my mother's behaviour, by her sudden aloofness after a friendship of more than three decades. Allegedly, my mother had been jealous of the girls at the boarding school who received love letters while she received none, so she started writing love letters to herself.

For the next four hours of the trip to Stara Pazova, my travel companion did not stop talking. I would periodically close my eyes and pretend to have dozed off. Or I would go out into the corridor for a smoke. But as soon as I returned to the compartment, she would resume her monologue. She mentioned a slew of names, listed toponyms, gossiped, related events, evoked Pula in the 1960s, showering me with a host of unimportant facts, from prices at the fishmonger's and the market to the names of doctors who easily prescribed sick leave. This concern about situating every silly detail, this crazy attempt to keep everything under control, reminded me of my mother. Was I looking at yet another member of the association of maladroit souls? In the darkness of my closed eyes, I followed the story of a scattered mind and could hardly wait to get to Stara Pazova and rid myself of my boring travel companion whose fate as a widow had already written her off.

I don't know what I would give now to talk to Radmila for just half an hour . From my present perspective, a lot of what she said was prophetic. For instance, that mania about writing letters to herself. Four years later, my life was completely upended when I met a woman who plugged every crack in our relationship with lies which I very naively accepted as the truth. For, everything that happened between us was destined to be – that is how she explained the strange coincidences we kept discovering at every step. The two of us were made for each other, and it had been just a matter of time when we would meet. But the key moment in our relationship, the last straw that gave me the strength to take a difficult decision and embark on a new life, was connected to a trip my darling made to Budapest. It was there, at an international symposium of sociologists, that she met someone who had had a long affair with a German writer I greatly admired and felt close to. It transpired that he had read translations of my novels, that he had liked them, that while they were together the two of them had often talked about me, and that the writer had even recommended me to his American publisher. This was all said in the letters that my darling had exchanged with this person.

A decade later, I would learn that she had invented the entire correspondence, and not just that, she had also lied about knowing the German writer's ex-wife, and, hence, about his praise for my novels. This detail was to play a crucial role in persuading me to start a new life. Because, since we'd been together, only nice things had been happening to me. The way she had managed to orchestrate the whole story, even obtaining envelopes with Berlin postmarks in Grunewald, with the dates clearly legible, is only to be admired. Of course, my darling had achieved her plan not only because of the vanity that had skewed my reasoning, but also because of the life of lies I had lived for so long in my childhood.

In my mother's world nothing was as it at first seemed either. Everything that happened had a hidden meaning. Nothing was said clearly. There were just allusions, mumbles, unfinished sentences, mind-shattering subjunctives. An array of passing blurred faces, silent footsteps, as if sneaking around us barefoot. She would immediately reinforce the truth of her words with true-life examples, lending an indubitable value to their usage.

When we were little, after our bath my sister and I would spend a long time rubbing down our hair with a towel. We had to sit by the tile stove for a whole hour, with my mother periodically running her hand through our hair to check whether it was still damp. For the umpteenth time she would tell us the story of how, when she was a child, one of her friends had gone out into the cold with wet hair, developed an inflammation of the brain and three days later he died. In the winter, if it was windy, she forbade us from talking outside, and if we did have to say something then we had to do it through our teeth and with our mouth closed. Warnings and dangers wherever we turned. For instance, never leave a wristwatch on a glass surface because the cold glass can make the spring snap. That was what the watchmaker Maleša had supposedly told her.

She was sure that one day my sister and I would realise how right she had been. But by then it would be too late for her to see with her own eyes that we had finally come to our senses because by then they would already be drawing lines on her body. She would depict for us the last scene of her existence. The body is laid out in the pathology lab. The pathologist proceeds to dissect the corpse with a scalpel. Horrified by the vision, she asked my sister and me to promise that when she died, she would be cremated.

She was incapable of presenting anything to us without mystification. Everything was final, with no possibility for corrections. Instead of an explanation, there would be a story. She didn't teach us how to think, how to see the relationship between cause and effect – she gave us ready-made solutions.

Deceptions and lies, desires and illusions, are all building material for madness; to destroy bridges to the real world and introduce an invented reality. My mother maintained her virtual world by engaging in mandatory activities, obsessed with unimportant details, constantly thinking up new rituals and ways to maintain them. The fact that the drawers in the wardrobes were impeccably neat, that the windows were sparkling clean, that every day was planned down to the last minute, was proof that her world functioned. She would say that even if she woke up in the middle of the night, she would immediately be able to find any object, happily boasting about it without ever wondering about the point of these nocturnal tests. For, this perfect sense of orientation in her own flat compensated for her difficulty in navigating the external world. Her doorstep was the border of her realm. The feeling of having a home again, a feeling she had lost as a child when she left for boarding school, filled her with quiet joy. She had an aversion to places where people lived in groups, be it a care home or a workers' holiday home. And a fear of moving, as if displacement could again lead to her losing a fixed point, her little universe where she set the rules.

I assume she never found her feet in the big world. Every friendship ended in disappointment and was suddenly broken off, with her being the injured party. I remember only too well those ponderous moments when she would wonder aloud why people who only yesterday had been friends were behaving strangely. The people from the beach were circling around us. Calm and selfish. My mother cried and didn't try to hide it from us.

In such situations I would experience the same shame and distress that I had felt at the beach in Stoja, when my mother, sister and I would be having lunch, sitting on our towels, legs folded, concentrating on the food on our plate, using cutlery and napkins, while everyone else was munching their sandwiches, relaxed, shouting and laughing. The whole time my mother would be telling us that before the war, the beaches in Opatija and Lovran had had parasols, deck chairs, small tables and benches. She would speak loudly, so that everyone around could hear the myth about the orderly Czechs in Crikvenica. Every so often someone would say something sarcastic. Without turning around, my mother would say something in French. My sister and I didn't know French, but we would smile approvingly at her every word.

We were like a little theatre troupe which, every day at the same time, put on a performance at the beach. I would furtively catch the curious looks of those around us, horrified when I saw a familiar face. I was afraid of encountering these witnesses when school started. There was no end to my joy when, after second grade, I was transferred to the school in Monte Zar which, a few years later, the Alfeldi twins, Doris and Noemi, also wound up attending. My mother transferred me because she got a job in the school's secretariat. She wanted to keep an eye on my sister and me. But primary schools had shifts, so every other week my sister and I enjoyed relaxed mornings without the usual pressure, much like our schoolmates whose parents worked. I so envied them the peace and quiet that surrounded them, the possibility of deciding for themselves what they were going to do. My sister and I were constantly under supervision, with no possibility of deciding anything by ourselves. Even something as banal as which notebook to use for which subject had to be approved by my mother. But now, suddenly, here was a chance to be on our own, relaxed, to move through a quiet apartment, without my mother's constant carping.

Unfortunately, our happiness was short-lived; it lasted only two months. My mother's job required her presence only in the mornings. She had hoped she would be able to persuade the director to let her change shifts for the sake of the children. But it was in vain. And so, after two months she quit her job, while we stayed at Monte Zar until the end of the school year. Gloom returned to our daily life. That year, my sister's grades dropped, and she devised several excuses to conceal it. One time, to put my mother in a good mood, she gave herself seventeen "A"s in her workbook. Naturally, Mum was suspicious and went to the school to check. Apart from learning the truth about the grades, she also found out that my sister had been telling her schoolfriends that she had been adopted from an orphanage. My mother came home in a state of shock. We had to listen to her lamentations until midnight. The whole town would hear about the scandal. Was that the thanks she got for everything she had done and was doing for us? Instead of having a good time like the wives of other men at sea, she had completely devoted herself to her children. She didn't even have time to see friends. So many of them had drifted away.

I don't recall if I already knew that it was she who had abruptly ceased communicating with them, but it didn't take me long to realise it. Usually it was because of some remark, piece of advice or comment that she found sarcastic, said to deliberately hurt her. She didn't argue – indeed there was no opportunity for her to do so because it took her a day or two after the fateful encounter to discover the hidden meaning and allusion in what had been said.

At some celebration, one of Dad's friends, a big charmer and Casanova, jokingly asked what Penelope did while her Odysseus was at sea. She stomached the allusion without saying a word. However, when she got home, she swore to us that she was done with him.

"What arrogance! What insolence!" she said, her cheeks red with fury. "And that's supposed to be a friend?!"

Actually, Mum realised that she wasn't very attractive and that any kind of courteous attention wasn't really meant to seduce. It was just a compliment, to be polite. That hurt her deeply. So she developed ways to guard herself against the constant temptation of promiscuity, as if, in her case, the danger was ever-present. She lived an honest life because she chose to do so. She could have lived differently had she wanted to. There was nothing easier than to put yourself out there. Skirt-chasers were waiting at every corner.

She would draw out the last syllable of the word in a trembling, almost menacing voice. Her eyes would well up with tears, and, for a second, she would close them. As if revelling in this imagined act of adultery. She would never use words like lover, or charmer or admirer. I suppose that, according to her criteria, such notions were more complex, endowed with subtler nuances, whereas a skirt-chaser is devoid of emotions, he's just a rascal whose attentions are more humiliating than flattering to a woman. A skirt-chaser has no warmth, it's just about the mechanics of satisfying an urge.

Her day-to-day life was such hell! She lived in an iron straitjacket of taboos. She constantly kept an eye on what was happening in the hold, in the hidden recesses of human communication, where she had no access because she did not speak the language of secret conversation. Always on the margins of naughty stories, never really knowing the context, a sad messenger conveying words of love. At boarding school she must have been so disturbed by the parade of her classmates' boyfriends, the stories of their adventures and pranks, the absence of forbidden thoughts and desires, their complete freedom, as if it were all a movie.

Mum's time for love came during the school holidays when the girls returned home. She would go back to the village. Roam the fields. In her loneliness, she would think up stories to tell and impress her classmates when she returned to boarding school.

Later, in the course of the year, she received letters. She even had a photograph of a young man in a sailor's top who was doing his military service. Her cousin, whom she introduced to her friends as her boyfriend, foreshadowed possibly the only man in my mother's life.

He would appear twenty years later, in the uniform of a lieutenant in the Yugoslav Navy. She was already approaching forty, but she still believed that she would escape the grim fate of spinsterhood. She consoled herself with the thought that it wasn't the worst thing that could happen to an honest girl. To be abandoned and left with a child out of wedlock, now that was a tragedy. Which is why she was intent on making sure that she would not be seduced and abandoned.

World War I had only just ended when Mum was born. It had left the Mačva region devastated. The wounds left by Austrian punitive expeditions were still fresh. Mum's father was the only one of his brothers to survive; he was the head of the family, to be more precise of the family cooperative that consisted of four widows and lots of children. He owned a huge property, an oakwood forest, a brick factory. One of the richest men in the village. He liked to drink, and when he did, he became short-tempered and nasty.

I know nothing about Mum's pre-boarding-school life. I'm completely in the dark about her decade in the village. She never talked about it. And yet those are the years when yardsticks appear which are later used to measure the world. She only made a point of saying that they had been rich: she would enumerate at length all the things they had owned, from horses and cattle to forests and fishponds. I once asked her why she hadn't inherited anything, and for a minute she fell silent. Then she said that she had renounced her inheritance in favour of her brothers and sisters who had stayed in the village. She was duty-bound to do so because she had been the only one of them to be schooled. In those days it wasn't unusual for heirs whose family had invested in their education to behave that way – in other words, it wasn't a matter of Mum's irresponsible generosity, but rather of an unwritten rule. I had my doubts about that story. I sensed that something was missing. The subject of her inheritance was not mentioned again.

Who knows what the night concealed in the villages of Mačva after the war ended and life resumed in those slumbering family cooperatives. The women stopped wearing black. Shadows swayed in the light of the petroleum lamps. Beds creaked. Bodies breathed under their quilts.

I peer into the dark. A convoy of relatives passes by. I recognise their rough faces from celebrations and funerals, from family photo albums and from gravestones. My mother was born in that darkness. It was there that she had spent the first ten years of her life, there that she had absorbed obsessive scenes, stories with lessons for every possible situation in life, there that she had adopted values that she never questioned, there that she had developed fears and phobias, and that tight smile with which she tried to charm everyone, to keep everything under her control. She was never completely relaxed, she moved with grinding brakes, like a train at the edge of a cliff. That tension that took hold of her whole body, was the most important element of her genetic code and she would pass it on to her descendants.

I am sitting at my desk, trying to figure out the motives and roots of the whole story, without straying into blind alleys, burying myself in useless words, afraid of the conclusions drawn.

It's wrong to believe that there is only one possibility, that all the others are false outcomes. What matters is not what Mum said, but what I believed.

Taboos at every step. I'm drowning in whirlpools of silenced stories. That is my darkness.

Constantly tense. I don't finish my sentences because that would be a definitive statement, with no possibility of changing the meaning of what was said if the other person did not approve of it. That other person is my mother. There is no way that the boy addressing her can know what he should say to please her: first, because her reactions are irrational, there is no logic to them, and also because she is never pleased. He has trouble speaking, trying with every word to find the right way to please his listener; he often stops, waiting for some sign, a nod of the head or a word showing that she agrees. He looks at her dismayed whenever approval is not forthcoming. And immediately asks: "Do you hear me?"

Discard the mother.

Leave the three-towel territory at the Stoja beach, climb onto the diving board and jump.

Be free.

17.

Another chapter at the window of the Skaleta hotel.

Everybody has to be somewhere.

How to resist this meeting point of the small family, here under my window, where Mum, my sister and I would wait for each other after coming out of the Istra cinema. Because my sister, too, sometimes managed to get lost in the crowd. We both dreaded Mum's comments to the undisciplined movie-goers who left behind trash. Repetitions of those scenes from the beach.

Later, on the way home, we would analyse the film in detail. Most important was whether the film had been instructive. According to Mum, anything that enabled one to recognise one's mistakes through the example of someone else was instructive. That was how one acquired experience. She was the incorruptible customs officer of our family universe where there was no place for negative heroes, for the irrational, for the triumph of evil over good. Justice always had to win in the end. Cheats always had to be punished.

How many abandoned women had paid the price of being naive simply because they hadn't paid attention to those little signs that betray a cheat. Right here, while walking down the deserted streets, our impressions from the movie still fresh, Mum asked us to tell her where her heroine had gone wrong. What should she have done to avoid the tragic end. I was more successful in these deliberations than my sister, who seldom managed to save the heroine from her fatal choice. There was always something that she overlooked.

"I can't believe you can be so naive as to think that Esmeralda would be happy with such a cunning fox as Harold," Mum says, dissatisfied with my sister's answer. "All he cares about is Esmeralda's wealth. But did you notice how little Patrick looked at her? Like an angel."

When my sister remarked that Patrick had a limp, was a head shorter than Esmeralda and also had a slight stutter, Mum came back at her with a torrent of irrefutable arguments: "Yes, he's got a limp, and so what? His soul is pure. Esmeralda would have had a happy life with him. This way, I don't dare even think what awaits her with that schemer Harold."

When it was my turn to propose a positive outcome for the heroine of the story, I didn't hesitate to shorten her adventure. Instead of a fatal love affair, I opted for the safety of waiting. Mum congratulated me on seeing through such deceitful characters. I became a great specialist who, behind a mask of solicitude and humanism, unerringly recognised a common-or-garden conniver.

Many years later, when the country where I had grown up disintegrated, all sorts of characters of varying abilities and ambitions, dispersed across Europe, focussed solely on their own interest. They were given honours and awards, sinecures and professorships, grants and pensions, speaking and writing the way their donors expected.

Like dampness, they crept into foundations, experts at relativising or magnifying crimes, depending upon the needs and taste of their sponsors. I encountered them at conferences and symposiums, always worried about the fate of the world, heroes of conformism, virtuosos of intonation, hirelings in the service of invisible centres of power. They won over the naive public of the West by expounding on the roles they played in their previous lives in the East. And that public opted, in no way naively, for naiveness. It decided to listen only to what it wanted to hear. The ones and the others playing their roles, creating a virtual reality of lies and manipulation.

Nothing is more lucrative and attention-grabbing than victim status. To acquire such a status is to secure one's existence for a certain period of time. The media market is hungry for victims, they assuage the conscience of the petit bourgeois. Victims represent capital whose value soars before a truce. The more victims, the more chips on the green-felt tables of peace conferences. That is why the warring parties in the Balkan hell did not hesitate to produce their own victims.

The people who produce such ideas are all the same! They differ only in terms of their sponsors.

The problem comes with those who do not accept manipulation, the division into good guys and bad, thus spoiling the tacit agreement to avoid anything that erases the border between the extremes. Because, if a world where profit stands supreme is to survive, it needs the constant driving force of a war. Only war ensures new cycles, gives impetus to science and technology, revives industry, stimulates accelerated consumption, whether of arms, medicines or the press. The only condition is that there is always an Us and a Them. And that as few as possible place themselves between the two, in that gap of the border.

In order for Us and Them to survive, intermediaries are needed, self-proclaimed spokespeople for the victims of war, who testify as they are instructed to. That is a job for professional peacemakers, for men of letters, for poets and publicists, for the travelling theatre of parasites who feed on victims. They address themselves to the ordinary little people, to those who take the line of least resistance, who lean towards Nazism and other totalitarian ideologies. These ordinary little people want to lose themselves in the masses, because that doesn't hurt, and they can then avoid being noticed, since that can sometimes be dangerous, especially when times are grim. They always want to be with the majority and avoid personal responsibility. They want to protect themselves behind the screen of cowardice, conformism and opportunism.

I grew up in a world of unusual ordinary people, who did not accept injustice, whether it happened to them or to people they didn't know on another continent. My mother was a prime example of such a person, a person who did not accept brute force; she had the courage to stand up to the crowd, be it a beach or at a cinema; she waged battles that were lost in advance and never gave up.

The decisive event of my childhood was when I read in an encyclopaedia that nearly twenty million Native Americans had lived in the prairies of North America before the age of Columbus. Four centuries later, that number had dropped to half a million, confined to reservations. That upset me. I swore to myself that one day, when I grew up, I would avenge them. That I would investigate and make a list of the crimes committed against them. That in my future novels, I would save these Native American warriors from oblivion.

I looked and I remembered. I spent a long time preparing to be a writer.

Mum believed in the power of the written word. Every book she ever gave me is inscribed with the dedication: *To Dragan from Mum*. She never failed to sign them, even editions entailing several volumes, which is how I have thirteen of her dedications in Proust's *In Search of Lost Time*.

To Dragan from Mum is also written in the eight volumes of Sigmund Freud's selected works. And in all three volumes of Karl May's *Winnetou*, bought in a bookstore in Ljubljana.

She would have written it on the logarithm table too if she could have. When I think of all the times she took that little dust-coloured hardback notebook from my desk and reverently read out the names of the authors!

"O. Schlomilch and J. Majcen," always followed by the same comment: "If anybody deserved to have their full names known, they did."

She was dazzled by columns of multiple-digit numbers. Putting order into the world with tables. Giving every day a number. That was her dream.

The morning before I left to take my math exam in my last year of high school, she solemnly told me their first names: Oscar and Juraj. Who knows how long she had kept their names to herself only to announce them at the precise moment when my self-confidence needed bolstering. She was so fascinated by coincidences that she often produced them herself. However, that did not call into question the validity of the event itself.

She created her own kabbalah, whose rules I failed to decipher. She boasted that when she was a girl, holidaying on the Adriatic coast, she knew in advance what her vacation would be like from the room number she was given at the hotel reception desk. She had her good numbers and her bad numbers.

Four decades after graduating from high school, Oscar Schlomilch's and J. Majcen's little book was on my night table at the Skaleta hotel. The triumph of Mum's kabbalah! Number four: the symbol of loyalty and discipline, of good organisation and prudence.

"Tell me, can that be a coincidence?" I can hear her say. "That Goran Ban should return your logarithm tables exactly forty years later?"

I dispute that. She's always imagining things, she has never faced the world around her. A fighter for the truth whose whole life has been one of lies and illusions.

"For heaven's sake!" she says, aggrieved.

She casts me one of those contrite looks she gets when for, a second, she exposes her real self, revealing her utter helplessness: her eyes are moist, her lips tremble, she is on the verge of tears, and with the palm of her hand she scoops invisible crumbs off the table. She seemed to retreat, accepting defeat, recognising her misapprehensions. But that was just part of her strategy, to tacitly obtain a time out from her interlocutor, so she could catch her breath before the final showdown.

"If that is true, then what are you doing here? Why aren't you in Belgrade? You're the biggest liar I know. You wrote all those books just to have somewhere to hide."

She went on, deftly taking advantage of my hesitance to contradict her.

"They did away with the cinemas. They closed down the department store. They abolished the trains. I can't recognise Pula anymore. The only thing left is the cemetery. There, at least, there's some order. What was once considered bad for your health, now turns out to be good. The world is spinning in a circle. There are more and more people, and fewer and fewer brains. Tell me I'm wrong. As soon as you can't find your size in a store, you're written off. And don't kid yourself that your shoulders have become narrower and your legs shorter. The simple fact is that there's not enough space for everybody. It's goodbye. If only you could do what I do, honestly, without calculating, even at the risk of losing everything. It's true, I couldn't stand the idea of strangers rummaging through my wardrobe. I took good care of the bed linen, the sewing box, the clothes, all those wonderful books, the cobalt blue glass violinist. Do you know that Viller's *Winter* stayed behind in Pomer as well? Nothing will be in its proper place anymore. From now on our house is the train carriage in Vinkovci. I'd rather not have it than witness all this chaos. I may be crazy but I'm not stupid. Departures are always final."

I can hear her voice in my head, the incessant noise of words. Scenes flash by. My mother, my sister and me running after the train. Looking for our seats in the darkness of the cinema. Everyone around us grumbling. At the Stoja beach, running naked between two rows of bathers. They laugh and make fun of us. The diving board at the end of the path looks like a gallows.

"Don't be upset, dear neighbour, Lizeta said to me that morning in Pula, after learning that we had been robbed. That's life. Me, I lost a whole city; you, you've lost just a few suitcases. What's in the suitcases doesn't belong to the house, she said. And you know, she was right. And you? You think I don't see where you're going? That's not investigating, that's falsifying! Where's your sister? Maybe she should be asked what she thinks. Let's hear what she has to say about your various claims. You're not the only witness. You just want to partly open or partly close the door, depending on what suits you. Why not for once open wide that door and then slam it shut so hard that the whole place shakes. Listen, what you're doing would only make sense if, in the end, you left here forever."

Her effort to conjure up answers in advance to questions from invisible opponents was admirable. Like a schoolgirl, she would repeat everything to make sure she hadn't forgotten anything. She always had alms ready at hand for beggars, bundles of old things for Gypsies, brandy for postmen. How empty her emotional life must have been for her to put such feeling into this nonsense! She laid a terrible trap for herself with her constant quest for love, to love and be loved. She had become a prisoner of the self-image she had created for others. She had ruled out the possibility of correcting it. Because her experience of the world had taught her that only women of dubious reputation polished their nails, went alone to cafés, smoked, drank hard liquor, spent more time with their female friends than with their own children.

I envied those children whose mothers were dubious and well-dressed and who left them at home alone in the evening. My sister and I had a childhood capped by our mother's constant worrying. She monitored and corrected everything. She had time for everything. She invested an enormous amount of energy in carrying out her daily duties. Our dress rehearsals lasted from morning to night. My sister and I rehearsed our lines, the movements and gestures of the imagined persons we were supposed to become one day, when we grew up and embarked on the sure paths of a planned life. I could hear Mum's voice coming from the prompt box.

And then, on our train journeys during the summer holidays, when in the crowded compartments friendships were struck up in just a few hours — Mum was a past master at that — I listened for the umpteenth time to her repertoire in these symposiums of Yugoslav Railway passengers. She invented incredible stories. She very quickly impressed everyone. Soon, hers was the only voice to be heard. I was surprised to discover the enormous difference between our life as it was, and the picture Mum painted of it for others.

My sister and I were her trophies. Our success was the purpose of her life. Whatever she had failed to do at the personal level, she tried to make up for through her children.

She was extravagant in her praise for us, predicting that we would have successful careers. Her fellow passengers looked at us with admiration. I felt as if I were at a slave market. They congratulated Mum on having such well-brought-up children. I was acutely embarrassed. On the train, like at the beach, we were a little family circus putting on a show.

Whole convoys of common references filled my ears. Even today, half a century later, I find myself tripping over the stupidities that stifle my every thought. I'm simply unable to block out how those trips affected me, the anxiety I felt from such closeness to people I didn't know, listening to their boring stories. Invisible borders existed even then, you could smell it in the air the moment the train left Serbia near Tovarnik, or after Zidani Most when it plunged into the pine forests of Slovenia. The houses in baroque towns reflected much more than order, cleanliness and the austere. The discipline and restraint of the north would disappear in the noise of the train tracks in the south. After Stalać, it was the breath of the East.

There were so many foreign countries on the domestic railway lines. But middle class passengers didn't notice it. Their country was all one piece. That's what they thought, whether they lived in Ptuj or Vranje, Zenica or Varaždin, Split or Kumanovo, stuck in the grips of realism; I try in vain to get off, to put a full stop, to move to a new paragraph, to open a new chapter.

The faces from the stuffy compartments of the Yugoslav Railways half a century ago have disappeared. They can't be found anymore, not even in novels. Literature is more interested in negative heroes than in the inhabitants of the monotonous everyday.

"Life punishes those who want to establish a bit of order, I know that," Mum says. "For centuries they burned us. The rabble is used to being indulged, it always finds justification and understanding for weaknesses and wrongdoing, it likes those in whom it can recognise itself, those who do not saddle it with lofty demands and moral principles. They are easy to follow and to love. Today, everybody is ashamed of goodness."

We passed Kanfanar, Divača, Postojna, Ljubljana, Zidani Most.

We passed Zagreb, Novska, Slavonski Brod, Vinkovci.

We passed Pazova, both Stara and Nova, Batajnica, Zemun, New Belgrade.

The last trip from Pula to Belgrade on a Yugoslav Railway train was a long time ago. But the directions are still indicated on signs. It's the same geography. Only the administration has changed. And with it, so have the flags, anthems, uniforms and, of course, borders.

Standing by the window of the Skaleta hotel, I take stock of a country whose regime I detested. This appraisal is by a person who, on a freezing cold January day in Ćuprija in 1978, his lips pursed, did not take the military oath; a person who never visited Tito's grave; a person who was never a member of the League of Communists, and, therefore, never had that magical attestation to moral and political aptitude, without which it was difficult to get a job; a person who spent five years looking for work, unsuccessfully applying for dozens of jobs in newspapers, on the radio and television, in libraries and schools.

And now, this same person would like to save from oblivion a period, no worse than the one that followed, when most people lived a decent life; to stand up to false patriots and profiteers, to those whose strong muscles of Croatdom and Serbdom were tattooed, in their youth, with the date when they entered the Yugoslav People's Army and ran in the relay race for Tito's birthday, only later to shamelessly revise their past; to put an end to boring stories about a time that could have come if only there had been less of the conditional and the subjunctive, for which the others were to blame.

No, gentlemen, there is no such time when you would be on your own, without those others, because of whom things are as they are, basically bad. Because, always and everywhere, it is you who are these others, regardless of whether your protector wears a *šajkača* cap and reeks of alcohol, or a green loden coat and leather lederhosen, yodelling in the beerhalls of the former Monarchy. You are never an individual person, you are always just one of many, crammed in the crowd, the weak in the strong embrace of mentalities. That is why you celebrate your ilk; like animals, you instinctively recognise one another. You speak the same language; you are each other's audience. You sense that it would take very little for you to change places, for you to be on the front pages and TV. For you to lead the pack.

That morning, standing at the window of the Skaleta hotel, I saw the novel I had in mind. They were all there, side by side: uncle Dragomir, the Hiterots, Vesko Krmpotić, count Milevski, Lizeta, the watchmaker Maleša, my mother, my sister, my father...And me, continuing the story that began in Mum's notebook stolen in Vinkovci. There where a given but never fulfilled life was chronicled.

There doesn't always have to be a plot. Nor the obligatory surprise ending. Or crucial changes. Experience says otherwise: no one has ever changed anywhere. One stays the same, always and everywhere. That, indeed, is the tragedy of life. A fool will never become wise, nor will a thief ever become honest. Goodness and wisdom are inexhaustible categories. So are evil and hypocrisy.

Mum says: "Thought is quicker than anything, and I can't escape that speed. That is why I don't wait for miracles to happen, I simply go on, I analyse every minute. I live in tune with the universe."

PART II

1.

He was almost sixty when he realised that old age did exist after all. And it wasn't far away either! He had finally found a fixed point. No more before or after, fast or slow, better or worse. Just the moment one finds oneself in.

He came to love life in reverse.

His discovery was preceded by an argument with his sister. How she had ever managed to read an excerpt from the novel published in a provincial journal had always been a mystery to him. She had never been interested in literature. In primary school he would recount to her the books they were supposed to read for class. Later, during her five years in music school, he would write her essays for her.

One afternoon, out of the blue, she burst into his flat unannounced and embarked on a monologue while still at the door. He should be ashamed of writing such lies. Of exposing his parents' private life. Was nothing sacred to him? And what gave him the right to mention her? No, she didn't care what *ich forma** was, what artistic truth was. In her world there was only one truth, the one that actually happened. What arrogance to doubt the official version! Anything that shouldn't be exposed to others but is exposed has the status of a lie. Yes, that's exactly what she thinks!

---

* First person narrative.

Otherwise, how was one to protect oneself against aggressive people like him? Everybody has the right to secrets that are never told to anyone. What would the world look like if everybody went around blurting out their confessions in a public square?

"You're a grocer! But, if you've already decided to settle accounts with yourself so ruthlessly," she continued without drawing a breath, "why did you keep silent about your time in the League of Communists? You were still a minor? So what? That's not a mitigating factor. Is your dirty laundry any cleaner than other people's?"

"True, in my third year of high school I was admitted into the League of Communists. The formal presentation of the membership card was the same day as my maths test. That was my only motive – to get out of doing the test," he says, justifying himself. "I never attended a single meeting and after three months they struck my name off the register."

"Then why didn't you say that in your novel? On the other hand, you didn't forget my seventeen "A"s. I was eight at the time, half your age when you became a member of the Communist League."

He says nothing. She continues.

"It's not Mum's fault that you're a poor swimmer. And you depicted us as mascots."

"But Nena, that's what we were…"

"Don't mention my name! Not anywhere! Understand?!"

Suddenly, the look on her face resembles my mother's – nostrils flaring in anger, lips pressed tight, head tilted to the side, as if aiming at a point in space. All that is missing is for her to scoop up the invisible crumbs from the table with her hand.

Why can't she understand that the truth is worth much more than just nice words? To invoke the spirit of the times.

Confront weaknesses, mistakes, illusions. Look at his own past without amending it. On the brink of old age, to discover the unsaid and suppressed, all those things that he had been deeply ashamed of all his life. Is there anything worth more than that?

She says nothing. He continues.

As if it were yesterday, he sees her on the black-and-white television screen. All their friends from Gupčeva Street had come to Lizeta's that Sunday morning to watch the "Children Sing – Zagreb 1964" festival. Her song is about a ladybug. She's wearing a little dress with tulle wings. Mum's creation. Not just the costume, but the entire staging.

"It was her idea for you to touch the edge of your dress while you sang, to gaze upwards every so often, to smile a lot. I remember how she would make you practice at home. You sang and she decided the movements you should make for each stanza."

"I was the best at the dress rehearsal in the Zagreb studio. I easily made it to the finals, but I didn't take first place, as everybody expected. I was third."

"Mum was devastated."

"Was she? You were there?"

"I remember how the two of you came back from Zagreb looking deflated."

"But we weren't devastated," his sister says. "What I found the most interesting was the hotel lift. I spent my time going up and down. And please don't talk to me about the symbolism of it. There was nothing surprising about it. It was the first time in my life that I had seen a lift."

"She should have let you look natural, instead of imposing her own scenario on you. She stifled your spontaneity."

"Maybe, in the damned finals, but so what? Anyway, it didn't get to me. I always did what I wanted. Unlike you, you did what Mum wanted. You're just like her, you know that? The spitting image. Once you sink your teeth into something, you don't let go. Imagine you remembering my finals from half a century ago. And you say Mum was devastated?"

"She was. Have you forgotten those train trips of ours when she couldn't stop bragging about us? She always made a point of saying that you took first place at the children's festival in Zagreb."

"Ok, so what's the difference between her lying about me winning at the festival and you keeping quiet about your three months in the League of Communists?"

She glanced at her watch. She had to leave, or she'd be late for the parent-teacher meeting.

"Mum was merely correcting the story of her everyday life in line with her own rules of justice. She wanted to make the world a better place. She wasn't a hypocrite. Or a loser," she says before leaving. "As for me, don't ever mention me again!"

2.

He arrived in Pula on a windy March morning on the overnight bus from Belgrade. He set out for the Skaleta hotel on foot. The wheels of his suitcase made an unpleasant noise on the short walk from the bus station to the hotel where, four months earlier, he had spent a whole week. It felt like a year since the Book Fair, when he had roamed around the city where he had grown up. Early in the afternoon he went to the main post office and at the Post Restante counter picked up a letter sent a month earlier.

He had started writing letters to himself while still in high school. A habit borrowed from the sovereign. Whenever Yugoslavia faced a crisis, Tito would address the working people. Once he did it in the form of an open letter, published in all the newspapers, saying that hard times lay ahead and that they could only be overcome with new reforms. He noted that great sacrifices would have to be made in the name of a better tomorrow for everyone. However, the reforms were implemented in a way that didn't bring about any significant changes. This show was performed for almost half a century.

His own was not much shorter. And it was still being performed.

Once a year, before summer vacation, he would draw up a list of his oversights and mistakes, make corrections, ranging from habits he needed to adopt — morning gymnastics and stopping smoking — to new strategies regarding girls. At the end came questions about the future. What kind of life would he be living in five or ten years' time? What town would he be living in? With what woman? Would he be in good health?

He would leave the letter between the pages of a randomly chosen book. The objective of this ritual was to be able, one day, to take stock of the road taken. Sometimes, he would discover his own voice from the past a whole decade later. All those unnecessary worries, mistakes, fears. Usually, things resolved themselves. He would note that he was still on the right road. Life lay ahead of him. The new toys from California were still waiting in the trunk.

He thought of himself in the third person.

One doesn't become crazy. One is born crazy. It's like having perfect pitch. Having the right intonation at every moment. Being aware of everything going on around you. There are no priorities. Everything carries the same weight. No one thing is more important than another.

Compulsory activities maintain continuity. To concentrate on maintaining hygiene. That is the weak point of amnesia. That is how one wins the battle against dementia. It is particularly important to protect oneself when travelling. To anticipate possible surprises.

To start with, it was with aspirin and an umbrella. Later, it was a change of clothes and a hair fan. It ended with an iron and a heater. No, it's not a question of being odd, it's a question of common sense. In between seasons, hotels can be very cold. A little portable heater solves the problem. And so, it became a permanent accessory on my travels.

He must have been German in his previous life. He'd suspected as much the first time he visited Munich. Never had he been more relaxed. Later, living in Germany, he found himself confronted with this logic, so close to him, of anticipating possible annoyances, and constantly trying to prevent them. He marvelled at this advance step, this need to predict the next moment.

The platforms at railway stations are divided into sectors; each has a departure board with details regarding the trains leaving from the given platform: the number of the train, the number of the carriage, the time of departure, the position of the carriages. If you have a reservation, you will know precisely where your carriage stops and which sector.

Only Germans have this aptitude to foresee everything. They love tools. They will buy a set of twenty screwdrivers just for that one screw that they may need to fasten one day. They love all sorts of useful aids which they then perfect, regardless of whether it is a shaver, a new generation of light-weight suitcases or a can-opener. They are so fascinated by anything that makes life easier that at a certain point it becomes unbearable. Take, for instance, the powered leaf sweeper. It makes a terrible racket while blowing dry leaves off pathways and concrete surfaces, which are then collected in piles and later loaded onto trucks. The noise these things make is worse than that of a lawn mower.

From his hotel window in Mainz he watched an employee in blue overalls use a big hose to blow away the fallen leaves from the parking area. He was wearing ear defenders against the noise. He looked like a pilot. The image was indelibly imprinted on his mind. That man from Mainz joined a rich collection of characters who had chanced to walk into his life. He remembered them, just the way the watchmaker Maleša remembered Kardelj's dark-jacketed security men standing in the August sun. Was that the way to save one's neck? A prescription for not participating in life?

In every madness there is a hidden desire for order.

Every trip he took invigorated his collection. Characters glimpsed in passing long ago resurfaced from his memory. Like the tipsy old man at the bus station in London's Camden Town. He had come up to him and asked for ten pence. Just then, the bus for Putney arrived. In his haste, he reached into his pocket and shoved an old twenty pence coin into the old man's hand. Getting more than he had asked for, the old man felt the need not just to say "thank you", but to make an extra show of his gratitude by excitedly declaring that the number 31 bus was very useful. It remained unclear whether this *useful* referred to the generosity of his benefactor, prompted by the sudden arrival of the bus, or to the 31 bus itself, which diagonally connected two distant parts of London.

The curtain fell. He forgot about the old man. Almost four decades later, while spending a few weeks in Péc, he inquired at the tourist office if there was a tourist bus to see the city. There is a little train which departs from the main square, the girl at the counter said in good English. Or he could take the number 31 bus which goes from the train station all the way up above the city, offering a wonderful view. A very useful bus, she said smiling.

Disinterred from the depths of his memory was the old man from Camden Town. The same word, in the same language, used in the same way. The same number – 31. Life is a weave of chance coincidences, inexplicable connections, secret signs. It was from such trivialities that he had built a dubious metaphysics and let himself fall captive to superstitions and witchcraft. In the street he counted his footsteps, in houses he counted the steps on the stairs, at night, before going to sleep, he did crossword puzzles. He was waging a preventative battle against dementia, following the instructions written in the notes left by the anonymous guest at the Garibaldi hotel in Venice, which claimed that enumeration was the best way to keep one's memory sharp. He would pick a letter at random and then, within the space of a minute, try to list twenty words that started with that letter, and that weren't proper nouns.

Leaving the post office, he headed for the Riviera hotel. There, on a stone bench dating from Italian times, his mother evoked the path taken. That was also the beginning of the journey that awaited him from the day that he had arrived at the Book Fair in the town where he had grown up. He returned four months later, this time incognito. He had grown a beard. He had lost a lot of weight since the winter. He smoked a lot. No one recognised him, not even his high school friend, Goran Ban, whom he had run into in Kandler Street one night.

3.

One humid August morning, the steamship Patras leaves the port of Trieste on the new Piraeus to Salonica line, with stops in Pula and Zadar. It is 1923. Among the passengers is a young woman with coal black hair and dark eyes. Her name is Lizeta Benedetti. Her Italian passport says she was born in Salonica on 11 November 1897 and resides at Via Cavana 34 in Trieste.

As the ship sails away from the coastline, she looks at the big hump of San Giusto, and the houses dotting the hills. Her eyes glide down the slopes. Trieste's steep streets open up like the pages of a familiar book. Her thoughts stop at one of them and dip into a paragraph – into the park in front of the City Library, or the steep Via Donata, above the Roman theatre excavation, she sees her first boyfriend, Ettore, with whom she had exchanged only kisses. Later the town would grow, in reverse proportion to the waning attention of her guardians who, after that August disaster – when flames raged for three days and three nights – had no one anymore to file a report to concerning their young relative. The uncertainty and hope that one of the Salonica cousins had survived the fire lasted for weeks. They searched for them via the Red Cross and Jewish organisations. The highest number of casualties was in the western part of the city, and by the sea, where houses had burned down to the ground. The family hotel owned by Lizeta's father was near the seafront, and in Egnatia Street his younger brother ran the biggest coffee trade in Salonica. None of the Benedettis survived the fire.

It was divine punishment, their Trieste cousin Mauro kept saying to himself; he was a spice merchant, owner of a coffee roasting shop and a regular visitor to the synagogue at the Piazza Giotti in Trieste. According to family lore, Ambroggi Benedetti of Ancona inherited a fortune after his father died. He went to Turkey and opened a hotel in Salonica. He did not care much about the religion of Moses. He married a Greek woman. In the course of a century, his descendants had mixed and mingled, including with the Turks, until they no longer knew who they were or where they came from. Not only did they not know, they never even asked themselves.

Lizeta, Ambroggi's only living descendant, heir to the Salonica Benedetti's shares in her Trieste relatives' coffee roastery, discovered the deception and, prompted by her lawyer, reached an out-of-court settlement. For a while she lived in the family house of the Hiterots, whose young daughter Barbara was her best friend. It was Barbara who was the first to question the amount of the inheritance Lizeta's guardian Mauro Benedetti was supposed to pay out to her.

A few years after the story of the inheritance, Lizeta is standing on the deck of the Patras steamship, the words exchanged by the sailors familiar to her ear. The ship is Greek. Its home port is Salonica. The epilogue of nine years spent in Trieste, with their many worries, a love affair that had let her down badly, several flirtations, friendship with Barbara, a complete break with her guardians after discovering that they had been stealing from her the whole time. But what has made her persevering and strong is her successful season in the Verdi Theatre chorus. She has been promised a permanent engagement, but before beginning a new life she has to put a full stop to her previous one. Actually, to the life that preceded the previous one.

With the end of the war, she found herself living in another country, without ever having moved from Trieste, just as, on the eve of the world catastrophe, her native Salonica had found itself inside new borders under a different flag. She had no idea that travel through nascent and disappearing countries would be the constant of her life. Over a period of eight decades, she would assemble a whole collection of documents: residence and departure papers, identity cards, powers of attorney, employment and health records, permits, wills and passports. And, like her father, she would be indifferent to flags and hymns, always wondering why the photographs of sovereigns weren't the size of postage stamps.

You can't let anyone leave without a declaration of departure, her father used to say.

He kept a scrupulous record of his guests. In the storeroom behind the reception desk were the family archives, going back to the days when her great-grandfather Ambroggi Benedetti, arriving from Ancona, opened the first European hotel in Salonica. Sometimes she would sneak into that windowless storeroom, with its lamp and little round table in the corner. She would randomly take one of the heavy tomes, spend a long time leafing through the yellowed fragile pages full of names, addresses, travel document numbers, arrival and departure dates. Everything was there. And yet, nothing was there. Just numbers and letters. The whole city was one big hotel, where there was a mixture of all sorts of languages, where children had two names, one for the street and the other for at home, and where no one was actually on their own territory. They all lived in a sort of no man's land, on planet Salonica.

That's why she felt reassured by documents, by the sight of her own name in her passport, on bank cheques, her residence permit, boat ticket.

Existence was unimaginable without a document that legalised one's presence, be it on a train or in a hotel. She hesitated until the very last moment about whether to bring the box of photographs with her on the trip – not because it would weigh down her luggage, but because of her superstitious belief that it was not good to part, even temporarily, with one's own past. In the end, she decided to confront what awaited her in the city she had left fourteen years ago, without those paper memories, which were her only firm territory. She entrusted the box of photographs to her best friend Barbara.

On the deck of the ship Patras she remembers travelling by train with her mother from Salonica to Vienna. The long wait at the Turkish-Serbian border. Then in Belgrade transferring onto the Orient Express. A hotel on rails. In Budapest, a man paid them a visit on the train. The man had a long conversation with her mother in the corridor. When they arrived in Vienna that evening, for a moment she thought that she saw the same man on the platform. Or was it an apparition, spawned by so many strong emotions during the trip? Before she moved to Mrs. Haslinger's boarding school a few days later, she had caught sight of a familiar face from the streets of Salonica in the crowd in Graben.

Vienna felt very quiet after Salonica. Her father's letters were long and detailed. Following the revolution of the Young Turks, Salonica was like a seething volcano. Explosions, rebellions, assassinations everywhere. Get as far away as possible from the Balkans, and the portent of future wars. A gesture by her father to protect her. He who, based on his customers' professions and the length of their stay, foresaw the times that were coming, said that what was in the offing was much more serious than all those Bulgarian and Macedonian terrorists who a few years earlier had robbed banks, planted bombs on ships and in hotels.

The hotel was her father's sanctuary. All his life, he had kept his own statistics. Most of the people who came to Xenodochion Egnatia were tradespeople and shipping agents who stayed in its spacious, reasonably priced rooms for weeks, sometimes even months, before moving permanently to Salonica. Those with more money would rent several rooms, bring over the family, and conduct their business from the hotel.

A whole century had found a place in the books of Xenodochion Egnatia, starting with the hotel's first registration under the name Albergo Benedetti. The history of arrivals and departures. Her narrow second class cabin on the Patras steamboat reminds her of the storage space behind the hotel's reception desk. On the tiny desk she finds a message saying that the person she will be sharing the cabin with will embark in Pula.

But before Pula there is Rovinj. Upon leaving she had promised Barbara that she would stand on the deck when the boat approached Rovinj, to make sure that she didn't miss seeing the island of St Andreja, the Hiterot family's patch of paradise where Barbara and her mother had been coming increasingly often and where they intended to install themselves permanently; and where they invited her to join them. Later she learned from the steward that the boat would not be sailing that close to the shore. The only thing she would be able to see from the sea was the belltower of Rovinj's cathedral.

Before the boat's arrival at the next port, the departure declaration needs to be completed. Like at the hotel. That's what she had told Barbara upon leaving.

And now here she is on the trip she had imagined so many times after having seen, on the front page of the newspapers, amidst news from the battlefront, the name of her native city. She hasn't slept for days. She is haunted by scenes of burned down houses. Half-asleep, she sees the silent faces of her father and mother. They float over the ruins like ghosts. When the Great War ended on the day that she came of age, Lizeta planned her departure for Salonica. In the meantime, thanks to Barbara and the Hiterot family's lawyer, she would discover that her guardians had cheated her by appropriating the dividends of her father's younger brother, who had also died in the fire, along with his wife and children.

Where, in fact, is she going? To face the disappearance of her parents? To finally expunge the Salonica inside her that hasn't existed for the past six years? To destroy the maquette, with all its hidden corners embedded in her memory. To make a declaration of departure from this spectral city. To make a declaration of departure from the family.

She can make a declaration of departure. But how can she face the disappearance? Disappearance is not an end; it is a black hole. It is a crater of uncertainty.

And whom has she got left then? The students at Mrs. Haslinger's boarding house. Her hypocritical Trieste relatives. Her world consists of cold dormitories, timorous touches, whispers, hoarse voices.

Twelve years in the safe shell of home. She discovers nearby streets, the cinema on the square in front of the Moreno department store, the shady paths of the Bechtsinar gardens. Gradually she learns that her father and mother are two different worlds. He, for whom the hotel was his life, who was afraid of crowds, who avoided walking through the market, always on the verge of fainting, terror-stricken by herds of people. And she, constantly looking for adventure. Under the pretext of keeping an eye on the staff, she would disappear into one of the rooms. Sometimes she would not be seen for two or three days, not in the hotel or in the house. At such times the whole apartment was filled with peace and gentleness, like a church.

They lived in a two-storey building opposite the hotel. From the window of her room, little Lizeta kept watch on the hotel, waiting to catch sight of a guest at one of the windows, or the familiar face of a maid. Sometimes she saw her mother.

On the dining room wall, a portrait of Ambroggi Benedetti; anonymous ancestors hidden in his long beard. On her mother's side, innkeepers from Thrace, a mixture of Greeks and Turks, who only in Salonica could live side by side in peace.

Standing on the deck of the Patras, *Lizeta observes the Istrian coastline. Before going any further she first must face the emptiness. That is all that exists. She carries in her memory the two people who conceived her. And that portrait of Ambroggi Benedetti. And all those numbers in the hotel ledgers in the storage space behind the reception desk. Who were the precursors in the long column of ancestors? She had heard about them from her Trieste cousins, who could reconstruct the family tree going back four centuries, from their flight from Spain when the Benedetti family first stopped in Livorno, before scattering in the Apennines, all the way to Rome, and on the other side, towards Ancona, Venice and Trieste.*

Her cousins were surprised by her ignorance. Although she understood Ladino, she knew very little about her ancestors' religion. Amongst themselves they called her la piccola Turca.

To look at the waves from the deck of the ship is to look at the past. At history. At her father's letters. At Salonica which boiled like a cauldron. After almost five centuries under the Turks, the town was retaken by the Greeks. Gendarmes and judges arrived from the Peloponnesus and Crete in order to Hellenise it as quickly as possible. Six months later, in March 1913, King George was assassinated during a visit to Salonica.

Fortunately, her father writes, the assassin isn't a Muslim, but rather a mentally disturbed person. However, during those few hours before the municipal authorities issued an official statement, Turkish tradesmen panicked, closed their shops and withdrew into their houses. The city fell quiet in anticipation of a pogrom against the Muslim community.

Although there was no pogrom, the exodus of the Turkish inhabitants would continue. When World War I broke out a year later, Salonica was inundated with Serbian refugees. Military camps soon appeared. Salonica became the base of the allied armies.

Her father writes that the city is overcrowded and cramped. It's like living in a matchbox. There's no room for even a needle. Soldiers, adventurers, vagabonds wherever you look. Salonica is like a big lower category hotel, like an inn where there are no declarations of arrivals and departures.

At the window of Mrs. Haslinger's boarding school, in the Vienna neighbourhood of Ottakring, history is making Lizeta tremble. The whole world has been shaken by the assassination in Sarajevo. Some students leave the boarding school overnight. Parents and telegrams arrive every day. Her cousin Mauro Benedetti gets in touch. Lizeta, carrying an expired Turkish passport, moves from Vienna to Trieste. It is still one country. The train stations along the way are chillingly silent. In Udine, newspaper boys cry out the latest headlines: Austria-Hungary attacks Serbia!

Having arrived at her guardians' house in Trieste, Lizeta begins making the round of consulates. Thanks to her Trieste cousins' connections, she obtains a Portuguese passport, which will be her only valid document throughout the war. She meets Barbara Hiterot and the two become inseparable. And then, in overcrowded Salonica, where there is no room for even a needle to fall, a spark allegedly caused by negligence in the French military camp, makes its way. Within a matter of hours, Salonica is in flames.

After leaving her guardians, Lizeta lives with the Hiterots for a while. She and Barbara talk late into the night, confiding in each other. Five years after the war, when Lizeta sets out for Salonica with an Italian passport — because she is now a citizen of the Kingdom of Italy — Barbara sees her off at the pier. The previous night, she told Lizeta her big secret. Before Barbara was born, her sister Hana, who was seventeen years older and near the end of the war had married an Austrian count and lived in Innsbruck, had spent five months in a women's monastery in the Tyrol. Later she lived for a long time on the island of St Andreja. From time to time, she would come to Trieste, and after the death of their father

Georg, she moved to Vienna. Hana was actually her mother. And her supposed mother Mari was her grandmother. She knew it. No one ever told her. But ghosts exist. They told her.

And Lizeta? Does she have a secret?

The trip from Belgrade to Vienna on the Orient Express. An unknown man on the station platform in Budapest. Her mother's return to Salonica took several weeks. She knows that. Nobody told her, but she knows.

Barbara takes her hand between her two palms and squeezes it; she kisses her on the cheek. That night they fall asleep together.

4.

He is sitting on a stone bench in the park at the foot of the Arena, at a safe distance from the sea. His fear of water is at the root of all his other fears. It has made him incapable of standing up to anyone. Having no response to authority, he has adopted the naive belief that by assuming his responsibilities he can protect himself against anything threatening him. Hiding his own heresy, he was ready for the final reckoning. He relied on patience. He allowed whole cohorts of the idle to enter his being, was suffocated by this emptiness but, like a born missionary, persevered in conducting exhausting debates; instead of isolating himself, not needing to prove anything to anyone; instead of being what he is: a poet.

Listening to the pavements. Gazing at the glass ball of time. He sees and hears those who passed by here before him.

Whole lives enter a single verse. Centuries, between two commas.

At the beginning of the pier, barely a hundred steps from the stone bench dating from the Italian era, there is a bollard, installed a century earlier at a time when Austria was building the port of Pula. It had been there in September 1949 too, when his mother, waiting for the bus to Rijeka, had walked to the edge of the sea. At one moment, she caught sight of that bollard, the same one that the tank carrier ship of the Yugoslav Navy had been moored to two years earlier. Standing on the deck was a young lieutenant. He was overseeing the sailors as they moored the ship. A decade later, that same person – this time dressed in civilian clothes, wearing a trench coat and a hat, like someone stepping out of a Melville movie – had his arms around a little boy perched on the bollard. Father and son in a black-and-white photograph, with the following inscription on the back: *Pula, 27 November 1959.*

The exodus of Pula's inhabitants, mostly Italians, started from this pier at the end of 1946. In the course of the winter, the ships *Toscana*, *Pola* and *Grado* transported refugees to Trieste and Venice. It was not just the living who were leaving Pula, it was also the dead: some families had exhumed their dead to take them to Italy.

Half a century later, a ship carrying the families of officers of the Yugoslav Navy will set sail from this same pier. But not all non-Croats will leave. Many will stay, change their documents and continue to live in this new yet still same territory. The most numerous were divided families – some stayed, others left – thus creating unexpected combinations of personal stories.

Here at this same pier, his thoughts will drift to the ship *Patras*, and he will continue the story of Lizeta that he had promised his mother on one of his last visits to the care home in Karaburma, and that he is now writing in fragments, rummaging through his own past. That bollard is a barely visible punctuation mark on the musical score of the town where he had grown up. Life is indeed a puzzle, a collection of artefacts, premonitions and obsessions, of seemingly unimportant moments registered by the whims of memory.

Grandma Danica's loose hair like Ambroggi Benedetti's long beard.

The round windows on the building of the cinema in Raša.

The note written by the unknown guest about Alzheimer's on the notepad bearing the logo of the *Garibaldi* hotel in Venice.

The mocking smile of Aleksandar Tišma on the platform of the train station in Hamburg on a January day in 1993 upon seeing the huge suitcase he was lugging. Three years later, the same smile would arouse the indignation of the audience and participants at the "Yugoslav Labyrinth" discussion organised by the Tivoli Cultural Centre in Graz.

The idea behind the symposium was to bring writers from the former Yugoslavia face to face, but Professor Aleksandar Flaker of Zagreb walked out at the very beginning of the discussion in protest over Tišma's remark that the main motive behind the participants' decision to come was the decent fee they were being paid to attend. The audience reacted loudly when the Novi Sad writer accused the western media of cynicism and hypocrisy regarding the break-up of Yugoslavia, while trying to hide their combat uniform under the habit of Mother Teresa.

But on that humid August day in 1923, as the *Patras* steamboat is mooring at Pula's pier, Tišma was not even born yet.

There in the crowd at the port of Pula is a lady about forty years old, wearing a beige suit and a wide-brimmed hat. Her name is Matilda Kesinis. A healer and stargazer, the mistress of Count Milevski. The previous day, at Pula's hospital, she had arranged for them to provide medical treatment for her mentor, who was languishing in the castle on the island of St Katarina near Rovinj. She had left her thirteen-year-old daughter Diona with him, as a guarantee of her return. She has a ticket for the boat to Piraeus and a good amount of money, a generous gesture on the part of Count Milevski. In Piraeus she will share with her brother the inheritance left them by their uncle, the owner of a rebetiko bar, and himself once a virtuoso on the bouzouki.

Matilda is not just the count's mistress and carer, she is also his sole connection with the world, for he has been living in total isolation for years now. He receives no visitors. His elderly servant Sashenka and a dozen dogs guard the island against the persistently curious, among whom are phony heirs from Lithuania and Poland. They also come from Crackow, Vienna, Verona and St Petersburg, all the places where Count Milevski had spent time, changing mistresses and nationalities. He still lives in the conviction that only the war had stopped him from turning his island into an elite sanatorium, a paradise like the nearby Brioni islands.

On the deck, Matilda meets the woman with whom she will share her cabin. The ship has barely left the bay of Pula and the two ladies are already telling each other their life stories. To their mutual delight, they speak in Greek. Matilda, ten years older, assumes the role of advisor. An hour later, the characters are in place. The scene is set, the elements of the story are pieced together.

A third person appears, Matilda's thirteen-year-old daughter Diona, present in a photograph, who, a decade later, after marrying a clarinettist with the Pula garrison's naval band, will replace her melodious last name Kesinis with the brusque name Fažov. But that afternoon she is playing with the count's dogs and strolling around the island, taking advantage of the last days of her summer holiday. Because in two weeks' time, when her mother returns from Greece, they will be going back to their dark, cramped flat in Tradonico Street near the Pula shipyards. She does not remember her father. He disappeared in a shipwreck near Corfu a year after she was born.

Times have changed, Matilda tells her travel companion. She should have no illusions that she can return to Salonica. Greeks from Anatolia have settled there now. Police from the Peloponnesus are maintaining order there. It has been very chaotic since the fire. Jews are not allowed to rebuild their destroyed houses, and most have moved to France, Portugal and the US. The fire is said to have been deliberately set with a view to ridding the city of the Jews and Turks. It was their neighbourhoods that were the worst hit.

With the long summer twilight, they retire to their cabin. Lizeta's still fingers lie on the palm of Matilda's hand while the fortune-teller's right index finger traces the line of fate. Later, she will confirm her prophesy by consulting the cards. She is quite definite about what the cards and the lines on her palm say.

He is no less definite as he hurries towards the Skaleta hotel, wanting to register his thoughts on the computer as quickly as possible. Finally, the figure of Matilda Kesinis has emerged, the mother of the piano teacher Diona Fažov from Ribarska Street, killed during the allied bombing of Pula in 1944. Her portrait had hung on the wall of the small sitting room. The distinct line of the nose, which would be evidenced if shown in profile, was discreetly hidden in full face; thick eyebrows, sensuous lips, and eyes that sparkled with life.

Whenever he went with his sister to that dark, high-ceilinged flat, he would go to the living room and, through the wide-open door, listen to his sister and the teacher Fažov rehearse the ladybug song for the festival *Children Sing – Zagreb 1964*. Lying on the low dresser was a baglamas, a small nacre-decorated string instrument with three pairs of strings – a relic inherited from Diona's great uncle who, as a child, had come with his parents to Piraeus from Smyrna. That was one of the stories the teacher Fažov had told. After the lesson, they would drink tea and eat halva. Never, in all his later travels around Turkey and the Greek islands, had he tasted halva like that. She made it the way the Greeks of Asia Minor do, with lots of cinnamon and rose water.

The living room windows looked out onto the Byzantine Chapel of St Mary Formosa and the park with its archaeological excavations. Once upon a time, this was the poor part of the old city – a dense web of narrow streets dotted with inns and bars, stretching all the way to the Forum. During the allied bombing in the last year of World War Two, most of these buildings were razed to the ground. After the Anglo-American administrators left the city, the local authorities decided to turn the site into a park.

One afternoon, after the tea and the halva, Diona surprised them by inviting them to come with her to the park. They walked between the pine trees and archaeological excavation sites. She explained that the main path, which cut diagonally across the park, followed Tradonico St. She had grown up in that street. She showed them where her house had once stood. Now, along the very edge of a parking lot, there was a Roman sarcophagus. Her mother had died at the front door, coming home from the market. The house was only partly damaged, and their ground floor flat was left untouched. Later, the entire neighbourhood was evacuated. Diona was sorry there were no benches in the park, because if there were, she would have dragged one to her old flat.

Her words stayed with him. Several weeks later, when his mother and sister left for Zagreb and the *Children Sing* festival, he would move to Lizeta's and discover on the walls of her bedroom an entire vanished city and people who were no more. That was when he understood, or sensed, that memory revives past worlds, even when they are physically gone. The world is indivisible. The old strings of the baglamas still bear traces of the fingers of Diona Fažov's great uncle, the laundry room of the Villa Maria echoes with the footsteps of English officers, and in the lobby of the Terapija hotel in Crikvenica one can hear the voices of Czech tourists.

His sensitivity to the noise of pavements, and awareness that all beings, things and happenings are connected, date back to then. Which is why, later, every time he walked through the park between the Forum and the Byzantine chapel of St Mary Formosa, he would see in the grass, by the Roman sarcophagus, the outline of Professor Fažov's bench.

5.

After three days and three nights, the Patras sailed into Piraeus early in the morning of the fourth day. During the long voyage, Lizeta was plagued by bouts of seasickness. Somewhere in the Ionian Sea, after Corfu, they were hit by a storm. She threw up. Matilda gave her some ginger. It didn't help. It was not until dawn, when the sea had calmed down, that Lizeta's stomach settled down as well. The coast of the Peloponnesus was in sight.

That entire sleepless night, Matilda had tried to distract her. She had sailed by ship so many times that she knew all about seasickness. Opium would do her good, but where would she find opium? She tells Lizeta to move her head to the rhythm of the rocking boat. That sometimes helps. The next time she goes somewhere by ship, she should take along some rose water. Lizeta laughs. Where was she to find this elixir? Matilda promises to give her a small bottle. Every year she makes some to put in the halva, the way they do in Smyrna.

The next day, Lizeta went to see the ship's doctor; he gave her atropine tablets, which were certainly more effective than ginger. She learned that the trip would take ten hours longer because the Corinth Canal was closed to navigation. There had been landslides in the wake of the recent earthquakes. Only rowboats and small boats were allowed passage through the canal.

Although the sea was calm around the Peloponnesus and they arrived in Piraeus as if transported on a magic carpet, after her experience with the storm around Corfu, Lizeta had made up her mind that she would never again go on a long journey by ship. She had been wise to buy just a one-way ticket. Of course, the reason for returning to Trieste by train rather than by ship wasn't seasickness, which she hadn't even thought about at the time, it was the desire to see once more the regions she had crossed with her mother fourteen years earlier. Except this time, she would be going only to Belgrade and then, instead of taking the Orient Express to Vienna, she would catch the Simplon Express on the Istanbul-Paris line and get off at Trieste. Four years earlier she had gone with Giorgio to the official welcome of the Simplon Orient Express at Trieste railway station. That evening he had promised that they would get married as soon as he finished his military service. They would go to Rome, to meet his parents, and then sail to Salonica for their honeymoon. On their way back, they would take the train to Venice. She had taken that trip so many times in her mind. But Giorgio left her; he simply disappeared after finishing his military service in Trieste. He went back to Rome. Or who knows where. From the beginning, Barbara had been suspicious of his southern accent, which he had allegedly picked up in the army from the Sicilians and Calabrians. They were unusually numerous in the Trieste barracks. After five centuries of Austrian rule, the dream of joining Italy had come true. Trieste had to be well protected.

At nine o'clock in the morning, the ship leaves Piraeus for Salonica. The sea is calm. Piraeus sparkles like a huge jewel. Lizeta returns to the cabin. She looks long and hard at her palm where Matilda had read her fortune over a period of three days. Her life-line is very clear; it is continuous, unbroken by illness or accidents. Her life will be long, over ninety years in all. She will be less lucky with love than with her health. The cards say the same thing. She will not have children. She will lose money and then suddenly have money. But, as Matilda told her when they parted, the dark and the light side are always equidistant. It is up to her to decide which direction she will take. Two simultaneously existing worlds.

"The choice is always yours," she hears Matilda's alto voice say. But she had never chosen – not going to boarding school in Vienna, not living with her cousins in Trieste. True, she had chosen Giorgio. That day she had come early to the rehearsal of Smareglia's An Istrian Wedding. She was having a cup of tea at the bar when he appeared. A sailor at the opera. That's how it all began.

He wasn't the first. Before him there had been Attilio, twenty years her senior. She had let herself get involved with this cousin of Barbara's even though she knew that he was engaged. And that he had already been married twice. At first, she was amused by his secretiveness, and by their excursions to Grado in his car. He knew all the secret places around Trieste, the inns on the Karst Plateau, as if he had always had forbidden affairs. After Attilio got married, they saw less of each other. And then Giorgio appeared, a sailor at the opera. And so, she stopped seeing Attilio.

However, he often went to the opera with his wife. She knew that he was watching her when she appeared on the stage with the chorus. He enjoyed the darkness of the theatre, sitting hidden somewhere in his loge. Attilio couldn't do without such thrills. She thought of all those times they had made love on the floor of the hotel corridor, in front of the wide-open door of their room. And then, at the sound of the lift or footsteps on the staircase, they would roll over like seals into the safety of their room.

Her mother withdrew in the same way behind screens and curtains, disappearing into the dark like a ghost. And in her wake, a stranger would always appear for a few seconds. Like that time on the Orient Express between Belgrade and Budapest. He wasn't a figment of her imagination. That man her mother had spent time talking to in the corridor of the train carriage in Budapest reappeared that evening on the platform of Vienna's railway station. The next day they passed by him in Graben. Once Lizeta ran into him near the orangery in Schönbrunn. Sudden encounters with familiar faces also happened to her in Trieste. Sometimes she was tempted to go up to them and ask if they had ever stayed at the Xenodochion Egnatia in Salonica.

She couldn't bear solitude. She often had panic attacks. She would wake up in the middle of the night drenched in sweat. She avoided busy streets. She remembered that her father avoided Salonica's marketplaces. And he didn't like going down to the port when one of those big cruise ships arrived. Like him, she would feel dizzy whenever she was in a crowd.

After Giorgio left, she lived for a while with the Hiterots again. Barbara had a whole floor to herself in the family villa in Farneto Street. She persuaded Lizeta to leave the flat she was renting and come and live at her place. Barbara was fascinated by the sea, loved to go sailing, like her late father, Baron Georg, after whose death the family fortune quickly petered out. Her mother took over his business affairs. At the suggestion of her lawyer, she changed advisors, which quickly proved to be a catastrophic mistake. Her older daughter Hana did not want to join in running the family's business. After marrying, she moved to Innsbruck.

Lizeta found Hana's aloofness from the family strange; it was as if she didn't belong to them. She seldom came with her husband to the family island of St Andreja, where the Hiterots owned a hotel. Once a year, they would gather their relatives and friends. The baron's two sisters would come with their families from Germany. Barbara once confided to Lizeta that Hana was a bit odd because when she was two years old her parents had entrusted her to her grandfather, Baron Georg's father, while they were away in Japan and Hong Kong. They returned only two years later. Hana didn't recognise them. Later they went only on short trips, which in their case meant an absence of two to three months.

Lizeta met the Hiterots four years after Baron Georg's tragic death – he committed suicide, allegedly because of his debts – but at home they talked about him as if he were still alive. Never in the past tense. And the domestic staff did the same. As if he were away only temporarily, on a long trip.

His portrait, by the Trieste painter Vittorio Saba, hung in the living room of the villa in Farneto Street. Lizeta had looked umpteen times at that face with its short beard, pale watery eyes and purple lips. It made her think of her great-grandfather Ambroggi, though she remembered only his long grey beard and piercing eyes. One had to be patient, which she never was, and wait for him to blink and signal his presence. Unlike Ambroggi, Baron Georg had the face of a dead man. It wasn't even a face; it was a death mask.

As business went from bad to worse, because her mother was not adept at dealing with creditors, contracts and bills of exchange, Barbara slowly felt her father's entrepreneurial blood take hold of her. She was the true heir of the Hiterots' faltering empire. She imagined moving permanently to the island of St Andreja near Rovinj, and continuing what her father had started, gradually turning the small fishing town into a tourist destination. She had the support of her friend Massimo Sella, the director of the Institute for Marine Biology in Rovinj. They were planning to set up a company for the exploitation of truffles in Livade, near Poreč.

Barbara was full of plans. She suggested to Lizeta that next summer she come with her and her mother to the island of St Andreja. The night before Lizeta's trip to Salonica, the two of them were sitting alone on the terrace of the villa, talking. That day Barbara had had a huge argument with her mother. It was over her mother's decision to sell both yachts so that she could pay off her accumulated debts.

That's the logic of a loan shark, Barbara repeated on the terrace that evening, topping up their glasses with wine. The greatest sin is cowardice.

And while Barbara kept complaining about her mother, who was terribly selfish and egocentric, even blaming her for her father's premature death – since she had been the initiator of many trips which had exhausted his already frail organism – Lizeta wondered how one could be discontent in this Hiterot paradise. Because, for her, the Hiterots were an island of safety and calm, an Arcadian territory outside of the chaotic world of constant catastrophes and wars, where empires and entire eras disappeared overnight. How could one be discontent when surrounded by the exotic things and objects Baron Georg had brought back from his travels? When there were so many relatives and friends. When letters arrived every day from all over the world.

It was all so different from Lizeta's own childhood, inhabited only by solitary people, even on Sunday walks in the Bechtsinar Gardens. Her parents led separate lives. She couldn't remember them ever arguing. She would spend hours in the storage space behind the reception desk of the Xenodochion Egnatia, reading the addresses of the hotel guests in the register. That is how she created a picture of distant worlds. She had her favourite cities, whose names she would say out loud: Smyrna, Odessa, Marseilles, Haifa, Venice, Malaga, Genoa. They were all by the sea.

Shortly before midnight, after a good deal of wine, Barbara confided to Lizeta a terrible family secret. Hana was her mother, and the mother Marie was actually her grandmother.

What about the father? Who is the father, Lizeta asked.

Count Milevski, from Katarina Island.

It was Hana's revenge for her parents' absence from her life. For her not belonging to the world. Hana had concealed her pregnancy until she was in her fourth month. By then it was too late for an intervention, so they sent her to the nuns in a monastery in the Tyrol. The mother assumed the role of the pregnant woman – far from the curious eyes of the neighbours – isolated on the island of St Andreja.

My birth certificate says I was born in Trieste to Marie and Georg, said Barbara. And so my grandparents became my parents and my real mother became my sister.

She fell silent, casting a veiled look at Lizeta.

Lizeta was completely taken aback by this inane story. The first thing she thought of was the box of family photographs that she had given Barbara the day before for safekeeping. Somebody with such a biography could not be rational. Who knew what could happen to Barbara while she was in Salonica. Living with such a secret was like sitting on a volcano.

In return, Barbara wanted Lizeta to tell her a secret of her own. Every family has secrets. There are no healthy people, there are only sick people, she kept repeating, more slowly. Lizeta promised to tell her a secret but only when they went to bed. A long trip awaited her the next day.

When they went to bed, Barbara wrapped her arms around Lizeta. She listened attentively to the story of the passionate Greek woman from Thrace, Lizeta's mother, who even after marrying an Italian of Jewish origin, continued to frequent rebetiko bars, spending entire nights enjoying hashish, the music and men. She didn't hide her dissolute life from her daughter or husband. Sometimes she would disappear from the house for days. And the father? Barbara asked. The father only cared about the hotel. That's my memory of him. He had a limp, the result of polio. He was two decades older than my mother. Over forty when they married.

Before Lizeta could embark on the story of her train trip from Salonica to Vienna with her mother, Barbara was already fast asleep.

The following day she complained that she had had too much to drink the night before. And when she did that, she always talked nonsense. That was her only comment regarding the terrible story that she had told her friend.

As they parted at the port of Trieste, Lizeta promised Barbara that the following summer, as soon as the season was over at the Verdi Theatre, she would go with her to St Andreja. They could open a music school in Rovinj.

Better a cabaret, said Barbara.

Late in the afternoon of the fourth day, Lizeta saw Salonica the way it had looked a year earlier on the screen of Trieste's Minerva cinema, without minarets and houses crammed together along the seafront. The only thing she recognised was the shape of the White Tower.

She felt vaguely dizzy when, suitcase in hand, she found herself on the pontoon bridge. Taking short, hesitant steps, she made her way towards the pier. In the crowd, several liveried porters waving flags cried out the name of the hotel. A young man with a limp, wearing a dark blue uniform and pushing a trolley, approached her. Her heart suddenly started racing when she read the gold lettering on his cap: Bristol Hotel.

If the Bristol Hotel hadn't burnt down, then miracles were possible. Her father always said that compared to the Bristol, most of Salonica's hotels were just ordinary inns.

She followed the porter through the crowd, with the group of travellers whose luggage he had piled onto his trolley. He told her why the Bristol had survived the fire: being situated on a big square, it had been easy for the firefighters to access it. Everything further on, inside the area, towards Bara, had burned to the ground.

A few minutes later they arrived at a two-story corner building, with tall French windows and narrow balconies. This was not what she remembered from her childhood. The hotel had been completely renovated.

The resplendent lobby reminded her of the Savoy in Trieste, where she had once spent the night with Attilio.

She filled out the registration form at the reception desk, leaving her date of departure open. They gave her a room with a balcony, overlooking the street. By the time she stepped off the lift on the second floor, the bellhop had already brought her suitcase to the door of her room. She gave him a tip. Alone in the spacious suite full of antique furniture, she felt as if she'd been taken back to the luxury of the Hiterots. She walked out onto the balcony. Instead of the rows of masts in the port that she remembered from her childhood, now the huge smokestacks of steamships painted with flags reached up towards the sky. They were mostly French, Italian and Greek ships.

Two hours later, she went out into the street. She headed for her old neighbourhood, which, given the location of the port, had to be somewhere nearby. But two streets further on, she had to stop to get her bearings. This was no longer the route she remembered from her childhood. For half an hour she kept turning in circles, trying to recognise at least part of the road she used to take to her music school in Kuskura Street. New roads had been built and they no longer followed the same path as the old streets.

She continued to wander around. The closer she got to the Mevlevi Tekke,* the more she encountered barren fields and remains of the fires. This was now a completely different city, without the familiar facades, without the streets she remembered. Next to the ruins of the synagogue she saw a huge tent, and children playing around it. Standing at the entrance to a half-demolished mosque, which had no minarets, was a group of women, Greeks, who obviously lived here. The words she heard as she passed by were Greek, but the intonation was harsh. That's how the tradesmen from Anatolia who stayed at the Xenodochion Egnatia talked. Whereas the Turks of Salonica, those of Lizeta's childhood, spoke Greek as if they were singing, their vowels clear and soft.

* A monastery of the Mevlevi Order, an Islamic Sufi sect.

The farther she plunged into the neighbourhood where she had spent her childhood, the wider the streets became. The names on the signs were different, written only in Greek. The small squares, the crooked little streets with their small single storey houses had disappeared. Suddenly she found herself standing in the direction of Egnatia Street. She trembled when she recognised the church near the house where she had grown up. The church was there, under scaffolding, but the house was gone. Across from the house that was now no more, had been her father's hotel. It too was gone. There was nothing left across the street because there was nothing that she remembered. She trembled as she walked up and down, trying to locate at least one touchstone.

The humid August afternoon was suffocating. Wide new streets, construction sites, hordes of people moving in all directions. She walked aimlessly, just to keep moving, carried by the crowd, hoping that she might feel she belonged to the city, if only for a moment. As she approached the port, she recognised the warehouses, those huge concrete buildings. It made her happy to see these grey halls because it meant that not everything she remembered had been devoured by the fire. As she approached the open door of the hall, she saw countless people lying on the bare concrete. A silent image. She didn't hear any voices. She just saw smoke from a chibouk pipe, the looks on exhausted faces, and children dozing on small bundles of clothes.

She fled the painful sight, going back the same way she had come. At least that's what she thought. But it wasn't the same road, and it wasn't the territory she remembered. Every return is an illusion, whether after a period of years or just an afternoon. She would come to understand that years later, not at once, but bit by bit, during those long, drawn-out days in Trieste, Rovinj, Pula. Every new disappointment made her stronger, more determined to give free rein to her nature, to her father and mother inside her. To cast off the chains left from her days at Mrs Haslinger's boarding school in Vienna.

In Salonica, she let loose: she began to smoke, heavily, she frequented bars. One evening, at an inn by the port, she was listening to a trio of male musicians and a female singer perform rebetiko music. When they sang the song Edirne, Edirne, she thought of her mother. Maybe this was her favourite song? She never heard her mother say the name of her native Edirne in Greek – Adrianopolis, it was always in Turkish – Edirne. Lizeta stayed at the inn until the morning.

Returning to the hotel she thought of Barbara. Her yearning for a healthy life was so sad and comic in the context of this terrible story. Even if she had invented it, she still would have had to find the material for it within herself. But it was all written on the purple lips of Baron Georg, on the portrait of the Hiterot family's death mask. Lizeta was no less clairvoyant than her fellow passenger on the ship, Matilda Kesinis of Pula.

She was to learn from the receptionist at the Bristol Hotel that all those people huddled together in the halls at the port, and all around, in the abandoned warehouses in Salamis Street, were Greek refugees from Asia Minor. It was a year now that they had been sleeping in rags, on the concrete floor, because there was no room left in the surrounding villages of Salonica. They were all full. There were more Greeks who had come from Anatolia than Muslims who had left for Turkey. And these Greeks did not want to go up into the mountains, they wanted to stay down by the sea. Because they had always lived by the sea, back there in Turkey. That's what she was told by the receptionist, the first person who spoke in the soft accent of Salonica, obviously a native.

After three nights on the ship, she finally had a big soft bed to lie on. But for a long time, she couldn't fall asleep. It wasn't the ship that was rocking, it was an entire city. She was constantly followed by those silent, exhausted faces with chibouks, and children who didn't cry and didn't laugh.

The next day, when she set out on her expedition to the archives, trying to find information about the people who had perished in the fire six years earlier, she panicked as she stood in front of the walls of city offices, cadastres and bureaus. Over the following two weeks, she encountered nothing but unpleasant staff. She had to bribe them before they would agree to tell her where to start. First, she needed to hire a good lawyer. There they were helpful, even offering, for an extra tip, to find her one. Why had she waited six years?

She didn't trust any of these corrupt employees. She didn't recognise herself in these Greeks of Anatolia. She, an Italian Jew on her father's side and Greek with traces of Turkish blood on her mother's, remembered a Salonica that had disappeared the minute its Turks and its Jews had left it.

The city suffers from the pack, the city gnaws at the pack, she repeated her father's words to herself. And that is why the pack takes its revenge and destroys cities.

But these unhappy Greeks from Anatolia, from the cities of Asia Minor, roaming around Salonica as if lost, are not a pack, the old receptionist at the Bristol told her one evening. They were driven out just like Salonica's Turks. Driven from their towns in Turkey, they are now wandering around a foreign Salonica.

Graves were moved. Some were ploughed. No traces of them are left.

Just a marble plaque saying that buried here are the unidentified victims of the fire of 18 August 1917.

In the evening, Lizeta stood on the balcony of her hotel room, smoking. She listened to the sounds and bustle of the street. She heard the sirens of the steamboats sailing out of the port, taking to Turkey thousands of Muslims who had arrived that summer from Macedonia.

She looked at the palm of her hand and remembered Matilda's words.

That last day on the ship, as they were sailing around the Peloponnesus, Matilda had spoken at length about her lover Count Milevski, who had dreamed of turning Katarina Island into a tourist paradise. He had been prevented from doing so by Baron Hiterot from the neighbouring island of St Andreja, who had engaged in all sorts of intrigues to eliminate his rival, the honourable Count Milevski. Why? Jealousy! Unlike Hiterot, Carol Ignatius Corvin Milevski did not become a noble yesterday, Matilda had said, nor was he made a noble by royal decree; he came from a family that could trace its nobility back centuries.

Lizeta then mentioned that Barbara Hiterot was her best friend, that they were planning to move to the island permanently. For a few seconds, Matilda was speechless. Then she said, well, in that case they would be neighbours, because she sometimes stayed on the island of St Katarina, helping the count to organise his collection of objets d'art and old coins. Lizeta reminded Matilda that she would certainly come for the little bottle of rose water that she had promised her. She'd be there in April, when the Teatro Verdi would be performing Smareglia's Istrian Wedding.

During her first week in Salonica, not once did Lizeta see in the street, in a restaurant or café terrace a face she knew from fourteen years ago. When she went to the police station to ask for information about people her age whose full names she remembered, they told her that they had no records of such people. The archives were incomplete, most of their records had been destroyed in the fire. And after the war many people had moved away.

When she arrived at the music school in Kuskura Street, she waited in vain to hear the sound of a piano, a violin, an oboe or an aria. Watching her from the upstairs window were the same silent apparitions that had been in the halls of the port. She learned from the caretaker that during the war, the school had been turned into lodgings for refugees.

She was left without touchstones. Without her city. Without her geography. That evening she went to the Attica bar. There she met the violinist Andrej, a White Russian, who had been waiting a year for his papers to go to America. She spent the night with him in the room above the bar, returning to the hotel only the next afternoon. She walked around in an evening gown, a stray nightbird. She ignored the brazen looks and comments cast her way. The whole time she was thinking of her mother. Of their last meeting in Vienna. She asked her how it had all happened. Why was there always a force majeure? She hadn't seen Salonica in three years. How much longer were they going to spend their summers in Austrian spas? The smelly Carinthian lakes were no replacement for the Aegean Sea. Nor could her father's long letters replace Salonica. She knew only too well what was going on and that it was dangerous to return, with bombs and assassinations everywhere. The repercussions of the Young Turks' revolution were only now being felt. She should stay in Vienna. That's what her father kept telling her. The following summer her mother would take over running the hotel, and he would come to see her. And maybe there'd be a miracle, the situation would calm down, and there she'd be, in Salonica. Such a miracle was possible, Lizeta told herself, but not one where her mother would take charge of the hotel, not even for just a few weeks.

And then the Balkan wars broke out. The Greeks took over the administration of Salonica. After that it was the Great War, which, it was thought at first, would be neither long nor great. Lizeta moved to her cousins' in Trieste. In the end – and it really was the end – there was the fire in Salonica. Lizeta decided to take care of herself.

That morning, after her night with the violinist Andrej, she was her mother. She would also be her father, but later, in the hotel room of the Bristol, when she sorted out the remaining Banco di Roma cheques on the Hiterots' luxurious inlaid table. She would list the costs and start madly doing the math; how many carefree days would her account cover? Not in Salonica, but in life.

Yes, she had had to come to Salonica to assess the depth of her parents' rejection. Whatever the times were like, they lived the way they wanted. Only she could ruin their tacit agreement, so they sent her far away, all in the name of the better future they hoped for her. Her mother rediscovered her freedom and her father found his place as an observer. They must have visited each other occasionally in their separate lives. Did they at least burn together in the fire?

One morning, on her way back from Andrej's, for a second she thought she saw in the garden of the café across from the Bristol a waiter who looked just like her neighbour in Via Cavana. And over the coming days, she thought she also saw people from Trieste on her walks in town.

Lizeta's memory was as full of faces as a police filing cabinet. But unlike a filing cabinet, her memory contained only pictures, not names or files. Even ten or twenty years later, she still remembered the faces of people who had spent only a night or two at the Xenodochion Egnatia.

It was time for her to return. At the beginning of the third week, she asked at the reception desk for the timetable for trains from Salonica. Several days later she bought a ticket to Trieste, with a stopover in Belgrade.

She spent her last night in Salonica with Andrej at the Bristol. It was only when she was on the train that she realised she was missing several cheques. What would Barbara have said?

This time there would be no waiting at the Turkish-Serbian border, because that border no longer existed. The train would simply race past the remote station, where on that muggy afternoon fourteen years earlier they had waited for hours to continue their trip. She couldn't remember the name of the place, or why they had been held up there, but she did remember that they had *lunched at the station's restaurant. And that she had become very scared when her mother went to the ladies' room. What if she doesn't come back, she had thought. She remembered the street lamps by the platform and the stationhouse with begonias in the windows.*

6.

He reads his diary for days before leaving for Pula. Notes written in the hand of a high school student, a university student, a writer, revive moments that had nothing to recommend them. The idle succession of nameless days. But life lay in these very residues. He would marvel at the memory of a morning when he played hooky from school and spent hours with his friends at the *Chez the Hungarians* pastry shop, or of a boring afternoon at the canteen of the barracks in Ćuprija, eating wafers, drinking beer and spending a pointless year in the army that seemed to last an eternity.

The breath of the past was there at every moment, he felt the physical presence of the people mentioned in his diary. True, sometimes, as he moved through the greyness of the everyday, he succumbed to fatigue. The chronicler's effort to write down as many details as possible of the day gone by — because most of the writing was done late at night — deprived the diary of any literary value. A monotonous accumulation of dry facts, without any analysis. No conclusions anywhere, just decisions, pathetic promises that *starting tomorrow* he would be a different person. This *starting tomorrow* was the only running thread in all of his diary's twenty-seven notebooks. That and simmering discontent with his existing life.

He'd been following the flow of water in the water clock for almost half a century. He is not about to stop trying to change, and to finally find his true self.

And then, at the beginning of the fifth notebook of his diary, a name pops up. Ida Ronjić. It says that they met on New Year's Eve, waiting to celebrate 1974 at Uljanik, a discotheque in Pula. The next day they made love in an abandoned boathouse at Valkane. The next note in the diary is dated two weeks later. He is in Belgrade, studying for an aesthetics exam. He mentions a letter Ida Ronjić sent him from Ljubljana. And that is all that is said about a person he can't remember. He doesn't remember a single minute of that New Year's Eve; he doesn't remember that there was a boathouse on the beach at Valkane. He has never spent a New Year's Eve at a discotheque. And yet, the note is unmistakably written in his hand.

The New Year's Eve episode at the Uljanik discotheque four decades earlier, and the adventure with a certain Ida Ronjić the following day, incontestably attested to in his diary, completely threw him. He started waking up at night. Over the next few days, he was visibly unsettled. He read random articles about dementia on the internet. He tried to find the notepads from Venice's Garibaldi hotel, with the note the anonymous guest had written about Alzheimer's. All to no avail. However, the twenty-second notebook of his diary mentions the event, and there is even a short quote from the note saying that "according to some studies in America, people suffering from Alzheimer's are from childhood prone to record the world around them, to compile all sorts of lists, to keep a diary." Then he consulted a neuropsychiatrist friend of his, telling him that he needed for his novel a case of dementia where not only was an event erased from memory but so was everything that preceded it. This is common in later stages of dementia, but then everyday communication becomes a problem as well, his friend told him. At moments, the person doesn't know anymore who or where he is. Of course, forgetfulness can also be the consequence of a mechanical cranial injury.

None of this applied to him. He stopped reading his diary and went back to writing his novel. He abandoned the linear approach and started from various points of departure. This was the first time he was writing like this. He created a separate file for each character. Their paths would cross at some point. As for him, he was going to follow his own instinct. Tišma was right. Listen to the pavements. There are things to hear there.

Obsessions are guideposts to future discoveries.

It was with these jagged stories that he arrived in Pula. At the reception desk of the Skaleta Hotel they kindly offered to exchange his corner room for a suite. There had obviously been a misunderstanding. When making the reservation he had said he wanted the same room he had had when he was there four months ago. They immediately found his email on the hotel computer. He was wrong. There was no request for a particular room. He smiled, slightly lost. He quite clearly remembered the sentence that had magically disappeared from the text.

And so, from the moment he arrived, nothing went according to plan. He spent the first two nights in the suite, waiting for the corner room to be vacated. The hotel covered the difference in price. For the next two days, his suitcase stayed on the floor, unpacked. He strolled around town, following a map that was only in his head. Spotting a familiar face, he was pleased to see that his beard provided him with good camouflage. Even Goran Ban didn't recognise him when they crossed paths in Kandler Street.

He walked along the dimly lit street, the same street his mother had hurried down in the dusk of a September day in 1949. He had never felt her presence so strongly and so painfully, as if she were just a step away. For the first time, he did not move away from his mother. He would have embraced her if he could. She wasn't suffocating him anymore with her torrent of words. He wasn't ashamed of her need to always be the centre of attention, in the spotlight, an entertainer on the stage, totally unaware of the looks and muffled comments she was getting. He seemed to be the only one who saw and heard them. There was a burst of laughter in the crowded carriage. For the umpteenth time he heard his mother tell the story of how, right after the war, when everything was in short supply, she would smuggle eggs to her landladies in Sušak. A police inspection on the train. They ask her what she's got in her bag; eggs, she says. Just eggs? one of the policeman asks. Just eggs, she replies. The policemen laugh and leave. And the passengers in the carriage laugh. The ones in his mother's story. And those two decades later.

Walking down Kandler Street he remembers those long trips with his mother and sister on the night train of the Yugoslav Railways. The trains roll across future borders. The sleepy passengers try to read the names of the stations through the fogged up windows. They can't imagine that one day, within their lifetime, these places will again be abroad. That's a lesson he learned as a child in Rijeka, descending the steps of Trsat with his mother one morning. They would often stop at landings midway. Down below, deep in the canyon, he would see a narrow ribbon of road and tightly packed rooftops.

"All that over there once used to be Italy," his mother said, pointing to the bare rocks on the other side, at the foot of which was a factory.

Puzzled, he couldn't take his eyes off the grey buildings and smokestacks. He had imagined Italy differently, like the country in animated films and in the quizzes on Lizeta's television screen.

"What are you looking at like that?" she asked, laughing. "Rijeka, Opatija, the Quarner, all of that used to be Italy." And then she added, almost to herself: "Countries are like people, they are born, and they die."

He and his mother are now on the same side. Together they are filling up the notebook stolen in Vinkovci. Why had it taken him half a century to realise that he shouldn't hide his emotions? Not be afraid of freedom; be who he is; pay no attention to the milieu. Understand that evil is not a fault, it is a choice like any other, an option which makes it easier and surer to acquire honours and wealth. It is a safe, well-trodden road, much more so than the sinuous, perilous paths taken by those who believe in divine justice.

It is only in fairy tales that the good triumph.

So think people who do not believe that lead seals on the doors of freight wagons are as secure as padlocks. Padlocks are not a sign of mistrust in the train-travelling community, or an insult to the Yugoslav Railways; rather they reflect doubt in the flowing bloodstream of so many unknown blood groups.

So thinks his mother while berating the people on the beach at Stoja, defending the territory of our three spread out towels. Like the Greeks at the battle of Marathon, encircled by the Persians' vast army.

Hence, a lead seal is not enough, it simply says that the carriage isn't empty, contrary to what is believed by the lieutenant of the Yugoslav Navy, captive of a group of small, simple people amongst whom he had grown up, at the old Ristovac border station where his father, the youngest stationmaster in Skopje, veteran of the Salonica front in World War I and recipient of the Albanian commemorative medal,* wound up. Given his fondness for alcohol, he was quickly demoted, and retreated with his family to increasingly marginal stations, finally finishing up as a rail track guard in Sićevo. There he would remain until he retired, still going at the crack of dawn to check on his sector, from the Sićevo power plant to Ostrovica. When he died, found on the shelves of his cellar was a whole collection of things carelessly tossed out of the trains.

The most valuable object in the collection was a leather wallet, inlaid with the head of a shark, which an employee at Station House no. 15 had found by the yard fence one August morning in 1941. He immediately recognised it as belonging to his elder son. Inside he found a brief note saying that they were being taken to Germany, that after being captured he had spent three months in a concentration camp in Bulgaria, that he was okay, that they shouldn't worry.

The convoy of captured officers of the Kingdom of Yugoslavia crossed the Sićevo gorge at night. Huge padlocks secured the carriages. When the composition slowed down just before the bend after the Sićevo dam, the young lieutenant managed to fling his wallet out through the crack under the door hinge, certain that his father would find it the next day when making his rounds.

He had come to the city where he had grown up, this time to leave it forever. He wasn't going to contact anyone. He would visit all the places where he had lived for decades as a boy, a boy whose sole dream was to leave. He had lived there in a permanent state of absence, at the mercy of thoughts that

---

* The medal commemorates the retreat of the Serbian army across Albania during World War I.

took him far away from this city. He knew that it was the wrong city in every respect. And that the houses he would live in, the women he would love, all the things that would happen to him, both good and bad, were in some other cities. This wasn't his story. He just happened to find himself caught up in misunderstandings that weren't his.

Sixty-five years ago, his mother too had walked around this city. He wished he could go back to that day and see all the places she had passed by. Was he already then fighting to come into this world from the void of non-existence? Or had the struggle begun earlier, when the young lieutenant of the Yugoslav Navy chose not to become seriously involved with the Italian woman in whose flat he lived? Or even before that, when the Serbian prisoner of war at the Barbek 1 labour camp, near Bremen, refused to stay in Germany after the war? Yes, that was a possibility, given that during the last year of his captivity he had become close to a woman, a cousin of the man who owned the farm where he worked by day. In the evening, he would get on his bike and return to the building of the dance school where the inmates slept.

So many dangers and hardships on the roads taken by those who were to give him life! But everything worked to his advantage, especially the panicky fear of sex felt by the woman who worked for the Directorate of the Northern Adriatic Port, due to the long nights spent in the village without candles, with a dog barking in the distance, while from the depth of the rooms came the rustling of restless bodies on straw mattresses, and an occasional muffled groan ending in a smothered cry. To be followed by another menacing silence.

He wasn't inventing a thing.

Whenever he found himself in Raša, a small mining town halfway between Pula and Rijeka, where the bus drivers stopped for a break, he felt as if he were enclosed in a cage, surrounded by dream-like scenes. Everything on the square where they stopped was surreal. It was like stepping into a drawing rather than a space. The square was always empty because it wasn't in the town centre, it was on the edge of town, beyond the comings and goings of its invisible inhabitants. The tall arch of triumph with its streamers and banners in praise of Tito and socialism, linked it to the nearby smaller square, which was also deserted. The whole square was closed off by a succession of vaulted buildings and the horizontal lines of balconies. A film set, blank facades with windows and doors painted on them. When the bus arrived, the square was filled with extras, who quickly dispersed towards the restaurant. To the left of the restaurant, the neon sign *Raša Inn* glowed day and night. The dark curtains on the upstairs windows were always drawn.

A shadowless desert in the square of dreams. A church shaped like an overturned miner's cart, with a wide porch and broad steps in front, a bell tower with straight lines reminiscent of a miner's lamp, the cinema building with its round windows. In the middle of the square a fountain.

The end of the world. The muteness of eternity. Raša — the town without a cemetery.

Raša appeared on maps two years before the outbreak of World War II. This mining settlement, one of twelve new modern towns envisaged to represent the power of the fascist regime of Benito Mussolini, restorer of the Roman Empire, would be built in 547 days. The principal architect, Gustavo Pulitzer Finali, from a Jewish family of Trieste, had spent years designing the interiors of transoceanic ships. Hence the round ship windows on the front of the cinema. In the first phase, Raša housed two thousand people, just half of the intended number. In the lower part of town were houses built for the miners; in the upper part, alongside the row of family villas for the managing technical staff, was a burgeoning development of one-story houses with gardens; this was where qualified workers lived. Raša had its own water system, public lighting, telephone exchange, hospital, Olympic-size swimming pool, cinema, hotel. The only thing that hadn't been envisaged, deliberately or not, was a cemetery.

This he was told a long time ago by a friend from music school who was a few years his senior. A boy with two names: Marijan and Milevoj. They used to make fun of him, asking which was his first name and which his last. He played the trumpet. Twice a week he would come to Pula from Raša by bus. Marijan once told him that his parents were older than the city where they lived. And that they would never die because Raša didn't have a cemetery.

In the spring of 2012, he started working on the case of the woman employed at the Northern Adriatic Port Directorate and came upon Daša Drndić's book "April in Berlin". The part that mentions Raša made him think of the trumpet-player with two names. In the meantime, Marijan Milevoj had become the guardian angel of his town, a reliable chronicler. His books could be found on the internet. He didn't live in Raša anymore, he now lived in nearby Labin where his son ran a bookshop. He decided to look him up at the first opportunity. That was a quarter of a century ago. Meanwhile, the country where they lived was gone, like the Raša mine.

"Raša – Arsia, the youngest of Istria's small towns. The workers' houses, each consisting of four two-room flats, lined up in two rows, surrounded by gardens of identical size, are today dilapidated and greyish. Raša started dying early, while it was still young and healthy. Its death was long and painful, it was betrayed by everyone who governed it, by the fascists and the socialist self-managers, only to be finished off by the new savage Croatian capitalists. Raša isn't producing coal anymore, they said; Raša is like a cow with no milk left, like a barren woman, it's time to close its eyes. The mine is dead and buried. Raša today is a spirit, a skeleton evoked only on the little square by the Church of St Barbara, the patron saint of miners who are no longer there."

St Barbara, the patron saint of miners, mentioned by Daša Drndić, brought to mind another saint, his mother, employed at the Northern Adriatic Port Directorate

Santa Violeta, the patron saint of orphans. That's how she saw herself from the age of eleven when she left her home in the village of Uzveć, a family cooperative of more than twenty members, for the boarding school in Šabac. She saw her departure for boarding school as a rejection on the part of her mother. The rest of her life was to be in search of a home. The ensuing years were spent alone in rented rooms, boarding houses, hotels.

She never forgave her mother for sending her away to boarding school. That was clear from a recurrent dream she had: her mother would ask her for a glass of water. If, in her dream, she did as her mother asked, something bad would happen in real life, even if it was just a minor annoyance. If, in her dream, she refused to give her mother a glass of water, it portended a happy event, often in the form of financial gain. That is how her subconscious settled accounts with her mother. Justice is implacable, even in dreams.

In the notebook that was stolen in Vinkovci she didn't write down just the names of the hotels and lodgings where she stayed, or the stories and fairy tales she invented; stirred by a strong sense of justice and the truth, she also recorded her dreams. Always in a dressing room, maid's

225

room, servants' room, where people dropped their voice. Where shadows never stood still. Where there was a constant succession of giggles, sobs and sighs. An in-between space and in-between time. And the remnants of other people's lives, evoked in the absence of a life of one's own. And all these creatures of God, these servants and gardeners, maids and cooks, working in other people's houses, were orphans looking for a home, for love.

7.

When, after his third day at the Skaleta, he left the suite and finally moved into *his* room, he took the morning Autotrans bus to Raša, in search of a part of his past. After turning towards Barban, the bus started to make its way down to the Raša River valley. He recognised the landscape, the angles where you could see the surrounding hills, the bare cliffs and swampy plains covered in reeds and aquatic plants. The bus abruptly braked at a sharp bend in the road. On the slope, close to the top of the hill, he saw huge letters spelling out TITO. They were still there after half a century. Somebody had obviously been maintaining the memorial sign, regularly cutting the grass, refreshing the chalk on the letters to keep them visible from far away.

It seemed like only yesterday that they were in the Fiat Topolino, on their way back from Rijeka after viewing the flat near the Governor's Palace. He and his sister were sitting in the back. His mother kept up a running commentary on what was wrong with the flat, his father occasionally agreeing with her. Yes, the flat was in poor condition, renovating it would require a big investment. That was the final word.

His vision blurred. The whole world had collapsed. He would never be an inhabitant of Rijeka, that big city where at any moment one could sink into anonymity, make a new start without any witnesses, commence a successful *as of tomorrow.* He would come up with the right word at the right moment because this was a real city. He would be relaxed when he approached girls. He wouldn't be speechless when the prompter inside him went mute and he turned red and retreated to his fallback position on the three towels spread out on the beach of Stoja. It was only in Rijeka that he could be himself, be who he was. Have a girlfriend. A new version of himself would be born in Rijeka: cheeky, brave, successful, a *bon vivant.*

With every kilometre, Pula became closer, and the anticipated life where he was neither shy nor insecure slipped that much farther away. He would remain in Pula, a captive of a small, boring town. In the autumn he would start high school. Everything would be as it was before in this sad town where everybody knew each other by sight.

Farewell, Fiume.*

The Fiat Topolino barely made it up the steep climb before the big curve in the road. In the Raša valley, the sun had already set, the blush of twilight persisting only in the distance, occasionally casting glints of light on the huge letters of the sovereign's name.

That was decades ago. He's now again in the square in Raša, a town that is only sixteen years older than he is. This is where he took his first step. This is where the twists and turns of his mother's story began, which meandered for half a century at an all too familiar rhythm. These are the same genes; he makes the same use of camouflage to avoid confrontation. He thinks of all those times that his mother would interrupt her story, always at the same place. The bus breaking down near Raša on their way back from Pula, the security agents

---

* The Italian name for Rijeka.

arriving in Baroness Hiterot's black limousine, she continuing her trip to Rijeka in the company of the agents and a girl. And then, *deux ex machina*: dinner at the hotel in Raša, the bus reappears – having been miraculously repaired in the meantime – and she manages to extricate herself from the company of the tipsy security agents. In the end: "The girl from Opatija stayed with them."

With that sentence, the curtain closes on the entire episode. Or on what could have happened had she not succumbed to fear, fear built up late at night in the village, and later in the boarding school in Šabac, fear imprinted on the genetic code of the offspring. Nothing was ever said to the end. All options were on the table. The story remained open-ended. Freedom of choice came to her only towards the end of her life, in the refuge of dementia, after eight decades of fighting the demons of her childhood. Forgetfulness liberated her from the discipline she had imposed on herself to fulfil senseless demands as conscientiously as possible. No more would anything be kept under lock and key. Finally, she could breathe. Without worrying about conquering another day, establishing her power anew in her anything but propitious everyday life. Gone was the anxiety, that contorted smile that had embarrassed him when he was a child. When she moved to the care home, she became calm and gentle, she stopped peppering him with peremptory advice. In conversation she would make long pauses, thinking before starting a sentence. And her walk changed too. Being relaxed made her small figure move with a sway. There was something distinguished about this calmness. It reminded him of the mother of a friend from his youth, Gianfranco, in whose house there were no taboos.

Hence, on his rare visits to his mother in the home, that feeling that he was talking to somebody else. When death is near it erases differences between the living and the dead. Through the memories of the living, the dead continue to participate in life. And that is comforting in old age: the knowledge that the world is indivisible and one.

She would smile gently when he disputed her version of some event he had witnessed. She would mention people he had never heard of before and give them decisive roles in her life or endow those close to her with odd traits. She maintained that Grandpa Milan knew Greek. She had heard him speak it several times with Lizeta. If he didn't believe her, he should go and ask the watchmaker Maleša. Grandpa Milan also spoke Albanian. What do you mean how come? He spent all those years on the railways working with Albanians in the backwaters of Macedonia and Kosovo. That's how his children knew Albanian too. They started school in Kačanik, in southern Kosovo. Later they moved to Zvečan, again in Kosovo. How could he not know that?

Before leaving for Pula, after discovering Ida Rojnić in his diary, a person he had no memory of, he worried that the erasure process had already begun. He paid another visit to his neuropsychiatrist friend and confessed that he himself was that literary figure who was losing his memory. They talked for a long time. He didn't know how to answer when the man asked if his mother merely had a severe form of old-age dementia or was suffering from Alzheimer's. She refused to undergo any unpleasant tests. No, she had not had an MRI. He didn't even know if she had ever been to see a dentist.

An MRI is the only sure way to establish if it is Alzheimer's, his friend told him. He'd arrange an appointment for him if he wanted.

He did want. But not now. When he got back from Pula. Yes, he was going there again. Last winter, it had been too short a stay. He needed at least a month to finetune the idea for the novel he was writing. What was he writing about? Well…about his mother.

That night he couldn't fall asleep. He tossed and turned in his bed until the morning, when he finally dozed off. It was more an impression of sleeping than the real thing. He kept hearing the voice of his friend the neuropsychiatrist. He talked about demanding ancestors who, after their terrestrial life, continued to fight for a presence in their descendants through genetic messages. He vividly explained the Hungarian psychoanalyst Leopold Szondi's theory about the family unconscious. Ancestors, present in their descendants in the form of latent recessive genes, unconsciously influence the choice of lover and spouse, friends, ideals, profession, types of illness and death, thus steering their fate.

Because dreams, too, are inherited, his friend told him as he was leaving. And that is why, when examining a person's genetic code, it isn't enough to take into consideration only the inner family circle; all the people who inspired love and friendship in the said person and in the latter's closest blood relatives, must be considered as well.

That last sentence followed him like an echo for the entire trip on the Belgrade–Pula night bus. What an abundance of possibilities! Dozing off, he saw his ancestors silently passing by in a column. Led by Grandpa Milan. He waves his lantern as he marches along the Sićevo-Ostrovica section of the railway. After crossing Albania and the Ionian Sea, after the hospital in Bizerte, breaking through the Salonica front, posts in Macedonia and Kosovo, his life has been reduced to these ten or so kilometres of railway tracks that he regularly inspects. He knows every crosstie. They are his patients, he takes care of them, makes sure that the steel bolts are tightly screwed on the rail fasteners, checks the condition of the metal supports, and whether the wood on some crosstie has started to rot. He records irregularities, and, using a special counting technique, marks the position of the crosstie that requires an intervention.

There is no doubt about it. He had inherited from Grandpa Milan a love of counting, a dedication to routine activities, the pleasure of engaging in superfluous activities, whether it be arranging empty bottles and jars by size on the larder shelves or calculating how many kilometres he had walked the previous week. But more than anything, he had inherited from his Grandpa Milan a passion for walking, an activity that allowed him to push away the everyday and put it on stand-by. The moment he stepped out into the street, for some supposedly urgent shopping, or under some other pretext, he was freed of all the obligations imposed on him and life unfolded as he imagined it. Never in a dialogue, always in a monologue. But what he had not inherited from Grandpa Milan was resigning himself to the present situation, the blissful feeling that there was time, that the world was as it was, and that there was nothing to be done about it. He did not accept it as it was. He was constantly trying to go beyond that temporary form, to finally unleash, in one of those *as of tomorrow* moments, his real self.

And it wasn't just Grandpa Milan who walked. His son, too, had his beat — the Belgrade streets that he roamed, thinking up pointless reasons for having to nip out of the house for a moment. It started after he turned sixty, when he stopped sailing and returned to shore forever. He didn't know what to do with himself. He was unprepared for this other life waiting for him at home.

Some of his father's friends also walked, to be precise they wandered through the rest of their life.

And his friends did the same thing. He often wondered why that was. He had no answer.

And then, on the Autotrans bus to Raša, all these walkers flashed through his mind. He realised that they had chosen the kind of wives, the kind of houses, the kind of daily routines, the kind of lives – that they later ran away from. They had chosen the wrong relationships. Life with such women was like standing in stagnant water. It lasted for years, until one day it became too much and got to them. That's when the wandering began.

From his maternal grandfather, who died before he was born, he had inherited a penchant for promiscuity. And alcohol, of course. In that respect, his ancestors on both sides had been generous. It was a miracle that, in the meantime, they hadn't collapsed from all that alcohol, leaving their wives alone on the family tree.

In Raša, he and two other passengers stepped off the bus onto the deserted square. Only four people had originally boarded the bus. Such a pathetic number on the Pula-Rijeka line. The bus didn't waste time as it set off for Labin.

He looked around the empty square.

A space rid of people. An ideal town. An ideal life rid of relationships with others because relationships are always complicated. To have simply a framework for inscribing the life of one's choice.

Raša has become a dead end ever since that damned Istrian Ypsilon highway was built, said the old man sipping his beer at the counter of a small snack bar. He started up a conversation as soon as the stranger ordered a coffee.

There are no more chance travellers as there used to be, people you could always learn something new from. Only local buses stop here now. Had he maybe stepped off the bus by mistake? Out of habit! That would be a good one! What? He has never stayed in Raša for more than half an hour ?

After so many years, it barely adds up to a day.

He has missed a lot. Why has he come — to make up for it? The man knows several Marijan Milevojs. They're not related, but they all look like brothers. He played football with one of them at the "Rudar" football club. Toni Privrat, the best footballer Raša ever had; he had been their role model. He hasn't heard of Privrat? This Marijan Milevoj who writes books doesn't live in Raša. He's in Labin; his son has a bookshop there.

Suddenly he has an urge to show off. He takes out his identity card. He is the oldest inhabitant of Raša. He's the same age as the town; they were born on the same day. On the fourth of November he and Raša will be seventy-seven years old.

Looks younger.

Who? He or the town?

In the course of his twenty minutes in the snack bar, he learned that the cinema had burned down the previous year, that's to say, what they still called the cinema out of habit. For years the cinema building had housed a furniture store. The last film shown there was a quarter of a century ago. The old man at the counter had been the projectionist.

There had been nothing on in Raša for a long time. The Mona Lisa café was also closed. Two cafés were too many for Raša. Like in a western, there was only room for one. Everything had closed, except for the care home. There, the number of people kept growing. What do you mean Raša doesn't have a cemetery? The whole of Raša is one big cemetery.

He left the snack bar to wait for the bus, leaving the projectionist to unspool his monologue.

Back in the square, alone. On the set of a film that had long since been taken off the programme. Abandonment and despair at every step.

No more banners with *Long Live Tito!* on the Arch of Triumph.

Before Tito, it was Mussolini.

He stood there, like a ghost, for maybe a minute or a quarter of an hour. And then he had an idea. Raša was that missing image from the MRI. One look at the square gave him his diagnosis.

Arsia – Alzheimer.

Cinema. Hotel. Care home.

The archetypical matrix that had followed him all his life. It was as if he had been there that September evening in 1949, when the two security agents from Labin, accompanied by the woman from the Northern Adriatic Port Directorate and the girl from Opatija, arrived in Raša in Baroness Hiterot's limousine. The façade of the hotel still bore traces of its old name, *Impero*. But it was not under that name that his mother had recorded the biggest building in the square in her notebook when she arrived in Rijeka the following day by bus. The name, which replaced *Impero* and which the woman from the Northern Adriatic Port Directorate had carefully written down , had, in the meantime, completely disappeared. Because, when he had passed through Raša in the seventies, the illuminated sign above the entrance to the hotel had said: The Raša Inn.

So many possible scenarios for that September night in 1949. But only one was played out, the one he himself would have chosen. The only scenario that allowed her to protect herself, to resist dangerous temptation, not to ruin her life for the sake of a moment of pleasure. Every act of love can mean the beginning of the end. Entering a life that it is later impossible to leave. Trapped forever.

So many women lost simply because he had instantly glimpsed what life would look like afterwards. No condom, no abortion, no protection could prevent the worst from happening – imprisonment in a life that wasn't his. That was an irremediable mistake. Fear had protected him.

Fear had also protected his mother. She certainly didn't correct her mistake of going off with the security agents by inventing that *deus ex machina* – with the miraculously repaired bus appearing in Raša two hours later and her managing to slip away from the tipsy group and continue her trip to Rijeka. No, she corrected it by deciding to leave the restaurant during dinner and take refuge in her room at the nameless hotel. She had previously procured the key from the receptionist, giving him her identity card. She locked herself in her room. It was stuffy so she opened the window. Then, fully dressed, she lay down on her bed. Half an hour later somebody knocked at the door, persistently, calling out her name. Then they gave up. The next day she stayed in her room until Baroness Hiterot's car left the square in front of the hotel. Only then did she go down to the restaurant for breakfast, and around midday she was on the bus to Rijeka.

When he returned to the snack bar an hour later, the projectionist was still there. He was standing at the counter, stolid, a fresh glass of beer in his hand. The man waved at him as soon as he saw him at the door. That same moment, the local bus to Pula arrived.

He changed his mind; he wouldn't linger in Raša any longer. He would return to the Skaleta as soon as possible. Lizeta was already on the train, travelling from Salonica to

Trieste. It was time for the Hiterots to finally move to the island of St Andreja, for Barbara to continue the mission of her father, Baron Georg, in Rovinj, for the truffle business to kick off in Livade, for Lizeta to move into the house in Saint Polycarp, and start her romance with the young musician, for Diona Kesinis to become Professor Fažov of Ribarska St, for the Anglo-American administration of Pula to end, for new tenants to arrive in the Villa Maria, for the Yugoslav Railways to expand its network, for the watchmaker Maleša to clean Tito's watches in Brioni, for Goran Ban to return the logarithm tables to the person he had borrowed them from forty years ago, for Raša to die along with its dry mine, for Marijan Milevoj to write all those books about Labin, Rabac, Raša and Trget, for what must happen to happen, as Tišma would say.

He would open a new file and gather all the characters in one place.

The bus stopped in front of the café. Several passengers got off. The next bus for Pula wasn't until the early evening. He turned towards the projectionist, and, still at the door, asked him what the Impero hotel was called before the war.

The same as the restaurant. *Central.*

Impossible! he cried out. That name was never on the face of the building.

My name Mario Vončina isn't written on my forehead either, but all the same, that's who I am, said the projectionist, raising his glass in salutation.

8.

Lizeta had spent more than two weeks in Salonica and now it was time to prepare for her return to Trieste. Just as he had discovered, when searching the internet for his mother's Stuttgart method, that it involved not only tram corridors but also a certain gardener Ziegler, a park landscaping specialist who had visited Belgrade at the end of the nineteenth century, so now, in just ten minutes, he found much more than he had expected. Instead of the gardener from Stuttgart, he found Baron Maurice von Hirsch of Munich, one of the five richest men in Europe at the time, who had built and owned the concession for the Eastern Railways, which included the Salonica-Belgrade line that Lizeta and her mother had taken in the summer of 1909 to travel from Salonica to Vienna. Fourteen years later, Lizeta would return to Trieste on that same line.

He found an article about the official opening of the railroad line.

"On 19 May 1888, in the presence of many invited guests, the final tracks connecting Belgrade and Salonica were officially laid at the Ristovac-Zibevče border station (which was on Turkish territory). The Turkish ceremony was very original. The ritual slaughtering of

a ram was performed on the tracks, while an imam invoked Allah's blessing for the completed work."

A few pages further on – that's to say five years later – he found the statement made by Francesco Ancona, a merchant from Trieste, about the Zibevče frontier post: "The stationhouse is unprepossessing, the Turkish compositions are assembled with eastern slowness, and passport control takes a long time. While most of the Serbian employees speak German or French, the only way to communicate with the Turks is with a *bakshish*.* The traditional *"Javash, javash!"*** calms down the impatient. The Asiatic style is palpable everywhere. Ristovac is the crossroad between West and East!"

Two years after the line was launched, there was not a single direct train from or to Salonica. Passengers heading for Niš or Belgrade had to either overnight at a very basic *han* or roadside inn in Zibevče, losing a great deal of time, or take a fiacre to cross the border and stay at an inn in Ristovac. Since the latter inn corresponded with European standards for a hotel, passengers going to Salonica were at an advantage. This inconvenience ended in 1890 when direct trains started operating in both directions twice a day.

Underneath the text was a postcard of the railway station in Ristovac. A one-storey stone building that would have done any small European town proud, with large arched windows, planters under the metal canopy and lamps at either end of the building. Right next to the stationhouse was a smaller edifice, with a restaurant on the ground floor and rooms on the floor above. The Cyrillic inscription in the upper left-hand corner said:

---

*   Tip or bribe
**   Slowly, no rush. (in Turkish).

Greetings from the Serbian-Turkish border
Ristovac restaurant and inn
Manager Djordje Roš

The postcard didn't give the year. In front of the station-house, near the platform, were the dot-like figures of passengers.

The same scene, but without the passengers, as on a photograph he remembered from the family archive: a young railwayman with his wife and two sons.

A year after the Great War ended, twenty-eight-year-old Milan Velikić, recipient of the Albanian commemorative medal, Salonica veteran combatant, the youngest station-master in Skopje, would be transferred to Ristovac as punishment. It was at this station, which had lost all importance once the border with Turkey ceased to exist and where the rapid and international trains no longer stopped, that the demoted railwayman began a new life with his wife Danica, who was six years younger. It was in Ristovac that their sons Vojislav and Dragomir were born. They would grow up by the tracks, watching the trains pass by, waving at the passengers and moving down the length of the line as their father, with his predilection for alcohol, descended down the ladder of the railroad hierarchy, until, a decade later, he wound up in Sićevo, his title now track guard. Even after he retired, he continued to get up at the crack of dawn every day to inspect his sector from the Sićevo power station to Ostrovica.

There his grandson and granddaughter spent their summers. They came with their mother as soon as school was out and stayed until the end of August. Taking the night train from Pula to Belgrade, then transferring onto the rapid train for Niš, and then the workers' train, they would arrive in Sićevo at three in the afternoon. Grandpa Milan would be there on the platform waiting for them.

The secret ritual began on the very first day. As soon as he was alone, the grandson would take the framed photograph of his uncle Dragomir hanging above his grandmother's bed and compare it with his own face. The resemblance grew with each passing year. Grandma Danica was right: he looked more like his uncle than like his own father. The broad brow, nose, lips, gaze — his spitting image. But he was still a long way from turning twenty-one. That last year of his uncle Dragomir's life — when their resemblance should have been at its peak — seemed to him unattainable.

One day he donned the woollen vest with the three bullet holes in front that his grandmother kept under her pillow and went out onto the veranda. There was a scream and he froze. Grandma's face was chalk white. He took off the vest immediately. Echoing in his ears were the words: "That's a bad omen!"

Seven years later, despite everything, he survived a car accident near Vinkovci. He was twenty-one. After that, it was only to him that his face aged.

Was he really the spitting image of his uncle Dragomir, as Grandma Danica said? If he was, that was forty years ago, when they were the same age. Would they have looked like each other at sixty, had his uncle lived that long? Or was there something more intimate than physical resemblance that connected two people? Beginning with the impression of a resemblance. That didn't change. It was indelible, however long one lived.

The backdrop to his uncle's death became clearer to him when in the autumn of 2011 he participated in a literary meeting in Sićevo. A young man from the village told him that during the war there had been an Upper and a Lower Sićevo. The ones supported the partisans, the others the Chetniks. The demarcation line ran down the middle of the village. At first, everyone wore a *šajkača**, then, depending on the circumstances, some sewed on a five-pointed red star or a cockade. In the course of his four days at the Sićevo event, he grew closer to the young man. One morning they went to the isolated house perched on a slope at the foot of the cooperative. They noticed an old woman in the vegetable garden, bending over a salad patch. This was the woman his uncle, the commander of the Sićevo partisan detachment, had had an affair with. Discreetly, he took two photographs of her. Hearing the click of the camera on his mobile, the old woman suddenly stood up straight. Their eyes met. He moved away from the fence. The old lady bent over again and resumed digging.

He was digging too. He could see his grandfather, having been notified of his son's death, running to the village across the snow-covered roads at dawn. What was going through his mind as the dead body was being carried to the house, at Guardhouse no. 15? Would Dragomir still be alive had he stayed in Skopje, would he have advanced in his job, led a different life far from this backwater where he was stuck with his family?

For years, the official version of Dragomir's death was that he had been ambushed and killed by the Chetniks. Later it was the Bulgarians. There were rumours of a love triangle. Half a century later, when an ideology, and the country that had created it, fell apart, other versions circulated. Dragomir had allegedly been killed by his own men. All sorts of rubbish and crimes by false heroes surfaced. Ghosts were awakened again, leading thousands upon thousands of innocent

* Serbian traditional cap.

people to their death. Scoundrels and manipulators took over. Stories are always slightly different at the scene of events, stripped of derisory efforts to conceal greed, envy and evil under the cover of ideology. Later, the winners canonize the past in chronicles and school textbooks, encyclopaedias and lexicons.

The demonization of the winners of 1945 was overdone, so that the regret expressed for the innocent victims of their fellow fighters' intrigues served as a convenient pretext for the future crimes committed by hypocritical revisionists, who switched sides overnight. Their victory after the break-up of Yugoslavia would be the victory not of an ideology, but of a mentality, a reflection of the negative potential of human beings.

After visiting Raša and wandering around the streets of Pula, he was back in front of his laptop. The light in the second-floor room of the *Skaleta* hotel would continue to burn throughout the night. Scenes and people surfaced in some kind of higher order, which escaped him. The real event came only once it was over. You couldn't own dividends of the past and at the same time live your life to the fullest. While the event lasted, he was only partly present, because every detail had to be noted. It was only after going over it again that he realised what he had missed. That was why he lived in reverse. Just like his mother. The past is never finished, it is simply improved upon. Glimpses into other people's lives so embed themselves in one's feelings and thoughts that they become part of the life of the observer himself.

The photographs in Lizeta's room were just as much a part of his life as those in the family album in Guardhouse no. 15; the collection of objects found on the tracks running from the Sićevo electrical power plant to Ostrovica had the same kind of magic as all those scarves, silk stockings and shawls in Lizeta's wardrobe drawers. He was just as preoccupied with the tragic fate of Barbara Hiterot and her mother (or perhaps grandmother?) as with the death of his uncle Dragomir.

He felt the invisible presence of others all around him. Did he have just one biography or was he made up of several? Whose lives was he living? Why did he experience events that had nothing to do with his life as if they were part of his family history? Fixations and obsessions presaged seismological activities in his consciousness which, at a given moment, would bring together the seemingly incompatible. He couldn't stop thinking about his neuropsychiatrist friend's remark that genetic legitimation considers not only close family but also those who foster relationships of love or friendship with them. The possibilities were endless!

Was it through Lizeta that he felt this closeness to Barbara Hiterot? Identification with the defeated side, regardless of whether it's Native American tribes or a hostage to the family pathology who assumes the role of a lightning rod, redirecting the negative energy of his environment towards himself. Because the Hiterots did not hesitate to place their family crest on the portraits of other people's ancestors hanging on the walls of their residences in Trieste and St Andreja, thereby appropriating the false status of centuries-old nobility. The list of sins committed on the road to wealth is a long one, and the Hiterot dossier held many secrets, going back to the days when their ancestor Philip, a wool merchant from Kassel, arrived in Trieste in the middle of the eighteenth century.

Why did Barbara await the end of the war in that mouse-trap of an island? Instead of taking refuge in Italy and saving her life, like the daughter of the man who owned the Villa Maria, and thousands of others. It's not that she couldn't have. The monograph about the Hiterots given him by the director of the museum mentioned a letter titled *Plans for the Sale of the Estate*, which Barbara sent to Giuliano Ancelotti, her lawyer in Trieste, on 1 August 1938, just a year before World War II broke out. Perhaps there had been earlier plans to sell the island of St Andreja, when property prices were higher, and the shadow of a coming war had yet to appear? Had Barbara been against her mother's proposed sale to settle her own debts?

Barbara was the first Hiterot to blend into the life of the small fishing village. She was the guardian spirit of Rovinj. After an accident in the Rovinj quarry, she risked her life to pull a half-dead worker out of the pit. For this act of courage, she received a civic merit award from Rome. The Hiterots organised a party in Rovinj to mark the occasion. There was singing and dancing. Among the crowd in the square were the future OZNA agents who, twelve years later, on the night of 30 May 1945, would beat the Hiterots to death, thus putting an end to the investigation procedure against enemies of the people. But on that April day in 1933, when the whole town had gathered to celebrate in front of the Adriatik hotel, they were still just young men from poor Rovinj families. Some of them were already going out to sea to fish, sailing every day past the island of St Andreja, where the Hiterots' castle could be glimpsed through the pine trees. Over the years, stories about their wealth became legendary. And when in May 1945, Rovinj and the islands of St Andreja and St Katarina found themselves in the hands of the partisans, the Hiterots' wealth would decide their fate. It would be yet another story about the scale of human evil.

At this safe distance from historical cataclysms and turbulence, it is easy to say what should have been done at a certain moment. After all, hadn't he been the one, at the end of the 1980s, to oppose his father's idea, which had only his sister's support, to sell their holiday cottage in Pomer? One could already feel that the country was disintegrating, that dark forces were taking power under the guise of fighting for democracy and civil liberties. The press carried more and more adverts from Serbs who were selling their holiday homes on the Adriatic coast. Belgraders were leaving Rovinj. Gorski Kotar and Slavonia were being shelled, but he still lived in the illusion that, at the last moment, some *deus ex machina* would prevent a catastrophe. That made his behaviour all the stranger, since a year or two earlier he had been an avid reader of the memoirs and diaries of writers who had lived at the twilight of periods when revolutions and wars were breaking out. Even though he had this second-hand experience which unequivocally indicated what was to come, he could not accept the idea of selling the house in Pomer. Because that would mean giving up a space that was his native country, giving up a whole inheritance. He was not a tourist. He did not holiday in Pula. He lived in Pula. Even when he was physically absent for months and years from the town where he had grown up, he still belonged to it. Just as it belonged to him. Its imprint was in his novels. No land registry could refute this belonging.

With her pathological fear of moving, his mother supported his proposal to keep the house in Pomer. In the end, his father and sister accepted the status quo. On the 12th of September 1991 he swam at the beach in Pomer for the last time. The sun suddenly disappeared behind the clouds. Their shadow hung over the whole bay. He was gripped with fear. He started swimming towards the shore, only some ten metres away. He felt as if he was not moving, just treading water. Then, with relief, he felt the ground under his feet.

In the evening, he tidied his desk and the books on the shelf. The cobalt blue figurine of the violinist watched him from the display cabinet. The next day he took the last JAT flight from Pula to Belgrade. Two weeks later, his parents would hand the keys of the Pomer house to the Milićes. He never wondered how they must have felt upon leaving. He had been hurt by their decision to leave, rather than stay and keep the house. Wouldn't it have been nicer for them to be on the seaside instead of in a Belgrade high-rise? Even thirteen years after having moved to Belgrade, his mother still knew more trustworthy repairmen in Pula. They had so many friends there and people they knew. Anyway, they only spent the winters in Belgrade. He tried to persuade them to stay but it was futile. He attributed their decision to the egotism of old age, to the fear of finding themselves alone with each other, facing a final reckoning. They needed their children and grandchildren around in order to forget their old age.

Confined to a cramped flat in a high-rise, his father took to wandering around Belgrade every day. He invented reasons for having to go out. He missed the German tools he had left behind in the garage in Pomer. He died four years after leaving Pula.

His mother descended ever deeper into dementia.

At the beginning of December 1998, he returned to his city. It was for a meeting of cultural figures from the former Yugoslavia engaged in the arts, organised by the association *Homo*, run by the actor Igor Galo and his wife Mirjana. The guests were put up at the Riviera hotel. He was given a room overlooking the park. He stepped out onto the balcony and inhaled the night air. In the distance, the lights on the seashore twinkled through the trees. And he remembered the daughter of the owner of the Villa Maria, whom he had observed from his hiding place in the courtyard as she stood on the terrace of their flat. He did not remember her face, but the situation was the same: finding himself in his city after so many years. He was both observer and observed at one and the same time. He had finally entered the domain of loss. And the look in his eyes became bitter and hard.

Every story has as many versions as it has protagonists, in leading and supporting roles, as silent witnesses or as obsessive narrators in secret collusion with the events that preceded them. That thought stayed with him while, in his hotel room, he travelled distances in space and time, and on his laptop wrote the story that had started long before the people who would give him life were born. It unfolded outside of any conscious decisions or intentions. Hence, the young stationmaster's transfer from Skopje to Ristovac, triggered by his penchant for alcohol, was actually the consequence of an ancestor's genetic donation, as the Hungarian psychoanalyst Szondi would say. It is impossible to establish with any certainty the origin of the obsessions that set the tone of an entire existence. In the case of his mother, the music score for our life was in that notebook that disappeared in Vinkovci one November night in 1958. However, its loss did not stop the already established mechanism. The oral transmission remained, regardless of whether it was about remembering the recipe for rose jam, the name of a hotel in Dubrovnik, or a fairy tale about the love between a bee and an ant.

Life is a great confusion, she used to say. So much happens out of simple despair, out of fear. The important thing is to never give up.

She did not give up. She persisted in having her own way. Even when her memory started going. She would spend hours looking for a word that escaped her and she wouldn't stop until she found it. That's how it was in the beginning, when there were still pathways in her memory. Later, the dementia spread like a flood, destroying bridges, turning the past into an archipelago of isolated islands. She mixed up the ijekavian and ekavian dialects. At their last meeting, she spoke in Fiuman.*

While looking out of the window of his room at the Skaleta hotel, he turned his head towards the corner of the street, where the little family would regroup after seeing a film at the Iskra cinema, and he clearly heard his mother's voice. This was where correcting the film's story began, seeking ways to avoid dangerous situations and tragedies. In response to his sister's remark that there would be no story if one could predict everything in advance, his mother said that temptations existed at every step, that there were more stories than people, which was precisely why there was always a choice. She did not doubt the existence of a perfect course of direction that would enable one to navigate any situation unimpeded.

He was looking for just such a course now in trying to bring everything together, to outline a plan for his life before another Ida Rojnić appeared and erased part of his memory. When one looks back over the decades, there are no enigmas on the road, everything is logical, one thing follows another. It could not have been otherwise.

In the city where he grew up, where living together with the Croats were all the other peoples of the then Yugoslavia, as well as Italians and a smattering of Hungarians, he and his sister inherited two Greeks. He got Lizeta, and his sister got Diona. A detail that might prove useful. So, he wrote it

* A unique dialect of the Venetian language spoken in Rijeka (Fiume).

down right away. By the morning, the desk in his hotel room was covered with yellow Post-its. He wrote random notes. His thoughts kept pouring out; he tried to group them, to put them in order.

Lizeta was his mirror. In her, he recognised himself.

Lizeta's memories of Salonica were his memories. It was what connected him to the world, what eliminated his fear. Infinity opened up before him.

Life was bigger than any story. It could not be reduced to a fixed number of characters and situations.

Women who own hotels and boarding houses in Hamburg, they have eyes like X-rays, they register everything, Tišma would say.

Silence. There is no one to pass down the street by the Skaleta hotel. The pavements have become mute.

9.

She took the morning train from Salonica to Belgrade, sitting in the half-empty first class carriage. She was no longer the same person who had disembarked at the seaside three weeks earlier. Not because that was where she had started to smoke – a habit she would try to conceal when she returned to Trieste, though with time it would become a passion – but because of the sudden feeling of freedom she found there. She had needed to come to her birthplace to reassure herself that everything she remembered had gone, so that she could free herself of the anxiety she suffered from. There had not been a time when she didn't feel a tightness in her chest, butterflies in her stomach before performing in music school, fear during those times when her mother briefly disappeared, dull despair during those first weeks at Mrs. Haslinger's boarding school, horror of German words that she found hard to get used to.

Anxiety and waiting.

Waiting for her father's letters, for her mother's visits to Vienna during the summer holidays. Waiting for the situation in Salonica to calm down so that she could finally go to her city. Waiting for the war to end, waiting to leave the Benedettis' home in Trieste, to hear news about the survivors of the fire in Salonica. Waiting for her cousin Mauro's final bill for the support she had received, which would significantly diminish her share of the inherited dividends. Waiting for something more than a kiss from the timid Ettore while they necked among the excavations of the Roman theatre at the foot of Donota Street. Waiting for the affair with Attilio to end by itself. Waiting to hear from Giorgio after he left Trieste. Waiting for an extended contract with the Teatro Verdi and, after two years in the opera chorus, being given a role.

And then, suddenly, in Salonica's Attica bar, she decided to stop waiting, to reject this slavish, life-warping discipline. Caution, which her father had venerated like a god. What had it done to him? Where had he found relief? In calligraphy? Where had the thrill of registering the arrivals and departures of his hotel guests taken him? He had lived his life like a moth, stuck to objects, his step slow, accompanied by the syncopated tapping of his cane. But there was no father anymore, and no century-old registers of the Xenodochion Egnatia's guests. What remained were his letters. They were mostly about the weather. It took more than a whole page for him to describe the sultry August heat. But there were only a few words about her mother or himself, saying that they were well.

She wouldn't wait for anyone or anything anymore. She would move forward. Just as the train moves forward towards the stations where it briefly stops. Polykastro, Gefyra, Idomeni, Gevgelija. Or it moves past stations where it doesn't stop. Those whose names flash by too quickly for her to read them.

Somewhere along here was the former Turkish-Serbian border. Would she recognise the station where she and her mother had spent a whole afternoon waiting? Where she had been so scared that she vomited in the restaurant where they were having lunch. Her mother had gone to the ladies' room and stayed there for a long time. Some men with beards sat down at a nearby table, speaking in an unintelligible language and laughing.

After Polykastro, the railroad followed the banks of the Vardar River. Water conjured up water. In her mind, Lizeta was on board the ship Patras. She remembered the words of her travel companion Matilda Kesinis. *Everything is written in the cards. The stars favour her, illness will bypass her. She will enjoy a long life.*

There was a crowd at the station. However, only the second class carriages filled up.

She was still alone in the compartment.

On the train she would discover that she was missing five Banco di Roma cheques. This wasn't the first time that a lover had robbed her. Giorgio had taken a lot of money from her before leaving. Only she knew how much. And so it would be in all those lives that Matilda had foretold. She would be alone. Live without witnesses. Not account to anyone.

Andrej, the blond violinist, the Russian émigré who had spun her the story that he was waiting for his papers to go to America, could have robbed her blind, even taken her jewellery, but he hadn't. With him she closed the book on Salonica. One of those lives that Matilda had foretold.

Her last night at the Bristol. How many nights like this had her mother had? Maybe she had been conceived on such a night? She was like her mother in build and looks. Like her father in character. Lost, she covered it up with rituals that instil order. Fear masked by patience. Nonsense! None of that was her. If she was like her father, then she would still be living as a prisoner of the Bendettis in Trieste. She would have stayed with Ettore's kisses. She was certainly like some father. But it was very unlikely that she had come out of Ambroggio Benedetti's beard.

"Edirne, Edirne", she sang to herself in her mother's voice.

They said that her mother had entered the Benedetti family in the uniform of a maid. The pretty Greek from Thrace caught the eye of the elder son of the Xenodochion Egnatia's proprietor, a withdrawn bachelor who ran the hotel with his father. The father suddenly died of a heart attack, and the son married. Three years later, Lizeta was born.

She never knew her mother's parents; they died early, in Thrace. They lived in a village near Edirne. That's all she knew. There were no photographs. Her mother's past was stowed away, hidden. In fact, her parents' lives were hidden. They lived according to a tacit agreement. They didn't argue in front of Lizeta, but they didn't show affection either. It had always been a boarding school life. Every now and then, her mother would disappear for a few days. Her father's answer was always the same: Mum is on a trip. On such days she would spend more time at the Bechtsinar Gardens with her governess.

The train was pulling into a bigger town. The station was coming into view. A long canopy at the front offered shelter to the crowd of travellers. It said: Skopje.

She was only a third of the way to Belgrade. The conductor said that the train was on time. She would have two hours in Belgrade that evening to catch the Simplon Express to Trieste. He repeated it several times, in poor German: "Belgrad Abend zwei Stunde warten." She asked him where the Turkish-Serbian border used to be. He looked at her perplexed and left without answering.

After Skopje, she was no longer alone in the compartment. She was joined by a couple travelling to Belgrade. He was a doctor; he had studied medicine in Vienna. He'd come this way six years ago; not by train, but on foot, with the Serbian army's sanitary service. They were breaking through the Salonica front.

He knew where the Serbian-Turkish border used to be. He would show her; it would take another two hours to get there.

Later, the couple dozed off.

When she was a child, she was afraid of people who were asleep. She was more afraid of them than of the dead. Because the dead were peaceful in their finality, but slumbering people were the moving dead.

The wife's head slipped onto her husband's shoulder; her breathing became louder. At one moment, he opened his eyes. He smiled at Lizeta. His wife was startled out of her sleep by her own snoring. Or had her husband discretely prodded her awake? She looked around sleepily, then rested her head against the plush headboard and closed her eyes.

Maybe she's embarrassed, Lizeta thought.

The husband nodded off again. They seemed very tired. Looking at them made Lizeta feel sleepy as well. She had barely slept a wink the night before. Sleep finally came just before dawn when Andrej left. When had he taken her cheques? She leaned her head against the curtain by the window. She was facing in the direction that the train was moving.

The dark side and the light side are always equidistant. Two worlds that exist simultaneously. You always choose. Those were Matilda's words when they parted in Piraeus. And Lizeta had made her choice.

Life is an unending score of music, full of unexpected passages and tonal changes. Life is the Atticas of this world, emigres waiting for the ship to take them to America, soft-hearted crooks, good fellows like her father – hypocrites who think that you can buy anything. For eight years, that moth wrote letters to his child. For eight years, his thoughts shaped her through his letters.

She smiled to herself at the pain of thinking about the life her father had led. Fearful and voyeur, marked by his withered leg. He never went to the beach. He was always in a fiacre. A collection of expensive canes. And hats...

She jumped at the touch of a hand. She had nodded off. The doctor told her that they were about to arrive at Ristovac, at the old Serbian-Turkish border.

The wife was asleep in the corner by the door.

Lizeta stood up to lower the window. The carriage stopped in front of a ground floor house with a garden full of roses. The stationhouse was all the way to the right. The streetlamps that she remembered were gone, and so was the canopy with the begonias. But the front of the building was the same as it had been fourteen years ago. In the end, it was no different from the train stations she'd seen all over the Monarchy. The windows were the same shape, arched above, adorned with red bricks.

There were only two passengers on the platform – they had just stepped off the train. And there was the stationmaster, with his baton. Waiting for the train to depart.

Just then, two little boys appeared in the garden, directly opposite the window where Lizeta was standing. They were holding hands. The older boy was no more than three years old. The younger one had only just started walking. They went over to the wooden fence and looked at Lizeta.

The whistle blew. The next moment the locomotive's valves hissed loudly, a cloud of steam rose up, the carriage suddenly jerked forward.

The little boys stood there immobile, like dolls. Lizeta waved at them. The younger one smiled and started to wave with both hands. The waving threw him off balance. The older one held him to stop him from falling.

Lizeta continued to wave at them. She stuck her head out the window and watched the station, the fence and the two little boys disappear into the distance. She would never see those little boys again. Because the old Serbian-Turkish border that the man on the train claimed was precisely at the spot they had just left, didn't exist anymore. Nothing can be repeated, and because of this realisation the world had suddenly become more accessible and less foreign. She promised herself that she would not be afraid of anything ever again. She closed her eyes against the increasingly strong wind, the smoke from the locomotive in her nostrils. She closed the window.

All the way to Belgrade she exchanged smiles with the woman, and from time to time talked to the doctor. When he learned that she had lived in Vienna, he recalled a few places, the beaches along the Danube, the dance halls, the theatres. Lizeta told him that a student's Vienna and a school boarder's Vienna were two completely different cities.

Her cheek pressed against the window glass, she absently watched the passing landscape. She thought of all the people she had met during her three weeks in Salonica, in the offices of the police and the land registry, in bars and restaurant terraces in the evening. She was only twenty-six. The world lay spread out before her, like on the palm of her hand. She carried strong emotions from her city. Salonica had a rough, but good-natured and clear face, like the face of Panayotos, the porter at the Bristol. The souls of cities reflect the souls of the people who live in them. And people move around, taking their cities with them. A Salonica was travelling with her to Trieste; Via Cavana would cross Kuskura Street; the facade of Xenodochion Egnatia would appear on the facade of some palace on the Grand Canal.

She was taking in her future life. In the spring she would go with Barbara to the island of St Andreja, she would go wherever her path took her, without a declaration of arrival or departure, strong, drinking in all the cries and muffled sighs of rebetiko. "Edirne, Edirne. Salonica, Salonica. Trieste, Trieste."

10.

A multicentric neurological study carried out by four Californian universities over a five-year period showed that 75% of the 1,265 respondents diagnosed with Alzheimer's had been obsessed since childhood with making lists, copying telephone numbers out of telephone and address books, and generally recording all and sundry. From an early age, the majority of the respondents had displayed a fear of letting information about the world around them escape. All their lives they had written down where and with whom they had spent their birthdays, celebrations, holidays. They also noted their plane trips and made lists of the books they had read. Over 80% of the respondents kept a diary.

Dementia is like the polar snow melting, Professor Eduardo Dalasco of the neurological clinic in San Diego explained picturesquely. The compact territory breaks up into islands. There is more and more water and less and less land. People with Alzheimer's become prisoners of the ocean of oblivion.

PART III

Mum,

I'm beginning to forget. I see people that I don't know. There are more and more names that I don't remember. I console myself with what you used to say, that the forgotten isn't lost, it's merely mislaid.

I owe you this letter. Because of our conversations. Because of Lizeta. Because of all those women, secret and silent, like Gianfranco's mother, whom I admired. Because of the shyness that preserved me like wax.

Because of the notebook stolen in Vinkovci, which is my baptism certificate.

That evening at the Slon hotel in Ljubljana, when you bought me the book *Winnetou*, I started my list of hotels in my notebook. From Ljubljana we went to Rijeka. After the Slon came the Neboder in Sušak. The following day we moved from the hotel to the villa of your former landladies, Milkica and Irma Car, at Vidikovac 4. It was my twelfth birthday. They gave me Karl May's book *From the Rio de la Plata to the Cordilleras*. And there, right at the beginning, it mentions a hotel. I immediately added it to my list. I thought of it as a way of giving life to your notebook. The lesson learned was that life can be found in books as well, that there is no separation between the two. The bee and the ant are in love, just like in the fable you used to read to me. I never found it again. I looked for it in the Grimm brothers, in Lafontaine, and in Andersen, but to no avail.

On my way to visiting you, as soon as I saw the Danube from the bus, I thought I was seeing the wide gulf of the La Plata. In the distance, on the Vojvodina side, I could make out Montevideo. You spent your last months at the home moving, changing hotels and towns. I will never know where you died.

What was your last vision? Some *veduta* of Selce, Crik-venica or Dubrovnik? Perhaps a tapestry picture, one from the series of mythological scenes woven in thirty-six shades of blue? Where did the cobalt blue glass violinist wind up? Not to mention the contents of Lizeta's dresser drawers. Or Professor Fažov's baglama?

You had your Hiterots as well. They weren't from the Red Island, they were from Obilićev venac in Belgrade. Right next to the Hotel Majestic. I never heard the story; I just guessed the gist of it. The look of deep hurt on your face. The moment when you lost faith in people, humiliated and helpless, like the time when that friend of Dad's asked what Penelope did while her Odysseus was at sea. Or, when you returned from the parent-teacher meeting and my teacher Mariza Šepić said in front of everybody that I had been given an undeserved "A". That evening we talked for a long time. You weren't mad at me. You said the hardest thing was to be yourself. Ever since, I've had two people inside me: the person I am, the student with an unmerited "A", and the other person I had to catch up with and become.

Meanwhile, the people from the beach have taken over the world.

They are everywhere now. At airports and on cruise ships, in banks and in parliaments. They have installed themselves in ministries, academies, universities, hospitals, film studios, theatres. The world has become a place of caricatures. The devil has become superfluous; fraud is now the norm.

This is no longer the city where I was born. In the mean-time — which means a whole lifetime — it has turned into a place of money launderers, with low brows and murky eyes, hired guns, fake donors, forgers of all kinds, those who buy building permits, birth certificates, marriage licenses, citizenship papers, diplomas and prayer breakfasts.

This is no longer the country where I grew up, it is a place where tricksters, bag snatchers and acrobats entertain the stupid crowd. I know, it's no better anywhere else. I came along at a bad time. There are centuries when Vandals, Huns and Visigoths rule, when people fall under the clenched fist of singlemindedness. When nonsense rules, when boors inundate the world. Because, in the end, it's always the barbarians who come.

I will never give up. Even after half a century, I haven't forgotten the beginning of *From the Rio de la Plata to the Cordilleras.*

"A cold *pampero* wind was gusting over the large La Plata estuary, which looked like a sea bay; it showered the streets of Montevideo with a mixture of sand, dust and heavy drops of rain. It was impossible to stay out in the street for long. Which is why I remained sitting alone in my room at the Oriental hotel, reading a book about the country I wanted to get to know."

Dear Mum,

Soon I'll start speaking Fiuman.

THE END